PRAISE FOR EVA CROCKER AND *ALL I ASK*

"Eva Crocker's stunning debut, *All I Ask*, eloquently depicts a generation struggling to gain self-determination in a climate steeped in societal deprivation, violence, and greed. Her characters, informed by progressive ideals and the optimism of youth, labour to overcome precariousness in all aspects of their lived experience. Housing. Employment. Love. All they ask of their home, by birth or by choice, is for some semblance of physical autonomy, emotional respect, and financial stability. Crocker implores we acknowledge the power inequity inherent in her city so that we might access an unknown store of compassion and empathy. Eva Crocker's *All I Ask* is precise and fervent storytelling. She is a fascinating, keen voice in Newfoundland and Labrador. This is a compelling novel and an impressive accomplishment from one of our most promising writers." —Megan Gail Coles, author of *Small Game Hunting at the Local Coward Gun Club*

"Crocker pulls off an ending that brings the drama full circle in a way that is both unexpected and satisfying...Comparisons to Sally Rooney and Eileen Myles have been made, but there's something in Crocker's forthright descriptions of physical bodies and their functions that feels closer to the work of Ottessa Moshfegh...It is Crocker's straightforward honesty and forthrightness that is most refreshing." —*Quill & Quire*

"There are novels that feel alive. There is no other way to describe it, because words like 'fresh' or 'current' are not enough. These novels are more than just a compelling plot or strong writing. They do more than tap into current events or debates. These novels offer access to something made animate on the page, and speak from a perspective that feels somehow deeply familiar and entirely unknown; Eva Crocker's *All I Ask* is one such novel...Refreshing as it is tense and sensual as it is sad, *All I Ask* is a sharp and absorbing read." —*Miramichi Reader*

Also by Eva Crocker

Barrelling Forward

ALL
I ASK

EVA
CROCKER

ANANSI

Published in Canada in 2020 by House of Anansi Press Inc.
www.houseofanansi.com

House of Anansi Press is committed to protecting our natural environment.
This book is made of material from well-managed FSC®-certified forests,
recycled materials, and other controlled sources.

24 23 22 21 20   1 2 3 4 5

Library and Archives Canada Cataloguing in Publication

Title: All I ask / Eva Crocker.
Names: Crocker, Eva, author.
Identifiers: Canadiana (print) 20190165464 | Canadiana (ebook) 20190165480 |
ISBN 9781487006075 (softcover) | ISBN 9781487006082 (EPUB) |
ISBN 9781487006099 (Kindle)
Classification: LCC PS8605.R62 A75 2020 | DDC C813/.6—dc23

Book design: Alysia Shewchuk

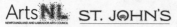

*We acknowledge for their financial support of our publishing program the Canada
Council for the Arts, the Ontario Arts Council, and the Government of Canada.*

Printed and bound in Canada

MIX
Paper from
responsible sources
FSC® C103567

For Jess Gibson

ONE

They took my computer and phone so they could copy the contents. They called it a mirror image. They said it was the fastest way to prove I wasn't the suspect and also I didn't have a choice.

There were nudes, there was a picture, taken with the flash, of a pimple on the back of my neck—swollen and inflamed. They didn't know when they'd get to it. The unit was really backed up. What was it called? Child Pornography? Digital Something? "The Unit." He said there were only three or four guys in the Unit. For the whole province.

There were emails back and forth with my mother, scheduling visits with my grandmother in the hospital. Emails where I said things like, *I have kickboxing but I guess I can go in if no one else is available—lessons are pre-paid.* There were rejection emails from casting directors.

All the stupid things I'd googled. Things I should have known. *When did Newfoundland join Canada? What is Brexit? Are most oven dials Fahrenheit or Celsius?* How much of that is in the mirror image? Reams of it.

These things take time. Couldn't tell you. A judge in Gander had signed the warrant. What were they looking for? Illegal digital material. What does that mean? And what does "transmitted" mean? Transmitted from my address. Is it the same as seeded? It's different than uploaded, I've seen "uploaded" in the paper. Footage of a slump-shouldered man with a windbreaker pulled over his head walking into the courtroom. A drawing in the newspaper of some sad-sack, evil piece of shit sitting beside the judge.

Who was combing through my hard drive? Picking through the digital traces, footsteps, shadows. Taking in all the un-deleted drafts, all the weird, unflattering angles. Three or four guys, taking their time.

WHEN THEY CAME to my house, my hair was greasy and I wasn't wearing a bra. I'd slept on my ponytail, it was sagging at the base of my neck, and I had glasses on. Normally I wear contacts; the glasses are an old prescription. I can't read street signs with them. I'd slept in a big T-shirt and a pair of bicycle shorts — no bra. I woke up to the doorbell ringing and a pounding that shook the house. Both at the same time — the doorbell and the knocking. It woke me up. I put my glasses on and went to look out the window. The plastic frames were cold on the bridge of my nose, it made my sinuses tingle. Someone was pressing the doorbell in and holding it down. I pulled the curtain open with one hand and leaned out of view.

I assumed the knocking and the doorbell was someone wandered up from downtown. When you live downtown belligerent people wander up. They yell and piss in the street and sometimes they ring your doorbell again and again. You turn off the lights and wait for them to go away.

The month before, my roommate Holly and I had moved into a house at the end of a short street. Our living room windows were street level and looked onto a small parking lot on the side of a church. A nurses' union and a row of group homes backed onto the lot, hiding it from the main road. The front of our house and the church enclosed the parking lot.

The top floor of the church had recently been turned into eleven bachelor apartments for low-income tenants. A clutch of people were always smoking near the church's side entrance, facing the house, or else on the fire escape that extended from the church's second floor. I left the curtains open and the living room lights brazenly bright in the evenings, even though you could see right in.

The church owned a dumpster that sat in the parking lot. Sometimes I'd slip into rubber boots and cross the parking lot with a garbage bag. I'd wear just my fleece bathrobe over a T-shirt and shorts when I ran out. The opening in the side of the dumpster screeched when I tugged on the handle. On cold days the side opening froze shut and I'd have to get on tiptoe and lift the dumpster's lid with one arm to heft a bag of garbage in. The unlocked dumpster felt like a luxury, to be able to rid yourself of anything whenever you wanted.

There were two windows in my bedroom; one looked onto the parking lot in front of the house and one looked onto the back of the church. Behind the church there was a yard surrounded by a chain-link fence with sign that said "Outdoor Play Area." There had been a daycare in the building long before we moved in. Now neighbourhood cats squirmed between the locked gates and used the Outdoor Play Area as a litter box. The shiny tape from inside a VHS was tangled in the branches of a tree just outside the fence. From my bedroom I could see the black ribbon moving in the wind, the plastic case knocking against the tree's trunk.

Each time they pounded on the door, the crystal lightcatcher I'd stuck to the window with a licked suction cup tapped the glass. I couldn't see who was on the step so I had to lean into the window. Four cops. Only two could fit on the step, the other two were standing below them on the sidewalk. One had a shiny bald head. I thought there must be a fire next door. I was thinking that fire-drill word, "evacuate." There must be a reason I need to evacuate. To be evacuated.

I opened the front door a crack and the bald cop put a hand on the door frame.

"We have a warrant," he said.

"What?" I said.

"Move out of the way, we're coming in, we have a warrant."

"Why? For what?" I held the door.

"You're going to have to move out of the way," the bald cop repeated.

"Why?"

"Because we have a warrant," he said. "Move out of the way."

"But why?" As I was saying it, I stepped backwards and let the door fan open. The bald cop walked past me into the house. The other three men crowded into the porch, leaving the door ajar behind them.

"The animals," I said, backing into the living room. "Don't let the animals out."

The three backup cops followed me into the house. Salty boots on the floor.

"What's down here?" one cop asked, opening the door to the basement. "Is there a light?"

There was a parade of white-and-blue cop cars in front of the house. I looked out at the parking lot. Three regular silver cars with cops inside were pulled up next to the dumpster.

The woman who always sat on the church's fire escape stairs — I could hear her coughing out there all night long — was on the bottom step, sneakers in the slush. The man who sometimes accompanied her was hunched on the step above her, a travel mug between his knees. Because of the out-of-date prescription in my glasses their faces were just pale smears above their collars. I thought they must be able to see the swarm of cops inside the house. Were they sympathetic? Worried about me?

"The cats," I said. "Please."

The last cop turned around and batted the front door shut.

"You have to lock it, it blows open," I said.

He paused before turning the deadbolt, deciding how much of an asshole to be, then walked into the kitchen and started opening the cupboards. The bald cop stood in front of me, legs wide apart. The cop who'd asked about the light made his way down to the dark basement, the fourth clomped upstairs in his heavy boots. Something fell in the kitchen, something plastic that bounced, I couldn't think what it might be.

"My roommate is in bed," I said, realizing. "Don't scare her."

"Is there a light down here?" the cop called from the basement.

"We have a warrant for the transmission of illegal digital material," the bald cop said.

"She's asleep, don't scare her." My voice came out loud but trembly. I saw the cop on the stairs hesitate before continuing up towards the bedrooms.

"Who's your roommate?" the bald cop asked.

"She's in bed." I felt the muscles in my thighs shaking like I'd just finished a long bike ride.

"What's her name?" the bald cop asked.

"Holly," I said.

The cop who'd been digging through the kitchen came back.

"Last name?" the bald cop asked. "Take a seat, sit on the couch."

"Holly Deveraux." I sank into the couch.

"What's your name?" the bald cop asked.

"Stacey Power."

"Do you know Natalie Swanson?"

"She lived here before us, I don't know her. We just moved in," I said.

Their faces changed. The bald man beckoned and three more cops came through the back door into the kitchen. How long had they been out there, waiting between our snow-covered bikes and the rusted-out barbeque? The last one shut the door behind him. The cats crouched amongst the cops' boots, tails wrapped around themselves, bellies close to the floor. Their heads jerked back and forth on scrunched necks as they took in all the strange people.

"There's no one up here," a cop called from upstairs.

"She must have stayed at her partner's," I said.

I was trying to count how many men were in the room but they all looked the same and they were moving around. Were they wearing guns? Yes. Also those extend-able sticks for beating people.

"Her what?" the bald cop asked.

"The person she's seeing," I said.

"What's his name?"

"I don't know—I don't really know who she's seeing."

"You don't know his first name?"

"We just moved in here, on November first," I said, hoping to summon the uncertainty I'd seen on his face when I told him I didn't know Natalie Swanson.

The bald cop looked at the cop beside him, a guy my age. The look suggested there had been a fuck-up and someone other than the bald cop was responsible for it.

"November first," the bald cop said, deflating. "Well, I'm going to need to see some ID and the lease."

Two cops let themselves out and stood on the front step. One of them squeezed the sides of a walkie-talkie on his shoulder and muttered into it as he left.

"The door will blow open," I said. "The cats."

"Those guys are coming right back," the bald cop said.

The young cop followed me into the kitchen. I dug around in the drawers; the lease had slipped down into a pile of kitchen junk the previous tenants had left behind. Beaters and fondue forks and blades for a long-lost blender. It was a carbon copy of the lease we'd signed; the landlord had taken the original when he gave us the keys. The thin pages were scrunched up and not in the right order. I found the sheet with our signatures and the date in faint grey handwriting and held it out to him.

"Got the lease here," the young cop called.

It was the young cop who followed me up to my bedroom to find my driver's licence. The two geraniums on my windowsill were in bloom: the petals on one plant were a deep, bloody red; the flowers on the other were searing fuchsia.

I had a cold, there were used tissues scattered around the bed. A roll of toilet paper on its side by my pillow had unrolled, leaving three clean squares flat against the floor.

"I have to follow you up here," the young cop said, taking in the unmade bed and phlegm-stained tissues.

I picked my winter jacket off the floor, the straps of my book bag were still tangled in the coat's armpits. I pulled my wallet out of the pocket and let the coat-knapsack jumble smack against the floor. I flicked through the receipts, movie tickets, and download cards for friends' albums. I saw the tiny, washed-out picture of myself. The young cop looked at my ID, then handed it back to me.

"Bring that downstairs and we'll show it to Sergeant Hamlyn," he said.

His boots were loud on the stairs but I could feel him giving me space, waiting for me to get two paces ahead before thudding down behind me.

"Got some ID there?" the bald cop asked.

The young cop nodded and I held the card out.

"We're going through with the search. We'll all be as respectful as possible," the bald cop said to the room.

"I'm going to read you the warrant," the young cop said, sitting at the kitchen table and pulling out a chair. "Just take a seat."

He was holding a couple of printed pages with something like a business card stapled to the top left corner. The other cops spread out, opening doors, tossing the couch cushions on the floor. I heard a crash from the bathroom; one of them must have opened the mirrored cabinet and all the makeup Holly had crammed onto the top of the case had fallen into the sink.

"Whereas it appears on the oath of —" the young cop began.

"You don't have to read it to me," I said.

"I have to read it to you," he said. "Take a seat."

WHEN THEY FINALLY left I went upstairs and put in my contacts. It felt like stepping out of the blurry chaos of the morning. I stood at the window watching the cops climb into their cars and leave the parking lot. They took my computer and cell phone but left a handful of flash drives—filled with old photos, papers I'd written in university, papers I'd edited for friends. They told me the flash drives were "cleared at the scene." They took an external hard drive from Holly's room, a slim silver rectangle with a thick cord wrapped around it. There was no way to text Holly and tell her what had happened.

She'd been sleeping somewhere else occasionally, maybe at Dave King's—she didn't talk to me about who she hooked up with. The cops had been in her bedroom, stripped the bed, lifted the mattress, gone through her drawers. I wanted to tell her in person.

One unmarked car lingered on the other side of the parking lot. Inside, a cop was touching a computer screen attached to the dashboard. Above his car, the sun was catching on the VHS innards snarled in the tree. The light made greasy rainbows on the tape as it stretched and drooped in the breeze.

MONTHS BEFORE THE COPS stormed our house, the plywood barrier that runs along Duckworth Street hiding an inactive construction site was spray-painted ABUSE OF POWER COMES AS NO SURPRISE. FUCK THE POLICE. The painter had held the can close to the plywood so the tall white letters dripped down the wall. The doors of the courthouse were covered in smashed eggs; yolks hardened on the wood and cracked shells littered the threshold.

The night before, a cop, Officer Doug Snelgrove, had been found not guilty of sexually assaulting a young woman he'd driven home in his cruiser. On the stand, he said he'd known she was drunk; he said that he had sex with her while he was on duty, while he was in uniform with a gun attached to his pants. The story was in the news for weeks. He admitted that he'd radioed in every other ride that night but not that one. He said he'd smelled alcohol on her breath but he didn't realize she was too drunk to consent, even though as a cop he was trained to recognize drunkenness, even though he'd testified about impairment at drunk driving trials. She told the courtroom she'd blacked out. She'd asked a cop for a ride home because she was too drunk to get home on her own. The woman's friend testified that she'd called him just before the incident happened and she'd been incoherent on the phone.

Snelgrove was more than a decade older and he'd been stone-cold sober.

The night the Snelgrove verdict was announced, people gathered outside the courthouse and howled "No justice, no peace" into loudspeakers pointed at the sky. The following day people stopped each other in the street to ask if they'd heard about the verdict, eyes glossy with tears, jaws clamped with rage. People asked, "Are you sure? Who told you? You actually saw the article? Who published it?" And then they said, "An appeal. There has to be an appeal. Did it say anything about an appeal?"

The bleak reality of the verdict settled on the city. Someone printed stickers that said "Hell No Snelgrove" and pasted them on parking meters and mailboxes. I passed ABUSE OF POWER COMES AS NO SURPRISE. FUCK THE POLICE. on my way to work and when I went to bars to hear music. Then there was the pounding that shook my house, four cops on my doorstep, more hiding outside the back door.

TWO

Everyone wanted to be Holly's friend when she first got here — she had so clearly just arrived from a big city. Everyone wanted to show her around. To have some of her fashion sense rub off on them. To wow her with a sweaty hike up to Soldier's Pond where you can take in Signal Hill from the opposite side of the harbour and swim in your underwear. To maybe make out with her because (if you grew up in St. John's and still live here) it's not that often you get to make out with someone you haven't known since eighth grade.

Me and Viv and Viv's boyfriend, Mike, were all living together on Patrick Street when we met her. Viv and I first noticed her waiting for a cab outside Sobeys. She was standing near a rolling rack of wilting flowers. She had tote bags full of groceries at her feet. Her hair was cut in a jagged bob and dyed a yellow that deliberately clashed with her dark eyebrows and made her pale skin look sallow. She had wide-legged jeans with a shaggy trim hanging around her ankles. Everyone in St. John's was still wearing skinny jeans with a clean, hemmed cuff and no one put their groceries in tote bags. She had plastic nails with neon green flames on the tips.

"You'd think they would put these on sale," Viv said about the flowers, smiling at Holly as we walked past.

"I was thinking the same thing," Holly said.

"They're half-dead." Viv stopped and rubbed the wrinkled petal of a violet pansy between her finger and thumb. The pansy was one of a bunch in a hanging basket hooked on the side of the rack. A mix of black and violet pansies, each with a splotch of yellow in their centre. The soil was wet but the leaves were brittle. Holly reached up and rubbed a leaf, unconsciously copying Viv.

"Everything is so expensive here," Holly said.

I was standing awkwardly by, Viv's silent sidekick. A cab pulled up and Holly climbed in with her cloth bags and shut the door. She waved to us through the window as the car pulled away.

"Do you know her?"

"Nope," Viv said.

We started across the parking lot, the handles of our plastic grocery bags digging into our palms. The wind whipped my hair straight up and across my face. A teenager in a safety vest pushed a long snake of grocery carts towards us. His chest was bent over the handles and he took slow, determined steps, fighting the wind to get the carts across the lot.

FOR A WHILE I was addicted to ChatRoulette, a site
that connects you with strangers via webcam and a chat
window. I don't know if it still exists — it might, or maybe
there's a new version. This was early 2000s, and I'd never
heard anyone use the phrase "revenge porn."

I was living with my first serious partner, Dan Kent,
in an apartment above a closed-down laundromat on
Alexander Street. We'd met in Corner Brook when I was
in university and had moved back to St. John's together.
We weren't having sex anymore and that was part of it.
The end of sex was slow and awkward. When he couldn't
stay hard I would cry into my pillow and he would rub
my back.

In the beginning I didn't put my face in it at all. Mostly
I clicked from person to person, unzipping a tight hoodie
to show I was only wearing a bra underneath. When the
person on the other end responded I would pause the
cam, zip the hoodie back up, and click to the next person.

Text at the top of the chat window told you where in
the world the other person was. Sometimes it would just
be the country and other times it would be more specific,
right down to the city. It was almost always men — lots
of men in England, lots in Egypt, occasionally men in
other parts of Canada. Once a group of teenage boys in
soccer jerseys, clinging to each other, filled the screen and
whooped at me. I clicked away from kids immediately.
Always. Once there was a man in Morocco, working at
a convenience store, a wall of cigarette packages behind

him. Occasionally other women, usually fragmented like me, hiding identifiable parts of themselves. Most of the women clicked away from me. Once a woman with long, pointed nails waved to me by wiggling her fingers before disappearing. She was lying on her side in a bra and underwear, and like me, most of her face was hidden. There was something conspiratorial in the wave.

I did it while Dan was at work. I smoked weed that I bought from the thirty-year-old skater guys who lived in the apartment above us. They had pet rats and their apartment stank. I kept the weed in an old sprinkles container, a clear plastic bottle with a bubblegum-pink lid. Rolling a joint was part of my ChatRoulette ritual. The men loved it when I blew smoke at the camera.

Eventually I started letting more of myself into the frame. I stacked couch cushions on the floor, balanced my laptop on them and then knelt in front of the webcam. I showed from my lips to the waistband of my jeans. Sometimes I dipped my hand into my underwear. Sometimes I put my fingers in my mouth and then slid them into my underwear.

Later I started wearing a pair of sunglasses I bought at the dollar store and showed my whole head. The glasses had big, square frames that covered most of my face; the lenses were dark purple at the top and faded to clear. I wore a frilly bikini top I got at a clothing swap. I would reach behind to undo the string tied around my ribs and then tug at the knot around my neck so the bikini fell into my lap.

You could turn on the microphone but I didn't. The

men spoke to me but I typed replies. The men begged to see my eyes in voices that were sometimes stern, sometimes whiney. At this point I was full-on masturbating for the camera, reclined on the floor with the laptop's webcam hovering above me on the wobbly tower of cushions. They would say, "Baby show me those beautiful eyes please," "Baby I need to see your eyes." The glasses weren't even completely opaque.

Once, a man in New York City wearing aviators and a baseball cap pulled down over his forehead appeared in the little window. He was holding a SMILE YOU'RE ON CAMERA sign, the kind you can buy from a rack with HOUSE FOR SALE BY OWNER and BEWARE OF DOG. He had a line of digital cameras on the coffee table in front of him and a silver video camera on a tripod. He smirked at me, this mean smile. I got up and slammed my computer closed. But after a few minutes I opened the page again. I agreed again to the terms and conditions. I smiled at a new man, a pudgy middle-aged guy rubbing the crotch of his grey sweatpants.

It was easy for hours to slip by, clicking from person to person. I learned how to angle my body to make it look the way I liked, and by the end of a session my back ached and my knees were strained.

Afterwards I'd feel like I'd been in a trance. Sometimes when I stood up my ankles had fallen asleep and I stumbled around on cold, bloodless feet for a moment. Then I would put the couch back together and delete my browser history.

⌒

A FEW DAYS after we saw Holly at the supermarket, we ran into her at the Wesley United Church sale. The sale happens once a week for two hours in the basement of the church. An older lady in a wheelchair sits at a table by the door with an open cash box. A piece of loose-leaf with 25 CENTS ADMISSION written in ballpoint pen is laid in front of the cash box. The same wrinkled piece of paper gets reused each week.

Usually there's hardly anyone at the church sale, besides the women who sit around the perimeter of the room in folding chairs. Sometimes elderly people come to shop. They lift up pieces of clothing with shaky hands and then slowly refold them. Young mothers come with toddlers and collect armfuls of bedding and dishes while their kids dig through a bin of toys in the corner. The children haul things out and let them clatter against the cement floor. A toy vacuum with coloured baubles that bounce when you push it, a rotary phone with painted eyes, a baby doll with a stuffed body and a hard plastic head. Every item has a handwritten price tag stuck to it.

Viv and I had rushed to the sale when I got off work—I was still working at the restaurant then. I was wearing my serving clothes under my spring jacket. A black collared T-shirt, a stretchy black skirt, black tights and ugly non-slip sneakers. I noticed Holly as soon as we arrived.

"That girl is here," I said, dropping a quarter into the cashbox.

Viv nodded.

For a while the three of us moved quietly around the room; occasionally me and Viv would hold things up for the other to evaluate. We were looking for kitchen stuff, cake pans or salad bowls or funny mugs. Most of the clothes had been donated by old people, or more likely by their families after they'd passed away. It was all either really big or really small because of how people tend to shrink or expand at the end of their life.

Holly held up a navy cardigan with brass buttons. Viv walked over to her.

"That's so great, is it hand-knit?" Viv asked.

"I don't know," Holly said.

Viv took the sweater from her and looked it over. "No tags."

"We met at the supermarket," Holly said.

"I recognized you, I thought I'd say hi," Viv said. "This is Stacey."

Again, I was silently useless between them. I smelled of sour fish chowder, coffee grinds, bleach.

"I just got off work," I said, trying to explain my clothes.

"Anyway, just thought we'd say hi, great sweater," Viv said.

"I just moved here," Holly said quickly. "I don't know anyone."

Viv invited her to a show that weekend. I bought four milk-white mugs with orange daisy chains around the rims while Viv typed her number into Holly's phone. The lady at the door took each mug in her lap and wrapped it in pages from a Pipers flyer.

It was sprinkling rain when Viv and I left the church.

I held the bag of mugs in my arms like a baby so they wouldn't bounce against each other and crack.

"It can be hard moving somewhere new, really isolating," Viv said on the short walk back to the house. "Especially a small place like this."

Viv had spent stints in Vancouver and Toronto and Montreal while I did my theatre degree in Corner Brook. She'd lived in punk houses, where she learned about making tinctures, washing the windows with newspaper and vinegar, making a bed frame by pushing a couple of pallets together.

She met Mike doing volunteer childcare at the Anarchist Bookfair in Montreal one spring. They spent a muggy afternoon sitting in new grass, reading radical picture books to kids. She slept at his apartment every night for her last couple of weeks in the city. He'd followed her back to Newfoundland and Viv invited me to move in with them.

Walking home from the church sale, I could tell she was getting wistful thinking about other places. I hated that.

"Who's playing that show at the Rose?" I asked. "It's on Saturday?"

"Don't you think she seemed nice?"

"Yeah, I guess."

THE MORNING THE COPS came I was scheduled to bartend a children's dance recital at the theatre where I worked part-time. When the last cop finally left, I turned the deadbolt on the front door and walked through the house, closing the drawers in the kitchen, stuffing the cushions back onto the couch. I got in the shower and then picked some clean clothes out of the laundry basket at the foot of my bed. I put a slice of bread in the toaster and leaned over the glowing slots, watching it brown. When it popped up I smeared it with hard peanut butter from the bottom of an almost empty jar. I could feel my pulse in my neck the whole time.

When I left the house, the unmarked car was still waiting on the opposite side of the church parking lot, nose pointed at my front door. The cop inside was absorbed in the screen on the dash. None of the people who usually hung around the fire escape were out smoking.

The kids who lived in the house next door to us were in their winter gear, riding in circles around the parking lot on bikes. The girl looked about nine and her younger brother was probably six or seven. Their puffy coats bunched around their hips as they pumped the pedals. They spent hours in the parking lot, chasing each other on bikes or bouncing a basketball off the lid of the dumpster. When it was time to come in, Fatima, their mom, would open the window and call to them in French. I saw her walking them to school each morning and home in the afternoon. We all fell in step one day when I was on my way to the theatre and Fatima put out her hand and introduced herself. Now I wondered if the kids had been out in the parking lot that morning when the cops showed up.

I speed-walked to the corner and then along Gower Street with my hair wet from the shower. The tips of my hair froze into upturned hooks. It felt weird not to be able to check the time on my phone.

I'd worked lots of these children's recitals, and I knew my shift would mostly be selling coffee and juice boxes, occasionally pointing the way to the bathroom. I got to the theatre twenty minutes early; I disarmed the alarm but I left the overhead lights off. I logged on to Facebook on the front desk computer. I knew Mike would be online. I asked him for Viv's number. I said I'd lost my phone, knowing Viv would fill him in later. I watched the bouncing dots that showed he was typing disappear then reappear. I could picture him sitting on the edge of their futon in his boxers, sleepy-eyed with a joint in his hand, waiting for the PlayStation to warm up. Finally he typed her number and a smiley emoji.

I called Viv from the front desk landline. The first two times I called, it rang through to voicemail. I could picture her too, looking at the phone, seeing a strange number and sliding it back into her apron. The third time she picked up on the first ring.

"It's me. Sorry, I know you're at work." A new email notification slid onto the screen, someone asking about comp tickets to a sold-out musical. I pushed the keyboard out of the way and rested my cheek on the particleboard desk.

"I literally have one second, it's packed here," Viv said. It was such a relief to hear her voice.

"The police were at my house, they took my phone."

"What?"

"It's okay, everyone's okay. Well, sort of, it's pretty fucked up, actually —"

"What do you mean? Where are you?"

"I'm at work now. I was in bed when they showed up."

"Why? What happened?" I heard a heavy door shut on Viv's end and the restaurant noise was replaced by static from wind blowing into her phone.

"I went to the door and I was thinking, you know how with cops they can't come in unless you invite them in?"

"They're like vampires," Viv said.

"But they were like, 'Get out of the way, we have a warrant,' and then three more of them came in the back door. It was like CSI."

"Are you okay?"

"Sorry, I know you're at work."

"There's three people on today."

"They wouldn't let me use the phone, they were like 'Sit on the couch,' I was just screaming, I wasn't literally screaming, but I was like, 'What's going on? Why? Why? Why?'"

"They wouldn't let you use the phone? Isn't that illegal? Don't you get a phone call?"

"I said 'Can I call my mom?' and they said 'No.'"

"Pricks."

"I shouldn't have said my mom, I should have said a lawyer. I should have called your cousin. But I was just totally overwhelmed. I was shaking. The whole time I was just thinking about the Snelgrove thing," I said.

"And Don Dunphy," Viv said. "And Kelly, those phone calls. What was his name? I think Sean, Sean Kelly. And Sergeant fucking Buckle with the BBM messages warning him they knew."

I could picture her standing in the snow outside the restaurant's back door in her waitressing outfit, the winter wind blowing her orange curls around.

"I wasn't even dressed. I didn't have a bra on. I was wearing a T-shirt and tiny shorts."

"They didn't tell you why they were there? Don't they have to give you the warrant?"

"They're so fucking incompetent, I don't believe anything they say. They were just bored of handing out parking tickets. They wanted to bash down a door in their bulletproof vests."

"They didn't say?" Viv asked.

"They were looking for illegal digital material."

"What does that mean?"

"I don't know."

"Is it, child porn?"

"I really don't know. They wouldn't say, I was thinking it could be like a credit card thing, or maybe identity theft. I'm just saying it's an invasion of my privacy. I don't want some man in my bedroom."

"You were there by yourself."

"What if I had a kid?"

"How did they get in the back door? Did they damage the door?" Viv was shivering from the wind, I could hear it in her voice.

"Or if I didn't speak English, if English wasn't my first language."

"Or if you were elderly," Viv said.

"An elderly person would've had a heart attack."

"I should get back to work, Stacey, I'm sorry."

"But you know what? They would have treated me a lot shittier if I didn't look like me, like a middle-class, cis white girl. By the end they were trying to make small talk. Being like, 'So are you from town? You grew up here?' And I was like 'Just get the fuck out of my house.'"

"Did you say that?"

"No, I was thinking it."

"I really have to go now, I'm sorry. I'll call you after work."

"I don't have a phone. The cops have my phone."

"Fuck," Viv said.

"It's okay, I'll call you. I still want to go to that party tonight," I said.

"We'll see how you feel," Viv said.

"I want to go."

"I'll talk to you later." Viv hung up.

I COUNTED THE cash at the theatre three times that morning before it added up properly. I was bent over, restocking the bar, when Krista Rice, the co-owner of Tiny Dancers, knocked on the plate-glass window of the theatre's lobby. I smashed my head off the top of the cooler. I stood up slowly and laid the cans of pop I'd been arranging on the counter. My scalp was throbbing. I felt my head for blood but my fingers came away clean. When I stepped into the hallway between the reception desk and the bar I saw Krista standing outside with a big Tupperware bin on her hip. I flicked on the fluorescent lights in the hall.

"Sorry, were you out there long?" I held the door for her.

She dropped the bin on the front desk. "There's programs in there, can we get them spread around, a few here, a few in the other room? Parents like to keep them."

The programs were a folded piece of yellow paper with a photo of all the child dancers in their leotards arranged in rows by height on the cover. Inside was a schedule of the different class performances with every child's name listed. I took a big stack and fanned them out on the front desk. Krista Rice walked into the bar and started flipping light switches. She turned on some music, a tinkling indie song with a broody-boy singer. As the space brightened up I felt that morning's invasion slide out of my body.

Soon parents and child dancers started arriving. The younger children wore tutus under rain jackets and winter coats; the oldest ones were nine and ten, they wore leotards, their hair in buns with sequined fascinators bobby-pinned to them.

The kids danced in rotation — the younger ones finished first and ran down over the stairs after their set. Then they waited with their parents in the bar for the after-show pizza party. They howled and jumped around the room, chasing and shoving. Some of them took their tutus off and flung them at the ceiling over and over. The layers of taffeta fluttered against each other on the way down. Lots of the parents were in their late twenties, just a bit older than me. I helped the dads unfold a row of card tables in the centre of the room. After the pizza I helped the moms pass out squares of sheet cake on paper plates.

I spent most of my shift making instant hot chocolate in Styrofoam cups. I dumped a tablespoon of crystals into each cup and poured water from the electric kettle over it. The dehydrated marshmallows softened as I swirled them with a spoon. I lost myself in the routine and the chaos of the kids racing around. My pulse slowed to a steady beat and I was mostly able to keep thoughts of the cops roaming through my house smothered by the thrum of familiar tasks.

A wave of downtown businesses had closed that fall. I'd lost my job at the restaurant. A lot of the storefront windows on Water Street got papered over with a collage of taped-together newspapers and flyers. Shops that had been open for half a century went under. People who could afford to leave the island were moving to the mainland in droves. I'd hated working at the restaurant, mostly because I was bad at it, but I cried after I got fired. Everyone and their dog was looking for a job.

Viv told me about the theatre—a friend of hers had quit to work at the front desk of an art gallery in Toronto and left an opening that wasn't advertised yet. I did the interview in the dressing room, me and Michelle Dodd reflected in a series of mirrors ringed in light bulbs. I sat on the edge of a tall chair with my jacket in my lap. Michelle was wearing a sundress with a hoodie zipped over it. She had a clipboard and a pen; she made a couple of notes and then looked up at me.

"So why do you want this job?" she said.

I had prepared for this question.

"I want to work in an arts space, a space —"

"I don't know if Alison told you, this job is just bartending and box office, the creative side, that's more the theatre company." Michelle's phone started vibrating in her lap. She picked it up and read the screen and said, "Fuck, sorry, I just have to, fuck, okay, I'm going to deal with that later."

She made the screen go dark and slid the phone into her pocket. "Sorry, it's a hectic day, what were we saying?"

"I like the idea of working in a space where art is happening." I was afraid I was sounding too touchy-feely-hippyish now. "A community-oriented space."

Michelle made a mark on her paper, still frowning from the message on her phone. "Right, good. Okay, and what motivates you?"

"What motivates me . . . in life?"

"Yeah." Michelle was focused on me now; she'd shaken off the text. "What motivates you in life?"

I felt the pause in the conversation stretching out as I tried to think of something to say. "That's a good question, great question."

Michelle nodded; her full attention was unnerving. I saw myself in the mirror behind her and straightened up. "I guess, I try to be a curious person, curious about life, so even if something doesn't seem interesting, I try to think of it as a learning experience, just learning about life, about how the world works."

Michelle made a tick mark on the paper.

"You have to be really detail-oriented for this job, there are a lot of details," she said.

"I totally get that, from my job at the folk festival. You

have to keep track of everything for when the final reporting comes up." I had prepared for this one too.

"Exactly," Michelle said.

"I have some administrative experience from the festival and also serving, my serving jobs are on the second page there," I said.

Michelle flicked the top page on her clipboard over and looked quickly down the list of restaurants and cafés on my resumé.

"It's just minimum wage, did Alison tell you that?"

"I'm not sure if she mentioned, but —"

"It's very flexible, it's all dependent on what shows are on, so some weeks it could be twenty hours, others it might just be ten, but the flip side is we understand people have other commitments," Michelle said. "Oh, the other thing is you have to close up by yourself, so some nights you could be leaving here at midnight or one a.m."

"That's fine, I'm fine with that," I said. The interview was going well. I felt proud of my what-motivates-you-in-life answer.

"Me too. I'm from Calgary and I always walked home alone at night," Michelle said. She got off her stool so I stood up too. We started walking towards the big, bright front entrance of the building.

"I mean, I understand people being freaked out but I've always lived downtown and I've always walked home alone," I said, feeling like we were bonding, two tough girls.

"I have a couple more interviews to do," Michelle said, but the way she said it meant I'd got the job.

A job — and I'd only really been unemployed for a week. It was a scrap of a job but it was a bit of income secured. Something to add to the spattering of cheques I got from doing Standardized Patient work and radio ads. Even if it was just bartending and selling tickets, I would be spending time at the theatre. I'd know what auditions were coming up. I'd be there on closing night when everyone got wasted and people fought and hooked up for the first time. I'd spring to mind when people were casting. I'd go to more shows, improve my craft by observation and osmosis.

THE YEAR AFTER I graduated from theatre school in Corner Brook I was in two plays. *Grease* and a play about the seal hunt. The one about sealing toured around the Atlantic provinces for a few months. I played the daughter of a fisherman who died on the ice. I got to ride a school bus through Nova Scotia, New Brunswick and Quebec with real actors, people who mostly just act for a living, who've been doing that for a long time. We ate chili together and shared hotel rooms. I didn't have many lines but I had a big moment: I learned about my father's death on my wedding day. I walked downstage towards the audience, emoting. I wore a white gown that smelled like basement and held a bouquet of plastic flowers against my chest. Wires stuck out of the bottom of the stems and I had to be careful they didn't get caught in the dress's crocheted sleeves. Every night I stood at the edge of the stage and let my eyes go blurry with tears. To make the tears I thought about visiting my cousin Gabrielle in the hospital after she was flung off the back of her drunk boyfriend's dirt bike. She had to ring a buzzer to get two nurses to help her out of bed when she needed the bathroom. Sometimes I felt guilty about using the memory; it wasn't even a good script.

I would remember hearing the nurses coaxing her behind the bathroom door, her half-eaten tray of hospital dinner, *Big Brother Canada* playing on the TV above the bed. People had paid to be in those seats. A real actor could make art with a bad script. Gabrielle would never know. At the edge of the stage in Halifax and Moncton and Quebec City I couldn't see the audience's faces but I could feel the energy coming off people. Some nights I felt a wall of boredom, some nights it worked. I believed I was going to spend the rest of my life driving around the Atlantic provinces touring shows, probably a lot of them mediocre, eating chili and sleeping on top of scratchy motel bedspreads. I was fucking excited about it.

But when I got back to St. John's, I found it hard to get in with the close-knit theatre and film crowd. I had people on Facebook and Instagram from my university class who'd moved to Toronto to pursue acting. That's the phrase they used, "to pursue acting," or, worse, "to pursue an acting career." Some of them were doing fancy commercials or had roles in important plays. One girl was in a new CBC series about time travel.

I still did some small things, my friends were always asking me to be in their short films. I was on a list for voice acting and every couple of months I'd get a call to record a radio ad for a local business. I did ads for a convenience store chain, a labour union, a bridal parlour, a tanning salon.

I also did Standardized Patient Testing gigs at the hospital, where you help train student doctors by reciting a list of symptoms and having them guess what's wrong with you. It's supposed to help them develop bedside manner. You don't have to be an actor to do it, they'll give pretty much anyone the job, but I received a lot of compliments about how believable I was.

You get paid more if you tick "yes" to "invasive" exams. I did a pelvic exam and insertion-of-the-speculum session once. There were eight student doctors in the room taking notes while one eased the speculum into me. They were all wearing paper masks over their mouths; my family doctor never wore one of those to do a pap. The student slowly cranked the speculum open, paused, and then did one extra, unexpected crank. I sucked in a breath and he looked horrified. One of the other student doctors looked away. When I left that day I asked to be removed from the invasive exams list but went back to clarify I would still do the breast exams.

ONCE I GOT into the swing of it I loved working at the theatre. I loved working alone. I loved wearing the swipe card that let me into every room in the building. I couldn't help feeling a bit important wearing the lanyard with the swipe card.

I started every bar shift by getting the grey metal cash

box out of the safe. I counted the money and did inventory, unloaded the dishwasher and moved tabs on the lighting board around until the room was dim and atmospheric. Just before people started arriving I'd put on some music and plug in the string of white Christmas lights that were thumbtacked along the outside of the counter.

I started being able to gauge which nights people would stick around after the show and if it was a wine or a beer audience. At the end of the night the two tech guys would come down and let me know they'd set the alarms upstairs and were leaving the building. When the last drinkers climbed into their cabs, I'd turn the music down. I tried not to be frightened by my own reflection moving on the framed posters across from the bar. I concentrated on getting through the end-of-the-night tasks without thinking about the cavernous space above me. Everyone agreed the theatre was haunted by a multitude of ghosts. When I got the job my grandmother told me her grandfather had helped build the theatre and died by falling off the roof.

"So he'll be looking out for you," she'd said.

Normally I didn't mind being alone in the theatre in the daytime. The morning of the dance recital, I was planning to call my mom at the end of my shift and tell her about the cops. But when everyone cleared out, I started thinking about Holly coming home and finding her bedroom torn apart, her hard drive gone. She would think we'd been robbed. I did a half-assed job of closing up; I stomped the pizza boxes down into the recycle bin and didn't unload the dishwasher. I jogged back to the house.

As I turned the corner onto my street, I slowed and tried to calm my breathing. The unmarked car that had been lingering outside when I left the house wasn't there, but I worried it might circle back. I wanted to be composed if I had to interact with the cops again. The small parking lot was empty except for the familiar cars that always parked behind the nurses' union. No one was smoking outside the church.

I let myself into the house. Holly's shoes weren't in the porch. I called out to her anyway but there was no answer. I closed the living room curtains. I checked the back door; it was unlocked but undamaged. How had they opened it? Maybe they had a tool or maybe Holly had left it open, sometimes she smoked on the back deck. I locked it.

I went up to Holly's bedroom. Snot and Courtney were sleeping in the sheets the cops had torn off her bed and left on the floor. Which asshole did that? The young one, probably. Probably his mother did his laundry for him. I scooped up my cats and closed the door on the cops' mess.

THREE

That fall had been cold, by September you couldn't go around the house on Patrick Street without a second pair of socks. On a day when Viv and I were both off, we got the bus out to Kelsey Drive. We wanted to nail a blanket over the doorway between the living room and kitchen, to stymie a draft that came in through the windows in the front of the house and swept through the whole downstairs.

At Home Hardware, we stuffed a couple of handfuls of nails in our pockets and bought a window insulation kit. Viv had gone to court over a coffee-table book on rooftop gardens a few months before and we'd made a pact to never shoplift anything with a barcode again. Unless we really wanted it. We walked back along Kenmount Road, stepping into the scabby strips of grass between car dealerships and fast-food restaurants to let people power-walking to work at the big box stores pass us. We waited at the light by the Halloween Spirit for four lanes of traffic to stop so we could cross over to the Value Village side of the road. The air was cold, and thick with exhaust.

Viv pointed out an inflatable pumpkin strapped to the roof of the Halloween Spirit. It was at least eight feet tall. An orange light flashed inside the undulating fabric. A thick cord ran from the pumpkin's base down the side of the building and in through the steel double doors on the front of the warehouse.

"Look at that. How much do you think that costs?" Viv said.

"The pumpkin? To buy?"

"To run it. Like, there's the electricity, and I think there's a steady flow of air being pumped in there too."

"Kyle Patterson works there."

"Holy shit, I almost forgot about Kyle Patterson. Doing what?"

"Driving a skid-steer."

"How did he get that job?"

"I think he worked there last year. It's seasonal. I guess he has some kind of special licence, maybe?"

"Just for Halloween?"

"For Halloween and Christmas — it turns into the Christmas Superstore after Halloween. He gets kept on until spring to clean the place out after Christmas."

At Value Village, we found a light blue wool blanket with a silky hem. We picked it because it was thick and wide enough and because we liked the colour.

At home I stood on a chair in the kitchen with a nail

between my finger and thumb, using the side of my hand to hold the corner of the blanket in place. I tapped the first nail into the moulding over the doorway. Viv passed the next nail up to me. When I got to the middle of the doorway I hopped down and scooted the chair over. Mike and his friend watched from the couch as I climbed back onto the chair and lifted the blanket to the opposite corner of the door frame, blocking their view. Viv handed me the final nail and I drove it in, cracking the white paint on the moulding. I stepped down and moved backwards to take in my work. Excess blanket hung down in a ruffle on the right side of the door.

"It's kind of like the curtain at the theatre," I said.

"It makes it darker in here," Viv said.

"We'll take it down in the spring." I went to the fridge and slid an open bottle of white wine out from under a bag of wilted spinach. Normally we would be able to see Mike and his friend from where we were sitting at the kitchen table; with the blanket up we could just smell the weed and hear the mumble of their conversation under the music.

"Are we going to the Rose?" Viv asked.

"We could stay here and hang out with the guys," I said. "We could do the window kit."

"I want to go," Viv said, emptying the last of the wine into my glass. "Finish this and we'll get dressed."

It was warmer outside than in the house. A wave of fall leaves scuttled down the hill around us. When we got to the Rose the guy at the door held my hand and drew a big smiley on the back of it in permanent marker. I could smell the fumes as soon as he uncapped the marker. The tip was wide and soft; he pressed it into my hand so firmly that black ink bubbled out of the sponge.

The bar was crowded and clammy. I kept losing Viv. I saw her dancing in the front and shouldered my way up there. I moved through the spread-out crowd nodding along in the back, into the denser, swaying crowd closer to the stage. The front was all girls who'd thrown their jackets into a pile on the floor by the PA. At indie shows girls dance with each other in the front and the guys in the band make eyes at them. It's different than at punk shows, where girls get elbowed out of the front.

I found a spot by Viv and concentrated on doing my one dance move in time to the beat — arms at my sides, head bowed, chest thrust forward, hips jutting side to side. I watched the bassist's tapping foot and tried to move with it. Between songs the guitarist asked if someone could bring him a beer; I went to roll my eyes at Viv about it but she was gone. I stood on tiptoe and looked towards the bar. I couldn't see her but I made my way back there anyway, the wall of bodies closing behind me as I went. I hauled open the door to the bathroom, startling a group of girls gathered around an upturned palm of pills.

"I'm just looking for my friend," I told them and let the door swing shut.

I found her outside, smoking with Holly.

"Holly came!" Viv said.

Holly smiled at me. "You look cold."

I'd left my jacket inside. Holly was wearing the

wide-legged jeans with the ragged hem and a silk, tiger-striped zip-up under a jean jacket. I felt silly in my tight dress.

"I was just looking for Viv." I turned to Viv. "I didn't know where you went."

"Just out here," she said, handing the cigarette back to Holly.

That night Holly stayed at our house. She slept in the freezing living room with her coat on. In the morning I passed by the living room and saw she'd pulled the folded quilts and crochet throws we piled on the back of the couch over herself. Her head was resting on a decorative pillow and her feet were sticking off the couch. She had on one powder-blue sock with a filthy sole, the other foot was bare. Her sleeping face was turned towards the door. I realized I was holding my breath, afraid of her waking up and seeing me. I left the doorway.

I went to the kitchen to make coffee and feed the cats. I moved around as quietly as possible, cringing when I had to pull the French press out of a jumble of dishes in the drying rack. I took the cat food out of the cupboard and the animals started mewling. The smell of tinned meat farted out of the can when I peeled the lid back, bringing my hangover to life. Meat water sluiced around a pale pink puck flecked with brown. I whispered "shut up, shut up" at the cats as I spooned the oily meat into their bowls. For a while I sat by myself in the quiet kitchen, scrolling through social media on my phone, exhaling hard through my nose to drive out the smell of cat food. The days were shrinking. The sun hadn't been up for long, washed-out yellow light streamed in the window.

When Viv came down I poured her a coffee and we talked quietly about the show. Who we'd talked to, how much we drank, did even one woman or person of colour play? No! Except, oh yeah, the bassist in the first band was a woman, right, but just her. All white people. Almost all cis dudes.

Mike came crashing down over the stairs, his footsteps loud in the hall before he arrived in the kitchen. I checked the time, twenty to eleven. He was going to be late for work at Long & McQuade.

"Is there coffee?" he asked.

Viv put a finger to her lips. I held up the French press.

"Holly's sleeping in the living room," Viv said. "A new friend."

He took a travel mug out of the cupboard. "I'm not taking the last of it on you?" he asked.

I shook my head. "All good."

"I think the lid for that is in the second drawer," Viv said.

Mike put the mug on the table and I filled it for him. He lifted his jean jacket off the back of my chair.

"I'm late," he said, and left with the uncovered mug. A couple of seconds later the front door slammed. We heard the couch creak on the other side of the newly installed blanket. We listened to Holly's footsteps crossing the living room.

"Hi," Viv said when Holly lifted the blanket. "Did we wake you?"

I got a mug and poured Holly a cup of coffee from the bottom of the French press. It was lukewarm and silty.

"I'll make a new pot." Viv took the cup from me and dumped it in the sink.

Holly sat down. "Thank you, I'm not really a morning person."

"It's almost eleven," I said.

"That's morning," Viv said, even though we both usually got up at dawn.

Me and Viv were going to an anti-austerity rally at Harbourside Park that afternoon. We were going to bike down but Holly wanted to come so we decided to walk.

"It's kind of a long walk," I said, as we laced up our sneakers in the front porch.

Viv said, "They cut the subsidy for the helicopter that flies food to Labrador. And they were talking about closing public libraries. Do you know about Muskrat Falls?"

"I definitely want to go," Holly said.

On the front step I turned my back to them to lock the door. The sky was bright blue but it was cold. On the way down Patrick Street, Viv explained how the Muskrat Falls hydro dam would poison Lake Melville with methylmercury.

"You've heard of Grassy Narrows?" Viv asked.

Holly told us she was from Ottawa, had been living in Montreal and moved to St. John's to do a master's in Gender Studies at MUN. She'd taken a basement apartment up behind the mall without realizing how far away it was from everything. Neptune Road. The bus never came on time, or sometimes it showed up ten minutes early and just went on if no one was at the stop.

"It's really hard to find a one-bedroom place here," Holly said.

"It's not really a rental city see," Viv told her. "Or town I guess. It wasn't built that way."

It was a smaller rally compared to the ones that we'd been to in the spring. There'd been a rash of big rallies in April and May, right after the provincial budget was announced. The unions showed up to those with speakers on tall spindly legs and played "We're Not Gonna Take It." Hundreds of people gathered at the Confederation Building and chanted "Hey, hey! Ho, ho! The levy's got to go!" The *Telegram* flew a drone overhead. Me and Viv watched the footage later and saw ourselves pumping signs we'd been handed in the air while someone from the St. John's Status of Women's Council talked into a megaphone.

This time, the last speaker was finishing as we arrived at Harbourside Park; the crowd was redistributing itself and moving into the street. We walked three abreast, chanting slogans that had become familiar over the past few months. "Shut Muskrat Down!" "Can't listen, can't lead! Dwight Ball, resign!" The atmosphere at rallies in St. John's was boisterous, almost joyful. No one got arrested for protesting in St. John's. Not like in Labrador, where cops were sent up in hordes to violently arrest Land Protectors.

After the day of the small rally, Holly slept on our couch all the time.

Viv was always saying, "You can't take a cab home, it'll be twenty bucks."

Often Holly slept until two in the afternoon, when the sun finally found its way over the houses on the opposite side of the street and into our dim living room. Her book bag was permanently slouched against the couch and her school books were always stacked on the coffee table between empties and weed crumbs.

Viv started talking about finding a place for the four of us, somewhere that wasn't so drafty.

"With four people, in a better-insulated place? Our bills will be so cheap. I can't afford another winter here," she said. "They're saying electricity rates are going to triple in the next two years."

"Because of Muskrat Falls?" Holly asked, dipping a chip in the guacamole Viv had made and set in front of her. Viv nodded.

I wanted to bring up the unopened window kit but I left it.

IN OCTOBER, JOANNA SPENCER, one of my co-workers at the theatre, had held a rock opera movie–marathon fundraiser at Eastern Edge Gallery. I'd thought it was strange that Viv agreed to go with me. It wasn't her kind of thing, and I probably wouldn't have gone either, except I was trying to make friends with Joanna. I knew her from school—we'd worked on a couple of projects together at Grenfell and gone to the same parties. In the three years since we'd finished school, her first short film had played at a festival in B.C. and she got funding to make the second one through a competitive first-time filmmakers' program that set you up with equipment and helped you find a volunteer crew.

I'd heard she was applying for money to make a feature about two women in an outport community: one works at the convenience store and the other is married to the owner. The employee is having an affair with the owner and in the second act the women learn they share a father. In the final act, the employee confesses about the affair and the women have a physical fight before reconciling. Joanna told me she thought I'd be a good fit for one of the roles but she didn't say which one, or how big of a part. The rumour was that things were looking good for the funding.

"It's supposed to be like gritty realism about rural life," I told Viv.

"She's from town, though, isn't she?" Viv's mom was from Roddickton, a tiny community on the Northern Peninsula.

"Yeah, but I feel like she has family somewhere around the bay?" I said. "I'm not sure."

Viv rolled her eyes at me. I wanted to remind her that she also grew up in town but I kept my mouth shut.

I'd heard cover at the fundraiser was ten dollars, or five with a costume. I let Viv borrow my sky-blue fleece bathrobe with the melted sleeve and she wore it over a pair of jeans and a bulky knitted sweater. She sat on the bed while I tore things out of my underwear drawer. I wanted to wear this frilly slip I got at the Salvation Army. I was pretty sure I'd seen it somewhere recently.

"Joanna Spencer pierced her own nipple at a party once, I was there."

"Holy fuck." I clamped my hands over my breasts.

"Well, she started to." Viv took a slug from her tall can of beer.

"Viv! Stop, that turns my stomach."

"Do you want to wear this bathrobe?"

"No, it's fine. I've got another bathrobe." I gave up on the slip and got an even rattier fleece bathrobe off the floor of my closet. This one was lime green and covered in grey nubs of dryer lint. "My aunt gives me one of these for Christmas every year."

Viv left her empty beer can on the overturned milk crate I was using as a bedside table. Downstairs, Mike was sitting at the kitchen table noodling on an unplugged electric guitar.

"We're going to this movie marathon thing at Eastern Edge now," Viv called down the hall to him.

"Cool," he yelled back.

Holly was in the living room FaceTiming with someone in Montreal. She had a pair of hot-pink earbuds plugged into her laptop. We called goodbye at her as we put our sneakers on. Holly glanced up and smiled, waving without taking the headphones out.

"That's just Viv and Stacey leaving," she said to the screen.

Viv and I were both wearing hip-length fall jackets, and the bathrobes fluttered around our thighs as we made our way down Pleasant Street. The air was warm and there were greasy smears of fall leaves on the sidewalk. It had snowed once but it hadn't stuck around long.

"Joanna said I could read the script, she asked me to

read it," I said, "for feedback. I feel like that's a good sign. She wouldn't do that if she wasn't seriously considering offering me the part. Do you think? I mean it might not ever be produced, but who knows."

"So you're networking," Viv said.

"No, gross."

"You are, though. That's why you want to go to this thing."

"I would never use that word," I said. "Anyway that's not why I want to go to the thing, they're showing *Jesus Christ Superstar*."

I threw my head back and sighed. I could see craters in the moon, the sky was full of bright, pinprick stars. I wanted to point out to Viv how clear and beautiful the night was but I was too annoyed with her.

"But that's the motivation for going, to talk to Joanna Spencer about this part you want."

"I can talk to her anytime, we work together."

"You're so defensive," Viv said.

AT THE GALLERY, me and Viv bought cocktails with bits of herbs floating in them and sugar on the rim of the ribbed plastic cups. There weren't many people there when we arrived. It was easy for the big space to feel empty. People were sitting crossed-legged on the floor and *Tommy* was being projected on the wall. There was a card table in the back with a restaurant-sized tub of Neapolitan ice cream, a dish of maraschino cherries sitting in their fluorescent syrup, a can of spray whipped cream and a few bottles of sprinkles. Joanna Spencer was behind the sundae table accepting handfuls of change and giving out Styrofoam bowls and plastic spoons.

At another table Christie Fleming was painting people's fingernails. She had a huge collection of half-used-up polish bottles spread across the table. Johnny Howse was sitting across from her in a folding chair, his hand flat on the table between them.

"Are you going to the sundae bar?" Viv asked.

"When I finish my drink. Let's say hi to Christie, you know Christie, right?"

Christie was brushing a pale coat of forest-green paint on Jordan's thumb.

"You're getting your nails done," I said. Jordan turned to look at me and Viv without saying anything; it felt like we'd interrupted a private conversation. I regretted inviting Viv down to the gallery. I'd hoped Dana, my co-worker and a friend of Viv's, would be there; she'd said she was going to go.

"Yeah! Five bucks, it's a steal, are you going to do it?" Jordan asked, suddenly warm.

"We're going to do a glitter top coat over this," Christie said.

"Not for me. I think it's a fun idea, though." Viv picked up a bottle of clear polish with hearts in it and shook it.

"What about you, Stacey?" Jordan asked.

"Maybe I'll circle back, I definitely want to go to the ice cream bar. I just wanted to say hi."

Jordan picked a top coat with star-shaped sparkles in it. Eventually Viv and I walked to the bar and ordered a second round of mixed drinks. We stood by the door in our matching bathrobes, watching people gather in front of the movie with bowls of ice cream.

"After this drink we can go," I told Viv.

"Don't you want to talk to Joanna?"

"No."

"Did I make you feel weird about it? I'm sorry."

"I thought it would be more fun here, I'm sorry," I said.

"It could be fun, if there were more people," Viv said. "The only good part of this movie is that Tina Turner scene, the rest is basically filler."

"I'm glad I didn't wear the slip."

"We came down too early," Viv said. "I bet it'll be really on the go later."

We crunched up the ice in our glasses and dropped the empty cups into a big recycle bin by the door. We hadn't been there very long but the wind had come up and it was colder outside. I balled my fists inside the sleeves of my jacket then shrugged them into the synthetic warmth of the bathrobe.

"We should've taken our bikes," I said.

"I have to tell you something," Viv answered.

"Yeah?"

"I think me and Mike might get our own place."

"Okay." I tried not to let my feelings show on my face.

"We didn't plan it, we just saw a place."

"Yeah, it's okay. I mean obviously, it's okay. It's nice. For you guys to do that."

"You and Holly could find a place, though, there's lots of two bedrooms right now." We were rushing because of the cold, the bathrobes streaming out behind us.

"Right, yeah. If Holly wants that."

"I love living with you, obviously."

So this was why she came with me. To tell me. And probably Mike knew. When he called out from the kitchen he knew we were going to talk about this. I thought it was always me and Viv talking about Mike but of course, of course, she talked to him about me too.

"I'm sure Holly will want that. Who else would she live with? She doesn't know anyone here. I actually saw a nice two-bedroom spot, I'll send it to you. On Coronation Street, it's cheap and there's a backyard," Viv said.

"You've been looking for a while?"

"We were looking for something for the four of us. We just didn't see anything. You know there was nothing."

"Sorry."

"Unless it was like out by the mall."

"It's really okay."

"This place is just really cheap. And there's a jam room."

"I know, I get it. I'm sorry."

Viv pulled me into her in the middle of the sidewalk. "It's not going to change anything."

I shrugged out of the hug and kept walking.

"You're going to come over all the time," Viv said. "Right? You'll come over?"

"I know, I'm okay." My chest was burning. "Look at the moon."

FOUR

In junior high I used to go to all-ages shows in the church hall by my house. At one of the shows the singer of a band called Sewer Standoff got duct-taped to a chair. The bassist walked in a circle around the singer, wrapping tape around his torso and the back of the chair. Then the bassist dragged the chair across the room and set the singer in front of the drum kit.

The wiener who'd organized the show was yelling about scratching the waxed hardwood floor. The bassist knelt and wrapped tape around each of the singer's calves, strapping them to the front legs of the chair. The singer could still bend his elbows — he held the mic up to his right shoulder and craned his neck to scream into it for two songs. At the start of the third song he kind of jerked around for effect and knocked the chair over.

The band kept playing and some older guys in the front

righted the chair. Three of them lifted the chair up over their heads; the crowd pulled away like a tide going out. But then someone passed the mic up to the singer and he started screaming along with the music and the crowd rushed back in. The older guys bounced the chair in the air, lurching the singer back and forth, and the crowd yelled along.

I was standing beside Candice Walsh and we were both shouting the words. When the mosh pit threw us together her big boobs would smoosh against my arm and we'd smile at each other like "what can you do?"

Then the chair came careening down. Somehow there was time for everyone to move out of the way. At first the band didn't notice that the singer had fallen. For a moment he was on the floor with the music rumbling over him, the crowd gone still around him.

When the band stopped, first the drums then the bass and guitar, one of the older guys held up a hand and told everyone to "back the fuck up" and then "get the fuck out." In the parking lot people were saying they saw blood, someone said he'd stopped breathing.

It wasn't dark yet; the sun was sinking on one side of the horizon and a pale moon was visible in the sky across from it. It was one of those strange times when you can see dark pits in the moon's face even though the sky is still bright. Someone said the cops were coming and people ran to stash beers behind the dumpster on the far side of the building.

There was a narrow driveway leading up to the church hall and the ambulance got stuck behind a stream of parents' vehicles. The siren wow-wow-wow'ed as clumps of kids piled into back seats and their parents' cars made tight U-turns to head back down the hill. I stayed and watched the paramedics carry the singer out on a stretcher. He was alive but there was blood all over his face. One of his bandmates walked alongside the stretcher going, "Oh my god, man, I'm so sorry. So, so sorry, dude." The paramedics were stone-faced.

That night when I got home one of the guys who'd been hoisting the chair added me on MSN Messenger. Jordan Nolan. He was in two popular bands. Tear Gas and Bad Guys. Viv had sewn a silkscreened Tear Gas patch on the back of her favourite fluffy pink sweater.

"It's ironic," she'd explained.

I'd sat with her while she sewed the patch on with dental floss. It took two hours. There was thread in her mom's sewing tin but dental floss was cooler. She kept pinning and re-pinning the corners to keep the patch from puffing away from the sweater.

"The sweater was always ironic, that I would wear a sweater like this is ironic, the patch makes it more ironic," she said.

I bit the round pearly tip of one of her pins. "Yeah, I get it."

I was jealous of the sweater. Jealous that she'd come up with the idea to sew the patch on it.

Jordan Nolan was one of very few people I knew as a teenager who had a full sleeve tattoo—it was of a space monster slapping a tentacle down in the middle of New York City. He was done high school, maybe he dropped out, but he was at least eighteen, I was around thirteen.

Sup, he messaged.

Not too much, you?

I was worried you got hit with that chair at the show

Nope

Cool, have a good night

I was using MSN Messenger on my parents' computer in their bedroom. The window was open, I could smell the lilac tree in our neighbours' backyard and the dirty socks in the laundry hamper next to me. I didn't want the conversation to be over.

Thanks for checking that's really nice of you

No problem

I stared at the green icon next to his name, trying to think of something else to say, until he slipped into the offline column. Then I ran downstairs to call Viv on the phone in the kitchen. She had updates about the Sewer Standoff incident and I let her ramble through them, savouring my news. It ended up the singer was pretty much fine, he had a concussion and three of his front teeth got knocked out, some broken ribs and a broken arm. We weren't allowed to rent the hall anymore. Sewer Standoff was planning to use a grainy photo of the singer taped to the chair for the cover of their new demo.

"Jordan Nolan added me on MSN."

"What?"

"To see if I got hit with the chair."

"He likes you," she said and I knew it was true.

The next day he sent me *Sup* again and told me he was helping organize a show to buy the singer dental implants. We chatted for weeks: I told him about studying for my first midterms and he told me about working at Tim Hortons. When I found out I was going to be playing the part of the Cheshire Cat in the school production of *Alice in Wonderland,* he wrote, *They should have made you Alice*.

I told him I wanted to be the Cheshire Cat, it was a more interesting role. I fantasized about inviting him to see me slinking around the stage in my black turtleneck and leggings with whiskers painted on my face.

Sometimes he'd say, *Too bad you're so young*, and I'd say *Why?* and he'd say *Never mind*.

One day I walked to his apartment. It was a long, hot walk from my parents' house. He told me there was a silver Boler trailer in the driveway, one of his friends was living in it. When I turned the corner onto his street the sun bounced off the trailer like X marks the spot. He met me at the front door and led me to his room. All of my friends lived with their parents; it was my first time being in a house where young people lived without adults.

His room was a skinny rectangle. There were two short bookcases filled with video games and DVDs. On top of one of the shelves there was a big glass tank with a lizard in it. Like most of my friends, his walls were papered with photocopied posters for local punk shows. Lots of shows I'd gone to and ones from before I started going to shows.

He sat on the futon. It was clearly his bed folded into a couch — there was a fitted sheet on it and two full-size pillows were tossed to one end. I sat down beside him. He used the remote to un-pause the movie he was watching. It was *Twister*. He was wearing cargo shorts and there was a white square of gauze taped to his calf.

"New tattoo," he said. "Do you want to see?"

"Yeah."

He lifted his foot onto the couch and peeled back a corner of gauze to show me a palm-sized tattoo of a wolf with three heads. All three mouths were dripping blood. I couldn't think of anything to say.

"It's still kind of puffy. It's shiny 'cause there's Vaseline on it. Do you want to touch it?"

"Does it hurt?" I asked.

"Yeah, a bit."

The skin beneath and around the tattoo was shaved. I put a finger in the slippery Vaseline and pressed down.

"Ow," he said, flexing his calf. I pulled my hand back.

"Sorry."

"It's okay, I told you to touch it." He smoothed the gauze over the tattoo and rubbed the tape, trying to get it to re-adhere.

"You're really strong," I said. "Like your leg is really strong."

Sunshine was streaming into the room. People on TV screamed.

"I've kind of been working out. Here, feel my bicep."

He tensed his arm, the one with the octopus-monster on it. I squeezed it and let my hand drop back onto the couch.

"Dave got the dental implants, they're so white you can tell they're fake," he said.

"Oh, that sucks."

"Anyway, I have to work soon," he said.

"Okay."

"So you should probably go."

I stood up.

"I'll message you later," he said from the couch.

I closed his bedroom door behind me. In the porch his cat rubbed against me as I tied my sneakers.

Another time I asked him to go to a movie with me at the mall. *The Hitchhiker's Guide to the Galaxy*. He'd already seen it once and wanted to go again. We arranged to meet in front of the movie theatre in the afternoon. I wore a pale blue T-shirt dress with a polo collar. Another long, hot walk from my parents' house.

I arrived first. I tried not to stare at the escalator. I looked at the blinking lights that showed the schedule of movies for that day. He was five and then ten minutes late. Finally I recognized the flop of brown hair that hung over his eyes coming up the escalator. There was no line at the ticket counter. No line at the concessions. He bought an extra-large pop and I didn't buy anything.

It was cool in the theatre. I leaned into his arm and he didn't move it away. I put my hand on the armrest and waited for him to take it but he didn't. The movie went on forever. When it was over I waited outside the bathroom for him to pee.

As we were leaving the theatre someone shouted his name. We both turned and four of his friends came walking towards us.

"Hang on a sec, just wait here," he said and jogged over to them. The group started walking back to the food court and he turned and yelled, "I'm gonna get a ride with these guys."

"Does she need a ride?" I heard one of them ask.

"Do you need a ride?" he called.

"No." I knew he didn't want to offer.

He turned around and slapped an arm around his friend.

On the walk home I imagined what it would have been like to go with them. Crammed into the back seat with the windows down and the music blaring. I tried not to look sad, because I thought they might drive past me.

ONE NIGHT AT PATRICK STREET, Viv organized a dinner party for her cousin Heather's birthday. I carried extra chairs up from the basement and Viv rolled out taco shells in the galley kitchen. We turned up the heat.

Heather arrived first. After stomping the snow off her boots in the front porch she went straight to the kitchen and started pulling packets of spices out of the cupboard. I leaned against the counter drinking gin and soda. Soon all four burners were in use. The girls reached around each other, stirring and sprinkling, flicking the oven light on and off.

When I asked how I could help Viv said, "Just keep us company."

Mike came back from the Great Canadian Dollar Store with helium balloons Viv had asked him to pick up. When he let go of their curly strings they swayed up to the high ceiling and bounced there.

People arrived in waves. A second load of chairs had to be carted up from the basement. On the way up the steps with a chair under each arm, I noticed I was drunk. During dinner someone brought up Jordan Nolan. Going to court for possession of child pornography. I swung around and tuned into the conversation. I googled and a VOCM article popped up. It was very short and there was no picture but the age was right.

"Are you sure it's him?" I asked. "The same Jordan Nolan?"

"I heard it's him," Michael White said. "It's sad, his life is so fucked up now."

"I haven't seen him in years, I thought he moved away," I said.

I flipped my phone over and googled again. There was nothing besides the VOCM piece. It was just four sentences long.

"Who told you it was him?" I asked.

Michael White's mouth was wide open, he was about to take a bite of taco but he laid it back on his plate.

"My sister, she knows his ex-girlfriend. It's sad, that girl is super fucked up. She got him into drugs and they just like spiralled into all this fucked-up stuff. He was really in love with her." He picked up the taco again.

It was never this warm in the house; we'd turned the heat up to twenty and now it was packed with people, plus the oven had been on.

"I don't think it's his fucking girlfriend's fault, what are you saying?" I felt people on the opposite end of the table turn their attention to us.

"I'm just saying, maybe if he didn't get into drugs, some people can't handle drugs." Michael shrugged, unfazed by how vicious I'd gotten with him.

I got up from the table and walked to the kitchen. I dumped my drink into the sink and filled my glass with water.

"We're going to do the cake now." Viv had followed me into the kitchen. She lifted the cake off the bottom shelf of the fridge. She'd made it the night before, coconut pistachio with swirls of rosewater frosting. She'd worked twelve hours on her feet and then come home to make this for her cousin. I watched her stab candles into the cake.

"Can you get the lights?" she asked.

I flicked the lights off and found my seat again, across from Michael White. Viv stepped out of the kitchen, the candlelight flickering on her face. We all sang. Someone turned the lights back on, and slices of cake were passed around.

ON THE DAY we viewed the house, Holly met me at Patrick Street. We were walking fast because Holly has very long, skinny legs. I'd worn an outfit I save for job interviews and had pulled my hair into a tight ponytail. Holly had on leopard-print leggings and a baggy windbreaker.

"Do you want to smoke some weed?" she asked me.

"Right now?"

Holly looked at her phone.

"We have time," she said.

I didn't want to smell like weed at the viewing but I wanted to seem like a fun roommate. All along Water Street and up Queen's Road, I'd been talking about myself, about a Standardized Patient Testing session I had coming up. This one was really like acting, I had to go to the doctor with the intention of telling him I was pregnant but then chicken out at the last minute and pretend to have a cold. The doctor was supposed to suss out what was really going on. The trick would be to seem more distressed than someone who only had a cold.

"Their professor will be in the room," I told Holly. "Or sometimes they do it with a mirrored window. It almost feels like improv; I need to help the student doctor understand the conflict in the scene without explicitly spelling it out."

"This looks like a good spot," Holly answered.

I worried I'd bored her.

We stepped into the alley at the bottom of Tessier Park to smoke. A tall fence built by the city hid the alley from the street, and a thicket of mile-a-minute separated the alley from the rest of the park. After the first puff the bamboo leaves shivering on their stalks behind us started to seem ominous.

Holly handed me the joint so she could show me a photo of the two pit bulls she'd left in Montreal. I brought the joint to my lips again without thinking and inhaled. Holly held the phone in my face: two giant heads with wide grins, the corners of their mouths loose and fleshy, bright pink gums and pointy shark teeth.

I was about to tell her about my aunt's pit bull, Burger, who had to be put down after it bit through her foot when she was mowing the lawn. My aunt thought it got confused trying to protect her from the growling lawn mower; she was heartbroken for a long time after the dog was euthanized. She kept his ashes on the hall table in an ornate tin. Once, I'd pried it open without knowing what it was and some of Burger puffed out and landed in the carpet.

I was going to use Burger to segue into a more recent dog anecdote, about how my co-worker's German shepherd bit through my hand. But Holly had started her own story.

Her dogs had been kidnapped. She'd tied them to a bike rack outside a Couche-Tard on Saint Catherine Street.

"Have you been to Montreal?" she asked, bending to scrape the joint on the ground before putting it back in her pocket. "We should get going now."

"I went once, to visit Viv." I followed her out of the alley.

"So you know Saint Catherine, right downtown, there's people everywhere and this was the middle of the afternoon."

She'd run in to buy a pack of Halls and when she came out the dogs were gone. She looked up and down the street, turning around in a circle like a bewildered cartoon character.

"But you got them back?" I asked.

"After like a week and a half."

"How?" I asked.

She'd papered the city with flyers of the very photo she'd shown me. Two big grins. Each poster was fringed with fluttering, easily rippable tabs offering her phone number. It had been a nightmare figuring out how to format the posters. And making a careful incision on each side of every phone number with a pair of hair-cutting scissors took hours. She printed and photocopied the posters at the library for twenty cents a page. Whenever she finished a shift at the tattoo parlour where she worked as a receptionist, she walked along Saint Catherine showing people the poster.

"That worked?" I was almost jogging to keep up with her long strides.

"I felt ridiculous, I didn't think it would work but I had to keep doing it because I had to do something," she said.

"Right," I said, and I did understand, because Snot had gone missing before. He didn't come home for three nights. Courtney sat in the window and mewled for his brother. I woke up every couple of hours and stood on the back deck in bare feet shaking the treats and yelling his name. One of my neighbours opened her window and shouted, "Can you shut up, it's four in the morning."

I yelled back, "My cat is missing," and more quietly, "you miserable bitch."

Eventually Holly got a text from a guy who said his ex-girlfriend had the dogs. She met him in a Tim Hortons and they drove together to the building where his ex-girlfriend lived.

"Were you scared?"

"No, that's why I met him at the Tim Hortons first, to make sure he wasn't," she paused, "scary, I guess."

"What about when you got in the car?"

"I trusted him, after talking at Tim Hortons," she said. "You just have to listen to your gut in those types of situations."

She'd waited outside while the guy talked the ex-girlfriend into handing over the dogs. The building where she lived was a skyscraper, the kind where you have to crane your head back to see the top of it. The guy told Holly his ex lived on the fourteenth floor. He took a missing poster into the building with him. Holly counted the windows up to the fourteenth floor. There was a row of twelve windows across the fourteenth floor but for some reason she felt like she knew which one belonged to the girlfriend. There were two forest-green lawn chairs on the balcony and, squinting, it looked like maybe there was a dog bowl on the ground. Maybe she imagined the bowl.

There were white curtains in the window, ones she recognized from the Ikea website. The cheapest curtains on the Ikea website; she'd thought about ordering them herself. They were white with a pattern of periwinkle or burgundy forget-me-nots.

Holly was watching the curtains, willing them to move and show the dogs, even one of them. Eventually the smudged glass doors on the ground floor of the building opened and the man walked out with her dogs straining at their leashes. She got out of the car and knelt on the sidewalk and they licked her face.

When her story ended we were still a couple of blocks from the house. I tried to think of a way to introduce my German shepherd incident and maybe show her the scar on my hand but we ended up walking the rest of the way in silence.

We turned down the short street and found the light

blue house at the very end. When we got to the front door Holly reached up, her skinny wrist sticking out of a baggy cuff, and knocked. I didn't notice the coughing woman then. I noticed the front of the house was draped in the shadow of the church.

"Should I ring the doorbell?" Holly asked, her finger already on the button.

The landlord was probably in his fifties, wearing a fleece vest over a checked dress shirt. He looked like a high school teacher.

"Welcome, welcome — sorry, I was in the basement," he said, ushering us into the house. In the photos on Kijiji the walls were all white. Now they'd been painted over in cheap rental-company colours, pale green, mocha, too-bright yellow — all chosen to conceal dirt. They were blemished with smears of plaster. The only furniture in the living room was a coffee table and a leather armchair with a rip on the seat.

The floors were the same as in the ad, though — soft wood, varnished that golden colour you see in people's cabins and full of half-moon dents. The same wood framed the windows and doors — wide yellow planks with dark whorls. I saw Holly run a hand over the glossy finish on the door frame.

"I can get you the records from the Newfoundland Light and Power but I have to tell you the girls who live here, they really went to town last winter. I think you could bring the bill down by at least fifty bucks a month if you just wore a sweater, or . . . I don't know what they were doing. This is some more storage here." The landlord pulled open a door to a crawl space filled with rusted tins of paint.

The house had been renovated by someone who didn't know what they were doing. On the ground floor, there was a strange, stunted hallway between the bathroom and living room. The doors were hung on a slant and some of them were sawed off on the bottom so they could close properly, leaving a space that leaked cold and light.

In the kitchen, the vinyl flooring was peeling away from the walls, revealing a subfloor covered in years' worth of dusty grime. But there was a big window. The cupboard doors were made from the same wood as the floor in the living room and slathered in a varnish that made them glow.

"This is a great kitchen," Holly said, like she was reassuring the landlord.

He didn't ask us any questions about references or credit history. Holly had shifted the dynamic somehow; he seemed eager to please us.

"Oh absolutely, look at the counter space." The landlord opened a cupboard and quickly shut it. "The girls will clean that out before you move in."

When the landlord flicked the light switch in the stairway nothing happened. We all looked up at the light fixture, a bell-shaped, frosted glass shade with a crack in it.

"The girls didn't change the lightbulb," he said. We followed him up the dark stairs to see the bedrooms. Both rooms had big windows and one of them had a window that opened onto the kitchen's roof.

Holly looked at me and I nodded.

"We're definitely interested, we'd love to take it." Holly held her hand out right above the landlord's belly. It looked like she might karate-chop him and he seemed to grab hold of it in self-defence. They were shaking on it. I felt a sinking feeling, the end of an era. I wished Holly wasn't coming back to the house with me so I could tell Viv about it on my own.

"I have some other people lined up but you seem like really nice girls, like a good fit."

Outside it was dark. The days were short and it got cold at night; the afterglow of summer had fizzled out weeks ago in a snap of frost. The weed had worn off and left me tired.

"I love all the windows," Holly said. "It's a lot of space for the price, don't you think?"

"Yeah."

"You didn't like it?"

"It'll be better without their stuff."

"We don't have to take it," Holly said. "If you don't like it."

"We should take it, we can always break the lease," I said. "It doesn't have to be permanent."

"Yeah, I mean we could look at other options but this is affordable and downtown," Holly said. "He doesn't mind about pets."

"We'll look around again in the spring," I said. "There'll be more stuff in the spring. At least we'll be right around the corner from Needs," I added as we walked by the glowing storefront, trying to offer something positive. One of the few pay phones left in the city was anchored to the front of that Needs.

I thought of when Viv and I were in junior high and we used to play with the pay phone in Churchill Square at lunchtime. We'd eat sitting on the curb outside the strip mall and then go in to use the bathroom. The phone was on the bottom floor, tucked behind the stairs next to a travel agency. We would try to guess which 1-800 numbers led to phone sex lines. We found that almost any vaguely dirty combination of a three-letter word followed by a four-letter word led to a sex line. 1-800 WET DICK. 1-800 HOT PUSS. 1-800 GOT WOOD. Me and Viv and sometimes Kyle Patterson would come up with numbers and test them. We'd gather around while one of us dialled — shielding the caller from passersby and watching for the security guard who sometimes came by saying, "Clear out, clear out, if you're not buying anything, clear out."

The slippery silver buttons would clunk back into the phone when you pressed them. 1-800 BIG TITS. Reaching out into the void. 1-800 GAY GIRL. If the number you dialled wasn't a sex line the phone would bark an angry dial tone in your ear. 1-800 SEX COCK. Got one! When you landed on a sex line a pre-recorded message poured out of the receiver, a woman purred a monologue about masturbating, interrupting herself with increasingly stern instructions to enter your credit card number. Every part of the pay phone was greasy: the phone's handle, the cups that rested against your ear and chin, the heavy coil that bound the receiver to the phone box, even the graffitied sides of the phone.

Just across the tiled hallway from us, middle-aged women would meet for lunch at the bistro-style tables outside Living Rooms. They broke apart tea buns and used plastic knives to smear butter and strawberry jam from little packets on the doughy insides. Sometimes they looked up when we got rowdy, howling with laughter, shrieking suggestions, wrestling over the receiver. 1-800 HOT HOMO.

We listened for as long as the pre-recorded messages lasted. Sometimes there would be different options to choose from: girls with accents, young girls, angry girls, gay girls, sometimes gay guys — we cycled through, listening to each performance in full. We huddled, shoulder to shoulder, next to a rack of pamphlets advertising tropical vacations. We listened to all the free parts of every phone sex line we could find. We stayed tuned in to the chorus of panting voices for as long as possible; I'm here, I'm horny, this is what my body looks and feels like, these are the things we could do together, pay me.

FIVE

I went with Holly to look at the bedroom set. The week before we moved in to the house by the church, the landlord texted to say the current tenants had asked him to let us know they were selling their furniture. Holly had hardly brought anything from Montreal; the place she'd sublet on Neptune Road was furnished.

Natalie Swanson opened the door in leggings and a tank top with a lotus flower on the chest.

"You can keep your shoes on," she told us. She was eating handfuls of trail mix from a Ziploc bag she carried up to the bedroom. Her hair was pulled into a high ponytail.

"We're leaving the province on the first so if you're interested in buying the bedroom stuff that would be great for us," Natalie said. "We're not taking anything, so if you like the armchair or the kitchen table ... we're going to sell everything really cheap, and you can just have the chair."

There was a rock-climbing poster on the back of the bedroom door; I hadn't noticed it when the landlord showed us around. It was a photograph of a woman in a harness clinging to a dusty orange cliff, one knee raised up above her hip. Natalie's sports bra hung off the doorknob by a strap. Weights that had been lined up on the dresser when we viewed the apartment were strewn across the floor.

"Do you mind if I try it out?" Holly asked.

"Go for it," Natalie said.

Holly took her shoes off and sat on Natalie's comforter, bouncing a little before swinging her body around and reclining. She put her head on the pillow. Natalie and I stood at the foot of the bed watching.

"Mmm," Holly said and shut her eyes. "Oh, it's really comfortable."

"Yeah?" Natalie said, sealing the plastic zip on her trail mix.

Holly opened her eyes and sat up, resting on her elbows, and looked at us like it was already her bed. Like Natalie and I were guests in her bedroom.

"I don't have cash, can I e-transfer?" Holly asked.

"Of course."

Holly put her feet on the floor and reached for her sneakers. "So you and your roommate are moving together?"

"Yeah, I just found out I got into grad school, I was wait-listed so I didn't know until the last minute if it was going to work out. Do you want that chair downstairs?"

On the way out, we passed the room that would be mine in a few days. I tried to imagine falling asleep in there, with Holly in the next room instead of Viv and Mike.

"I think we've got living room furniture covered, don't we, Stacey?" Holly said.

"We're good for chairs," I said.

ON OUR LAST day at Patrick Street, Viv and I scrubbed the baseboards, kneeling on either side of the living room with our backs to each other. Mike was allegedly sweeping out the upstairs bedrooms. Viv and I divided up the other jobs: Viv dealt with the litter closet and I cleaned the bathroom. It was the third house we'd moved out of together.

When we were almost finished, we cracked the windows and propped the front door open with a chair. Soon it would be time for that last walk-through. The final load of odds and ends had been packed into laundry baskets and reusable Sobeys bags.

Viv mopped out the basement. We fought over who would do it, both insisting the other had done enough.

"Do you think it smells like litter down here?" Viv asked.

"No, do you?" I was sitting on the dryer.

"I'm not sure, kind of." Viv twisted the handle of the mop so that all the strands of the mop head twirled together in the straining basket. I took the bucket upstairs and dumped the dirty water out the kitchen window into the backyard.

Viv stood on a chair and used the back of a hammer to haul out each of the nails holding up the wool blanket in the doorway between the kitchen and living room. I gathered it off the floor and pressed my face into it: it smelled of cooked food. The silky bottom was covered in dirt and cat hair where it'd swept across the floor.

I picked used Lysol wipes off the floor and dropped them into the garbage. "I think we have to change the bag."

We had already pulled the mouth of the garbage bag up out of the bucket because it was so full. Inside, a pair of my mud-soaked running sneakers teetered on a pile of almost-empty sauce jars Viv had cleared out of the fridge. She tugged on the edge of the garbage bag and I held the bucket. We wrestled the fat bag out together, the jars clinking against each other.

I held the opening of the bag in two fists as the contents relaxed out of the shape of the garbage bucket. I knotted it shut. Viv took the bag down the hallway, stooped by the weight of it. I raced through the empty dining room and living room to open the front door for her.

Once Viv had dumped it, we stood on the step for a moment, looking at the pile of garbage bags slouched against the telephone pole in front of our house. Soon to be someone else's house.

HOLLY AND I rented a panel van from U-Haul. I can't drive, so I sat in the waiting area while Holly spoke to the guy at the counter. When she finished filling out the forms, she spun around and held the keys up for me to see.

In the van she said, "Any requests, roomie?" before tuning the radio to Hits FM.

But then she couldn't find the parking brake. We sat in the cab of the truck for a long time while Holly fucked around with different levers and knobs sticking out of the base of the steering wheel. She bent and looked under her seat.

"Is it that thing?" I pointed to a lever.

"No." She said it like I was stupid. "That's for the window wipers."

One of the U-Haul employees was walking a couple over to the storage sheds behind our van.

"Want me to grab that guy?"

"No." Her voice was even harsher this time. The dance music flooding out of the dash was loud inside the van. I watched the U-Haul guy pop open the padlock on the front of a storage shed. Just as the door to the shed opened, the van started rolling. Holly had released the parking brake.

"Alrighty! Should we get coffees at McDonald's?" she asked, like she'd never snapped at me.

On the way down Kenmount Road, people bawled their horns at us every time Holly changed lanes. She would hold a middle finger up in the rear-view and then look to me for validation.

"Assholes," I said.

When she glided through the red light at the intersection by Carnell's Funeral Home, I involuntarily sucked in my breath.

"What?"

"The light was red."

"It was yellow. You're making me nervous, can you relax?"

I was silent until we pulled up in front of Patrick Street. We moved almost an entire house's worth of my furniture into the new place by the church. Then we went to pick up Holly's smaller load—all she had was a few suitcases, some books and a mirror.

Holly'd been living in a basement apartment below a bungalow with white plastic siding and a cracked drive-way. She led me around the back and down a short set of cement stairs. She'd gathered her suitcases by the door. I felt a surge of sympathy for her when I took in the lonely little space she'd been living in. The kitchen and living room were one room separated by a counter crowded with a dusty collection of wine-making equipment.

"That's not mine, it's been here since I moved in," Holly said.

I noticed a variety pack of instant oatmeal on the stove. I had assumed Holly was naturally skinny, like she just had a high metabolism, but now it occurred to me that she might not be eating very much, either because she was broke or depressed or both. She pulled open her bedroom door; the head and footboard of her single bed were flush with the walls. She stepped on the striped mattress in her sneakers and lifted a mirror off the wall.

"This is mine, I got it at Value Village and took it home on the bus." She grinned over her shoulder at me.

It was about four feet by four feet in a gilded frame, with a twisted wire on the back to hang it. Holly and I each took a side and walked the mirror out of the apartment, up the stairs and down the driveway.

"I guess we should lay it flat," I said when we got to

the van. We flipped the mirror so it reflected the grey sky and the bottom of our chins. We slid it into the van. On the drive over I tensed each time we rounded a corner.

When we got to the new house, I hopped out and opened the front door with a key we'd picked up from the landlord the night before. There was a woman in the living room with a mop. Natalie Swanson's roommate. She was sporty too; she wore sneakers with jelly soles and yoga pants.

"Sorry, I'm almost done," she said.

"It's fine," I said.

"Thanks for cleaning," Holly said.

We brought the mirror in first, leaving the van doors wide open and all Holly's suitcases on display. I was aware of the people clustered around the church's fire exit but Holly didn't seem to care. It was starting to rain — a few drops landed on the mirror and shivered themselves into rivers.

"I actually wanted to mention something to you guys, maybe Natalie already told you," the woman said as we edged into the house with the mirror. "We have this really great deal on internet, you could just take over our account if you want, then you don't have to wait for a modem and we don't have to fuck around with cancelling it."

"I've never heard of that," Holly said. "Taking over an account."

"You just call and say you're Natalie's roommate and you want to be added to the account," the woman answered. "Honestly, it would be great for us because then we wouldn't have to pay the cancellation fee. But it'd be good for you too, it's some kind of student deal they don't offer anymore, really cheap."

I left Holly to deal with the internet conversation. I lifted the mirror by myself, my arms fully extended so my fingers could clamp around either edge, and started walking it up to Holly's room.

"We don't need the account number?" I heard Holly ask.

"I'll write it down for you, hang on."

I set the frame down every couple of steps. It wasn't heavy but my arms were aching. In Holly's bedroom there was a nail sticking out of the wall above the long, low dresser she'd bought from Natalie Swanson. I lifted the mirror and slid it down the wall, lifted and slid, lifted and slid, until the wire on the back caught the nail. I could still hear Holly talking to Natalie Swanson's roommate downstairs. I leaned in and used my sleeve to rub away the streaks the rain had made on the glass. I stepped back and watched my breath disappear. Holly got the nicer room.

THE LAST CHORE on moving day was a trip back to Patrick Street to load up the cats and a sad, sunken loveseat that had been cycling through communal households for years before it ended up with us. A '70s-style velour couch with skinny mustard and forest-green stripes, coated in cat hair. The insides had given up. When you sat on it the cushion collapsed onto the floor and the wooden frame banged against the underside of your knees. The surprise of hitting the floor was like missing a step.

The cats were light enough to stay afloat on the cushions, though, and Snot had often spent the afternoon there. Guests who didn't know about the couch ended up with sore tailbones and a matt of fur on their pants. We posted a photo online offering free delivery with the caption "Still some life left in this relic" but no one had responded.

Viv and Mike helped me load it into the van and then we all threw the garbage bags from the heap outside the house onto it. Viv helped me catch the cats and force them into the large carrier I used for taking them to the vet. I put them in the front footwell and sat with my sneakers on top of the carrier, knees against my chest. Courtney was shivering in the back of the carrier, Snot kept rearranging himself and letting out awful howls.

I thought Holly would be annoyed about the trip to the dump because it was all my stuff. We were being charged for mileage on the van on top of the rental fee and gas. But she was in a good mood. Before we left Patrick Street she handed me the ripped corner of a flyer with a string of numbers written below the Shoppers Drug Mart logo.

"That's the account number for the internet. Do you want to call and switch it over? That girl said we can just add ourselves to their account," Holly said.

"It's Rogers?"

"Yeah. She said to say, 'I want to take responsibility for the account,'" Holly said. "You have to say that."

We hadn't discussed whose name the bills would be in. I'd already e-transferred the damage deposit to the landlord because Holly had been working the day it had to be sent. But Holly was driving, so I googled the Rogers number and dialled. I was on hold all the way to the dump. I put the call on speaker and dropped my phone in the cup holder, letting elevator music fill the cab. Every few minutes Snot wailed. I kept catching flashes of his yellow eyes through the ventilation holes in the side of the carrier.

At the dump I laid the phone on the back bumper of the van while we flung bags of garbage over the railing into the dumping port we'd been assigned. Dumpsters that got emptied throughout the day were lined up at the edge of each port; beyond them a sea of garbage was being raked by bright yellow backhoes. Seagulls circled overhead. I saw the blur of at least three grey rats swimming through the trash directly below us.

I climbed over the couch, leaving footprints on the velvety cushions. I got behind the armrest and pushed it to the doors of the van. Holly lifted the opposite end up onto the rail. I gave it a good, hard shove. The creaky frame rocked on the rail for a moment before sliding into the dumpster. I hopped out of the van and looked over the rail at that last piece of me and Viv's life, half submerged in puffy garbage bags.

It wasn't until we were almost back at the house that the music cut out and a voice came through the speaker, "Hello." The Rogers employee had a Newfoundland accent. I assured the woman I was a roommate of Natalie Swanson's, that we lived at the same address, and I said, "I'd like to take responsibility for the account." I heard the clicks of a keyboard on the other end as I recited my date of birth and social insurance number.

AFTER THE YOUNG cop had finished reading me the warrant, he'd flipped back to the front page and laid the papers on the table. I pushed my chair back and stood up.

"Oh, you can stay seated. Sergeant Hamlyn is going to ask you a few questions now."

"Can I call my mom?" I'd asked.

"No." The young cop stood up. "You're going to need to answer some questions for Sergeant Hamlyn right now."

The bald cop sat in the chair beside me, splayed his legs wide and flipped open a notebook. I couldn't believe he was taking notes by hand. I crossed my bare legs, my spandex shorts riding up.

The other cops were pacing around; the front and back doors kept opening and closing, letting cold air into the house. My arms and thighs were covered in goosebumps; thin hairs stood up in the puckered skin.

"Whose name is on the internet account?" the bald cop asked.

"Mine," I said, rubbing my arms.

"Is it password-protected?"

"Yes."

"Who has access to the password?"

"My roommate."

"That's it? Just you girls?"

"Yeah."

"No one else?"

"No."

"No one else? You can definitively say no one else has the password?"

"It's on the fridge."

"Here's a tip for you, keep your internet password private. Keep all your passwords private. We're going around to schools teaching them that."

I tried to keep the irritation off my face.

"People don't realize. And another thing we tell them, don't put anything out there you don't want traced back to you. The second you hit save or send or upload or whatever — it's out there just waiting to come back at you like a boomerang."

"I know."

"I don't do the presentation, Sergeant Leslie Brace does the presentation. The presentation is . . . the kids really respond to it."

He flipped back through the notebook.

"And this Holly, she's not on the lease?" he asked.

"She's on the lease."

"How long have you known her?"

"A few months? Less than a year. Neither of us are involved in this, whatever you're looking for."

"How do you know her?"

Over the bald cop's shoulder, I saw the young cop come down the stairs with my laptop under one arm and three or four flash drives dangling from his fist by their lanyards.

"What's he doing with that?" I asked.

"If I were you, I'd want to co-operate as much as possible."

"I'm co-operating, I'm just —"

"Because things can go a couple of ways here today. We all want this to go smoothly."

The flash drives had been in a compartment of the jewellery box I kept on my dresser. The jewellery box was filled with precious junk, letters from when Viv lived away, trinkets from friends and lovers, my grandparents' wedding photo. The flash drives bounced on their cords with each step he took.

ON OUR FIRST night in the new house I'd sat with Holly while she unpacked. She unzipped a suitcase, took out a wrinkled sheet and flapped it twice in the air. I helped her stretch the bunched corners over Natalie Swanson's mattress. The sheet was cream with butter-coloured roses on it. I was surprised by her soft, feminine sheet set.

"There's hangers here," she said when she opened the closet door.

"Take this down?" I asked, my hand poised over the rock-climbing poster still stuck to the back of her door.

"Oh yeah, please."

The glossy poster ripped in the middle as I tore it down. I picked four carefully rolled balls of tape off the door. I scrunched the poster up with two hands and tossed it into the hallway. Then I sat on the bed and watched Holly feed hangers into the necks of baggy sweatshirts.

"You know those bookcases people make with milk crates and zip ties?" Holly asked.

"Yeah." Viv had one when I first met her.

"I'm going to make one of those, I just need to find some milk crates. I'm getting my books shipped down here eventually — it's so expensive, though."

She held up a black velvet dress with wires in the bodice and a crinoline under the skirt. It was strapless; she wrapped the ribbons sewed next to the armpits around the hanger's hooked neck.

"No one dresses up here," she said.

"Not really, I guess."

"I miss dressing up. I'll probably never get to wear this here."

The heavy dress swayed in the closet.

"You could wear it," I said, leaning forward to smooth her creamy sheets with my palms.

"It's not fun if no one else is dressed up."

"Heather Canning dresses up."

Holly flipped the top of the suitcase closed on the rest of her dresses and unzipped a compartment on the front of it. She took out a plastic clamshell filled with thumb-tacks and laid it on the windowsill. Then she took out a tin and popped it open. It was full of skinny Polaroids taken with an Instax camera. She started pinning them to the wall in a cluster by the mirror.

The photo on top of the sloppy pile left in the tin was of Holly and a guy in bed topless. The guy was looking into the camera and Holly had her eyes closed, lips pressed against his cheek. It was so clearly staged, with her looking demure and adoring. It grossed me out. And Holly had become moody. I felt like she didn't want me in her bedroom anymore.

"I'm not connected to the internet," I said. "I'm going to get the password."

I'd left the scrap of flyer with the internet information on the kitchen counter earlier. The lights were off downstairs but it wasn't dark; a streetlight's swan neck curved over the dumpster, making it look like a prop in the middle of an empty stage. My things were strewn around the living room. Except my mattress—Holly had helped me push the mattress up over the stairs and into my room.

The couch was in the centre of the room and the cushions were piled next to it. The legless tabletop was face down in front of it. I felt a pang of pride that I'd put all the table screws into a Ziploc bag and taped them to the table's plywood underside. The chrome legs were bound together with sticky knots of packing tape.

I turned on the light above the stove and leaned in under the hood. I typed the string of letters and numbers Natalie Swanson's roommate had written in red pen below the Shoppers logo. The first time it didn't work. I spent a few frustrating minutes swapping out "5" for "S" and "0" for "o."

Me and Holly had ordered pizza earlier in the day. I wriggled a cold slice out of the box in the fridge. It was only 8:30 but I was exhausted from moving. I walked into the living room with my pizza, noticing the stiffness in my butt and thighs. I put two of four cushions on the couch and sat on it. "Incorrect Password" kept popping up on my phone's screen. I typed the numbers in again, extra slowly. Snot poked his head around the corner of the basement door and crossed the room, meowing at me. When he hopped into my lap I rubbed the glossy fur between his ears. Courtney was stretched out in the cool bathtub, sleeping. There was music coming from Holly's room, something gothy. I tried turning the Wi-Fi off and back on again.

I was mourning all the systems Viv and I had developed. There was an agreed-upon plan for which sauces went in the fridge and which went in the cupboard. Other people's mail slid between the posts of the banister. An understanding about how long the litter could go unchanged and dishes could be left in the sink unwashed. Borrowing books from each other without asking, but checking before wearing one another's clothes. Clean towels stacked on the stool by the bathtub. A psychic connection that let us know when we could wander into each other's bedrooms and when one of us wanted to be alone.

Finally, the curved bars in the top corner of my phone filled in.

I heard coughing so loud it sounded like it was right there in the room with me. I dropped my phone and clamped my hands down on Snot. I looked around the room and then out the window. That was the first time I saw the hacking woman at her post on the bottom of the fire escape. She had curly grey hair that hung down her back and wire-framed glasses. It looked like she was staring straight into the living room at me but I could tell by her expression that she was lost in thought.

SIX

As a child, I spent a lot of time with my grandparents. They often took me for long drives, usually to visit my grandfather's relatives who lived around the bay. I sat in the middle of the back seat, swaying back and forth as we drove the old road to Spout Cove. The old road is two lanes that wind past fish and chip shops and Chinese take-outs that closed down when they built the new road. The windows of the restaurants were smashed and covered with wet-looking plywood. My grandmother kept saying, "It's nice to take the old road and see the fall colours."

My great-aunt's house was on the side of the highway, across from a cliff that skidded into the ocean. There was a car parked in the tall grass beside my great-aunt's house, so we parked on the cliff side of the road.

"Be careful of cars getting out," my grandfather said. "They won't expect you."

I got dizzy looking over the guardrail at the drop into the choppy bay. My grandmother took my hand and we crossed the highway together. We walked between the house and my great-aunt's silver Sunfire to the back door.

"I should come out here and mow the grass on the weekend," my grandfather said. He called out to my great-aunt as he opened the unlocked door.

My great-aunt didn't stand up when we came in. She was wearing a turtleneck sweatshirt with a polar bear in a swirl of glittering snow on the front. I couldn't imagine a grown-up woman picking out that sweater for herself. Her shoulders curled beneath the fabric, dark purple veins snaked over her knuckles and up into her sleeves.

"Get the girl a bun," she said.

She pointed to a see-through bag of raisin tea buns on a white Styrofoam tray. My nan pulled out a chair across from my great-aunt, saying, "Have a seat, Stacey."

My grandfather ran a finger along the window ledge, checking for moisture. He walked into the hallway and bounced on the floorboards, flicked open the fuse box and looked over the rows of switches.

"How are you holding up, Alice?" Nan slipped the tip of a steak knife into the folded bit of red tape sealing the bun bag.

"What's that?"

"I said, how are you holding up?" The plastic bag twirled open in my grandmother's hands.

I heard the gentle knocking first.

"Gerard comes by every evening, bless him," my great-aunt said.

A bumping with no rhythm to it.

Nan turned her head towards the sound. "What's that?" The question was directed at my grandfather, out in the hall.

"Gerard comes by most evenings." My great-aunt raised her voice. She ran her hand back and forth across the vinyl tablecloth.

My grandfather, my nan and I listened. The sound was something soft battering itself against a hard surface.

"It's coming from the stove," my grandfather said, and he crossed the hall and pushed the living room door open. My nan put the buns on the counter and followed him. My great aunt watched her leave the room. I could see she was used to being out of the loop, she accepted that things would either make themselves clear eventually or not, it was out of her control. The thumping quieted and then returned in short urgent bursts.

I heard my grandfather in the other room saying, "It's a bird in the stove."

"I'm going to go see, I'll come right back," I told my great-aunt.

"Go ahead, get yourself a bun," she answered.

In the living room my grandparents were leaning over the wood stove.

"Shut the door and open the window, Stacey," my grandfather said.

"A bird in the house," my grandmother said.

"Louise," my grandfather said.

I twisted the brass door handle until it clicked and rushed to the window. At first I couldn't get the window open; I turned the lock on top of the frame and pushed but it didn't move.

"That's alright, give it another shove," my grandfather said.

I pushed as hard as I could and the window screeched open. I kept both arms over my head, holding the bottom of the window in case it slammed shut. I watched over my shoulder as my grandfather knelt in front of the stove and opened the door. A bird covered in ash shot out, smacked into the wall and fell behind the couch. It left a streak of grey ash on the pink carpet.

I let go of the window and backed away, watching to see if it would start to slide down. My grandmother and I looked into the dark space between the back of the couch and the wall. The bird had a cream-coloured chest and a brown body. A brown so bright it was almost gold in places. Its claws were curled up; somehow I knew that wasn't good.

"Dead," my grandmother said.

"Could be stunned." My grandfather stood, leaving the stove door open. He pulled the sofa away from the wall and scooped the bird up. My grandmother watched. He carried it across the room and dropped it out the open window into the tall grass growing alongside the house. He wiped his ashy hands in his corduroys.

"He might wake up yet." My grandfather put his hands on my shoulders and turned me towards the door. "Go keep your aunt Alice company."

In the kitchen, my great-aunt was still sitting at the table, looking at my empty chair. My grandmother was vacuuming the carpet in the other room. My grandfather walked through the upstairs, checking for leaks.

"There was a bird in the stove." I stood next to my great-aunt and said it loudly. "Flew down the chimney."

"A bird in the house is bad luck," she told me.

"It flew into the wall but it might wake up yet," I said, mimicking my grandfather.

"Have a bun," she said. "I bought them for you."

Before we left, my great-aunt Alice gave me a decorative spoon with a photo of the Pope on the oval tip of the handle. She'd bought the spoon when the Pope visited Newfoundland in 1984. She told me he'd held her hands and kissed her head.

"The Pope," she said.

"Imagine," my nan said.

Great-Aunt Alice pointed out the spoon on the decorative spoon display hung above the kitchen table and Nan took it down. It left an empty slot in the otherwise-complete spoon display. I would have rathered the spoon that said "Florida" on the handle and had a cartoon image of a palm tree bent over a pink sunset, or even the Nova Scotia one with a bright red lobster on the tip. But I could see that leaving an empty slot in the front of the spoon display was a sacrifice.

"I'll keep that safe until you're old enough to take care of it," my nan said. She polished the Pope's face in the hem of her shirt and put the spoon in a zippered pouch inside her black leather purse.

On the way out to the car she patted her purse and said, "That's a very special gift, you'll appreciate that when you're older."

"This car is going to rust out here," my grandfather said, kicking the tire of my great-aunt's Sunfire. All the grass beneath the car was yellow.

I scanned the side of the house for the bird but it had sunk down into the grass or flown away.

DANA, WHO I worked with at the theatre, told me there was a joint production between Newfoundland and Ireland happening, a feature-length film. A period piece with a huge cast. They were hiring people in both locations. Dana told me I should audition.

"You look Irish, you've got the dark hair and blue eyes," she said. "Worth a shot. You're busty, they love busty in a period piece."

That same night Viv's friend Clara made a post on Facebook offering free headshots — she was trying to put together a portfolio to get gigs like wedding photography and grad photos, to make money to support her real art. She used that phrase, "my real art."

For her last real art project she'd installed cameras in queer couples' homes and recorded them 24/7 for a week to capture moments of everyday intimacy. She made looped videos of things like a man laying a plate of fried eggs and toast in front of his partner. Or someone calling out from the shower to ask their partner to bring a towel. She projected five loops of small domestic gestures like that on the walls of the gallery. Audio of people saying "I love you," "What should we have for dinner?" and "Can you bring me a towel?" lapped over each other. Viv thought it was sappy and probably staged but I liked it.

When I messaged Clara about the headshots I hadn't quite admitted to myself that I was going to try for the historical feature.

"You could use them, though, she's good at portraits," Viv said.

Clara took my picture in her apartment above the record store on Water Street. I was nervous walking over there and sweated into the armpits of the white shirt I'd chosen for the photos.

"We're going to have to wait for that to dry," she said. She made a French press of coffee and we smoked a joint at the kitchen table.

"That's enough," she said. "I want you to be relaxed but I don't want you to look stoned. Do you look stoned when you smoke weed?"

"Sometimes." I passed her the joint; I liked her ordering me around. "How did you meet Viv?"

"I think at Decadent Squalor in Montreal," she said. "Come stand over here in this light."

She took my arm and moved me in front of the window. Then she put her fingers in my hair and tousled it.

"I thought you met in Vancouver," I said.

"Maybe it was Vancouver." She was close to my face; she had crow's feet around her eyes.

She had a fancy digital camera set up on a tripod. She dragged it across the room and got between me and the window. She directed me to lift and lower my chin, to smile with and without teeth, to cross and uncross my arms.

"Look sad," she said. "Not sad but solemn, we want a range of emotion."

Gabrielle and I struggling to regain a normal rhythm of conversation when the nurses helped her lower herself back into the bed after using the washroom. The smell of hospital, piss and plastic and floor cleaner. A single wool blanket scrunched up at the foot of her bed. The sky a brilliant, cloudless blue outside the window.

"Nailed it," Clara said. "Now laugh."

The guy who auditioned me for the joint production was younger than me and from Toronto. I'd heard there was a woman from the Ireland side of production in town for casting, so I'd been expecting a woman. There was a video camera on the table in front of him.

"You can stand there." He pointed to a strip of green painter's tape on the floor. "I'm Ryan."

"Nice to meet you," I said from the painter's tape.

"I'm going to turn this on now, if you're ready." He pressed down on the button. "Stacey Power reading for Aideen."

"Sorry, are you going to read Cathleen?" I asked him.

"Yup. Just begin whenever you're ready, we're rolling." He nodded at the video camera.

Earlier in the week they'd sent me three pages of a scene where Aideen's younger sister tells her she's pregnant out of wedlock. In the office at the theatre I had printed a set for me and a set for Viv. We'd practised in her kitchen while she greased her hands with olive oil and sculpted chickpea burger batter into patties. Viv kept telling me not to go overboard with the accent. Ryan read

Cathleen's lines without any emotion. The scene was done in about five minutes.

"Let's do it one more time, and this time read Aideen a little angrier, she's pissed that her sister fucked up." Ryan took a sip of coffee from a glass travel mug with a cork lid.

We did the short scene again and then Ryan pressed the button.

"Great, thanks very much for coming down, we'll be in touch."

After the audition I went to Viv's and she took out a Tupperware filled with stacks of cold chickpea burgers.

"How'd it go?" She took two plates out of the cupboard.

I went to the fridge and found a jar of bread-and-butter pickles.

"I hope you're right about the accent," I said.

"Have I ever led you astray?"

Viv ripped the buns open, she laid the patties inside and squeezed swirls of ketchup on them. I stuck my fingers in the pickle water and pulled out three slimy slices to drape over my burger.

"Are we just having these cold?" I looked around the kitchen to see if she had a microwave. "I know what you're saying about subtle is better but maybe those people don't feel that way."

"Yeah, I thought cold. Do you think you did a good job?"

"I don't want to jinx it."

"Don't say anything then," Viv said. "I want pickles too."

❡

THE DAY THEY searched my house and took my things,
I went out after work. Because I had been planning to
go out, and because I didn't want to sit at home alone
thinking about them going through my pictures and text
messages, maybe driving past my house in unmarked cars.
There was still no sign of Holly. I wanted to get wasted, to
wipe everything out of my mind for a little while.

That night, I met Kris at a party on Pleasant Street.

I arrived at the party a bit drunk—I had gin and soda
while I was getting ready, out of a short, amber-coloured
glass embossed with a swirl of fall leaves. From a set Viv
and I had picked out at the Wesley United Church sale.
I tapped the top of the soda can with my fingernail so it
wouldn't spray out. A big glug of gin and then soda up
to the rim. Normally I would play music from my phone
through a shitty Bluetooth speaker while I got ready, but
the house was silent.

I wore a white dress that I'd hung on to for years and
only took out when I got thin. Getting thin was always a
surprise. It didn't seem to have anything to do with my
diet or how much I exercised. Usually I thought of myself
as pudgy and mostly I didn't mind that. But every two or
three years my body morphed, hip bones rose up on either
side of my stomach and muscles shaped like the top of a
loaf of bread appeared on the backs of my calves.

When it happened I felt strong and competent. It felt
like having money in the bank.

When I was thin I would run my hands over my belly in

bed, feeling one curved hipbone then the other, tightening my stomach muscles and poking the skin on top of them. I knew it was a window. Soon the new space between my body and the waistband of my jeans would disappear.

Usually the thin phases lasted two or three months. When I felt a thin phase coming to a close I started skipping meals. But nothing had any effect on the transformation. It was like a spell, something to do with lunar cycles and shifting weather patterns. Or maybe I have an overactive thyroid. Once I found a bald spot the size of toonie on the side of my head. The doctor prescribed me a steroid cream but warned me not to overuse it or it could eat through my skull. For two or three months each evening, I'd sit on the edge of my bed with my head tilted and Viv would part my hair and rub the cream onto the bare stretch of skin.

When I settle back into being chubby — my thighs spreading out on the toilet seat, a bit of pudge hanging out of my bra by my armpit — I'm fine with it. I still feel sexy. People come on to me the same amount, regardless of my size. But on this night, the night after they had presumably started sifting through my hard drive, I happened to be thin and I put on the special dress.

The cats knew I was going out. Snot was turning tight circles on the bed, digging at the comforter with his front paws. He had already ripped a hole in the bottom of the blanket doing that. I'd stuffed the synthetic fluff back in and closed the opening with a bulldog clip. When I pushed him off the mattress he jumped up on the dresser with his brother. Their heads moved in unison, following me around the room.

The white dress had two layers of fabric, a silky layer that clung to my body and a gauze layer that hung loose over it. The top layer had gotten nubbly and there was a cigarette burn. I liked the burn, I thought it gave the dress a sexy Courtney Love vibe. I stood on the lip of the bathtub to look in the medicine cabinet mirror. I steadied myself by holding the shower curtain rod. I twisted my hips in the mirror, admiring how the flare of the hemline made my thighs look.

Snot jumped off the dresser to stand in the doorway of the bathroom. His eyes were saying *don't go don't go don't go*. I stepped down and lifted my glass off the back of the toilet.

"Lie down, Snot, go to bed," I said and finished my drink.

I picked a mascara out of Holly's things and dragged the wand through my eyelashes. I did the top lashes, screwed the tube together and returned it. Then I picked it up again and did the bottom lashes.

The plan was to meet Viv at the Pleasant Street party and then go somewhere else; there was another party and a show at Bar None. Normally I would wait for a text from Viv saying she'd left her place, we'd meet at a midway point and arrive together. But I didn't have my phone so I headed to the party alone with the neck of a bottle of wine in my fist.

I nodded to the coughing woman as I locked my door. She knew the cops had come that morning, she saw their big macho display. I tried to find a reaction to it in her face: judgement or commiseration or even curiosity, but she gave me the same neighbourly nod as always. The night was warm, the sidewalks were wet with melted snow and the air was damp and heavy.

When I got to the party Viv and Mike and Heather were in a tight huddle with a fourth person. A petite woman wearing her T-shirt sleeves rolled up around her shoulders and stiff jeans, big brown eyes. Her arms were thin but muscly, her hair was shaved on the sides with tight curls on top that flopped into her face and a messy ducktail in the back. I could see she was wearing a black sports bra under her white T-shirt.

I caught Viv's eye and she shifted to welcome me into the conversation. I edged into the circle. The new woman looked me up and down and said, "So this is who we've been waiting around for."

"Rude," Heather said and smacked her on the shoulder. The woman kept her eyes on me, daring me to say something saucy back. Viv introduced Kris before I could come up with anything: "This is Kris, she's a poet; this is Stacey, she's my best friend and an actor."

"I don't know if I'd call myself a poet," Kris said.

"Why not? You write poetry," Viv said.

"I work at Ready to Ride. I repair bikes, pedal bikes," she said.

I threw my coat on the post at the foot of the stairs and held up my wine. "I need a glass."

Viv followed me to the kitchen and tried to ask how I was feeling. I stretched up on tiptoe, reaching for the only glass left in the cupboard. Her eyes were too wide. She was high.

"I don't want to talk about that," I said. "And don't tell people I'm an actor."

"Okay."

"Is Holly here?" I asked. "Have you heard from her?"

"I texted her, haven't heard back," Viv said.

"Are you doing drugs tonight?"

"Yeah."

"Do you have more?" I filled the glass to the rim and hid my wine behind the bottles of olive oil and vinegar on the counter.

"Ask Heather," Viv said.

We all got too wasted to make it elsewhere. All night we were finding each other, gearing up to leave, someone was just finishing a cigarette and then someone really had to pee and then we'd be sucked back into the party. Hauled into a conversation or down to the basement where people were dancing to someone's favourite song, handed a fresh beer.

Kris lived around the corner from the party. Ostensibly we left to look for a pack of cigarettes. It was four in the morning and the stores were closed. There were people out front smoking and pissing on the side of the house. Kris's roommate, Frankie Castillo, had wandered up the hill after a drag show. I'd met Frankie in university out in Corner Brook—they were from Belize and had come to Newfoundland to study visual art at Memorial. That night they were wearing a yellow latex dress and a pair of hot-pink boxing gloves.

Frankie was beneath the neighbour's porch light circling the gloves above their head while someone took photos with their phone. People stood behind the photographer, leaning in to see the screen. The group directed Frankie in and out of the light, to the left and to the right, and Frankie obliged.

I felt the little crowd notice me and Kris leaving together. I'd jammed my feet into my boots and left without doing them up. I relished the laces slapping my calves on the way down the steep hill.

In her bedroom, Kris bent over, taking books and papers out of a knapsack. The room was very clean and almost empty. There was an expensive-looking single-speed bike hanging off a wall mount. There was a stack of thin books on the bedside table. *Autobiography of Red* by Anne Carson, *This Wound is a World* by Billy-Ray Belcourt, *Night Sky with Exit Wounds* by Ocean Vuong, *Chelsea Girls* by Eileen Myles. I sat on the bed, pulled the hem of my white dress down to cover the thickest part of my thighs and tried to think what underwear I had on.

"Viv saw Eileen Myles read in Toronto," I said.

"Cool." Kris straightened up, holding the cigarettes triumphantly.

"There's only three in here, though," she said when she opened the pack.

"Still," I said. I'd misjudged the mission. The soles of my tights were stiff with dried sweat, I worried they stank. I had assumed that because a gay girl invited me over she wanted to fuck me, but Kris seemed genuinely excited about the cigarettes.

"Let's smoke one here before we go back. Want to?" Kris said.

"Sure."

We went up a set of stairs and out onto a patio supported by tall stilt legs. Kris opened the door for me, stepped out behind me and then reached back in to flick a light on. The deck was slippery, the wood was dyed dark by disintegrating leaves. I could see into the backyard of the party, a couple of quiet gardens over. Figures filled the kitchen window, arms lifting beers, hands gesticulating.

Kris passed me a cigarette and her lighter; I noticed how much smaller her hands were than mine. Her nails were short and clean.

We smoked in silence. I'd forgotten about the cops for a long stretch of the night. At the party I'd had conversations about Heather's shitty ex-boyfriend and people walking out of the government's library consultations and more arrests at the Muskrat Falls site. When I'd caught myself slurring I realized I'd become too drunk for the serious conversations happening upstairs and went down to the basement where I danced until I could smell my armpits.

On the deck with Kris I felt sober and tired. I still hadn't seen Holly, I hadn't told her about the cops. There was a good chance she'd been home. She couldn't call or message me if she had. I watched people wander in and out of the back door of the party. Close enough to hear me and Kris if we called to them but unaware we were there.

I went home after the cigarette. Kris went back to the party with two beers from her fridge and the last of the smokes. When I got to my house I stretched out across my bed, on top of the covers in my underwear. I couldn't sleep because of the drugs. I kept wishing I'd gone home with someone so I wouldn't have to be alone in this vio-lated house. Every unfamiliar noise sent a jolt through me — *The cats, it's just the cats*, I kept telling myself.

I'VE SLEPT WITH lots of women. And one of them I loved. But even her, Nicola Stevens, we only slept together when we were drunk. We'd find each other when parties were thinning out or when everyone was leaving the bar in clus-ters. Once, at an overflowing New Year's Eve party where the host had covered the floors with ripped-up cardboard boxes, we'd made out in the upstairs hallway. My back was up against the humps of a hot-water radiator.

At midnight I'd gone out to the muddy backyard where people were lighting fireworks and passing around a novelty-sized bottle of Baby Duck with a bent straw bob-bing in the neck. I let Greg Locklear shoot a plastic water gun filled with tequila into my mouth and then Greg and I made out on the side of the shed. I invited him to come home with me and Nicola.

"Definitely, just let me know when you're leaving," Greg said, shoving the plastic gun into the pocket of his bomber jacket, muzzle pointing out into the night.

Back in the house the cardboard had turned to mush. I found Nicola in the kitchen talking to some guy.

"If they smell pee, they'll pee," she was saying. "So you're going to have to really scrub that part of the couch. I don't like chemical cleaners, I use diluted tea tree oil in a spray bottle. Just a drop or two."

I sidled up to her.

"Tea tree oil, okay, and where would I get that?" He was flirting with her.

She was wearing a sparkly off-the-shoulder sweater with a short skirt and army boots. I tugged on the hem of her sweater. The guy didn't acknowledge me at all. She smiled at me but kept talking. "The other thing is the litter box —"

"I scoop every day," he interrupted.

"There's fireworks in the backyard," I said, aware of the tequila on my breath.

"Is it covered? Some cats prefer covered."

I pulled on her sweater again. "Do you want to see the fireworks?"

"And if you can find a sort of private corner, they like that," she said. The guy was nodding.

"It's going to be over soon," I said.

"You guys go on, I'm going to the bathroom, I'll find you out there," the guy said.

When we got outside people were lighting Roman candles plunged in the snow. They'd bend over to light the cardboard tubes with a barbeque lighter and jog away. We joined a loose circle of people passing a joint around. The Roman candles made a hissing noise before spraying sparks and curls of smoke. Bright orange embers hopped on the snow. When the joint got to me I inhaled deeply and held the smoke in until it made my chest hot. I exhaled through my nose and got the spins.

"I think Greg Locklear wants to come home with us," I whispered into Nicola's hair. I thought I said it quietly but I'm a bad whisperer so who knows.

"Why?"

"He told me he did, that he wants that," I said.

I handed Nicola the joint.

"What do you think of that?" I asked.

"It's fine," she said, but she passed the joint on and stomped off into the yard.

When I turned around Nicola was swishing a Roman candle through the air. Her arm arced upwards, shooting flares of light over the fence, then down at the ground. The sparks burrowed into the snow leaving black craters when they fizzled out. People yelled, a combination of warnings and cheering. Nicola spun around and waved her arm back and forth across her chest. A rush of sparks hit the house; some ricocheted off the barbeque and back towards our semicircle.

I didn't feel anything but I slapped my palm against my face. I smelled burnt hair. I knew the smell right away. She dropped the cardboard tube and it spun itself in a lazy circle in the snow, sputtering out the last of its smoky guts. I combed my fingers through my bangs and singed bits of hair fluttered past my eyes. There was a wet spot on my forehead. I poked it and it stung.

"Am I bleeding?" I asked the guy next to me.

He got his phone out of his pocket and shone a light in my face. "A little bit, yeah."

Nicola came up to the bathroom with me. We both leaned into the medicine cabinet mirror. There was a raw pink circle the size of a quarter on my forehead. There were pinpricks of blood inside it that reminded me of the craters on the moon.

"I really didn't try to do that, I promise, I swear, I would never, I just . . . would never."

"My bangs actually look kind of cool."

Later Nicola, Greg Locklear and I ran through streets that were smeared in slush, back to my house. We passed a group of guys with their shirts undone who yelled "Happy New Year!" to us. When we got to the house we were laughing hysterically about how Nicola had wiped out and landed on her ass. I kept trying to shush Nicola and Greg because Viv and Mike were sleeping across the hall from my room, but then I'd succumb to a fit of giggles myself and we'd all be laughing loud together again.

In my bedroom, the see-through pink handle of the tequila water gun poked out of Greg Locklear's jeans pocket. We were all in the bed, kissing, still mostly clothed. I took the gun and pointed it at both of them, waving it back and forth. They opened their mouths. I pulled the sticky trigger, two squirts each. But the gun was almost empty and the alcohol didn't make it to them. Drips of tequila sank into my comforter. Nicola held up a hand for stop. "Don't you have any music, Stacey?" I shuffled on my knees to my desk and flipped open my laptop. I put on some sleazy seventies music. *What a lady, what a night.* I found us a string of condoms in the bottom drawer of my desk.

In the morning I woke up to Greg Locklear climbing over me to get out of the bed. He mouthed "Sorry" when he saw my eyes were open. The bed springs crunched as he moved. The room smelled of alcohol and sweat. He dressed quickly with his back to me. His freckled back and bare ass, the patch of long black hairs on the back of each thigh. I closed my eyes, my mouth tasted of tequila, my teeth were scuzzy. I heard him jog lightly down the stairs, a pause as he got on his shoes and then the front door opening and closing.

Nicola slept for most of the morning. I showered and lay on the couch in my bathrobe until she woke up. She came downstairs in her baggy sweater and short skirt. She'd left her tights upstairs. I sat up and she joined me on the couch. I pulled Viv's flannel blanket over her bare legs.

"I'm so sick," she said.

"Me too." I slid a hand under her sweater and rubbed her bare back.

"It's a new year," she said, looking out the window at the grey sky.

"Did you have fun last night?"

"Yeah."

"Yeah?" I asked.

"It was fine, I would have rathered just us."

She went to the bathroom and I heard her vomiting through the closed door. There were long pauses between the retching. It sounded like someone trying to lift a heavy piece of furniture. I worried again she would wake Viv and Mike. When she came out, her face was so pale that the dark bags under her eyes were frightening.

"I need to go home," she said.

"Do you want some water?" I didn't want her to leave.

"No. Could I borrow some pants?"

I hugged her goodbye at the door and watched her walk through a snowdrift in my jeans.

SEVEN

I woke up the morning after the Pleasant Street party, where I'd met Kris, to the loud beep of the garbage truck reversing. I liked watching the church dumpster get emptied. I stood up and took a couple of dizzy steps towards the window.

Huge metal prongs extended from the front of the truck and slid into handles on either side of the dumpster. The prongs lifted the dumpster up over the cab of the truck, leaving a wet square on the ground where it had been. The metal arms moved up and down, shaking the dumpster in the air above the truck; the plastic lid flew open and garbage rained into the truck's bucket. Then the driver slammed the dumpster back down in the parking lot. The crash made my dresser jump and scared the cats. The coughing woman stepped out of the side door of the church, an unlit cigarette stuck to the wet inside of her bottom lip, bouncing there.

The garbage truck beeped as it backed away from the emptied receptacle and retracted its prongs. The dumpster sat where it had always been. The coughing woman settled into her spot on the fire escape, patting her pockets for a lighter. I heard a key in the front door. Holly's voice in the porch.

I wanted to pretend I wasn't home. To listen through the wall as Holly and whoever she was with found the mess in her room. My legs felt tired going down over the stairs to greet them.

Holly and Dave were unlacing their boots in the wet porch. Holly was wearing a big black hoodie that hung to her knees and black tights. She had a soft guitar case over one shoulder. Dave King played bass and I'd heard Holly was going to play guitar in his new band.

"Oh no — do you have a dish towel or something?" Dave King said as I passed them on my way into the kitchen. There was a cloud of stale alcohol around them, they were just finishing their night.

"Why?" Holly asked.

"There's a dead mouse here," Dave said.

"What?" Holly said. "Where?"

"It was probably the cats," I said. "Where is it?"

Holly was always bringing people over to the house. They didn't make a racket so I couldn't say anything, but I hated having random people there all the time. When I went to make supper she was always at the kitchen table drinking beer with some folk dude. They left empties and beer caps on the table.

I looked under the sink for a J-Cloth; I'd seen some in a bucket of cleaning products the previous tenants left behind. I found the open package and slid a crisp, folded cloth out. When I straightened up they'd both come into the kitchen.

"I'll get it," Dave said, reaching for the cloth.

"It's fine, I can do it. It doesn't bother me," I said.

"Let him do it." Holly snatched the cloth out of my hand and gave it to Dave.

I went to the sink and squirted zigzags of neon green detergent over the dishes.

I turned on the hot water and used steel wool to break apart a crust of oatmeal around the top of a pot. Dave came back in and dropped the cloth into the garbage bin. I heard the mouse's body hit the bottom of the can.

"I need to talk to you about something," I said.

Holly pulled out a chair and sat at the kitchen table. Dave sat across from her.

"I'm exhausted. I'm going to bed, I just need some water," She folded her arms and lay her head down on the table.

"It's important," I said, still facing the sink working on the creamy scuzz in the bottom of the oatmeal pot.

"Okay. Do you mind getting me a glass of water? I literally can't get up."

"It's kind of intense." I wiped my wet hands in my jeans. She lifted her head off the table, her eyes were red. I filled a pint glass with water and put it in front of her.

Holly took a long drink, "What?"

"The cops were here yesterday. Did they call you?"

"No, why?"

"It's kind of disturbing. I had to give them your number, I'm sorry."

Dave King was flipping a beer cap over and over on the tabletop. It seemed dismissive, but maybe he was uncomfortable.

"Jesus. Can you just tell me?"

"They said illegal digital material was transmitted from this address. An image. They took a bunch of stuff—electronics. They took your hard drive."

"What does that mean?" Holly asked.

"You had an external hard drive in your room? A silver thing?" I said. "They took it, I'm sorry."

"Like child porn?" Dave King asked.

"I don't know," I said.

"Oh my god. What the fuck." Holly rubbed above one eyebrow with pinched-together fingers.

"I had to give them your number—"

"Fuck," Holly said.

"It's okay, it's just a mistake. It's going to be okay," I said. "I really think it's going to be okay."

"Someone made child porn here?" Holly asked.

"I don't think they made it. It was transmitted. It might not even be a porn thing. The warrant is over there." I nodded to the living room. "It doesn't really say anything, it's legalese. But listen, is there anything on your hard drive that might be bad?" I tried to make my voice gentle.

"Bad?"

"Something they would consider, like, evidence of cybercrime? Or illegal activity in general? Some kind of image?" I asked. I was waiting for Dave to say something, like, "Maybe I should leave," but he just sat there.

"I'm moving out." Holly said.

"Did the cops say 'cybercrime'? They used that word?" Dave asked. "I'm sure you're not the kind of people they're looking for, they're looking for some sleazy guy."

"Yeah!" I realized I was holding the scrubby in my fist, dripping grey dish soap froth on the floor.

"They said that?" Holly asked.

"Not really."

"What did they say?"

"They said they have to prove we're not the suspects. They said we should think about who might have access to our Wi-Fi." I was careful not to look at Dave while I said the last part.

"I'm going to stay at Dave's until I find another place." She turned to Dave. "Is that okay?"

"Yeah, totally, of course," he answered meekly.

"You don't have to worry because the internet's not in your name. They said that. They really did. The person who owns the internet is the suspect." I tried to keep my voice level.

"Why did they take my hard drive?" Holly asked.

"They couldn't clear it at the scene. They kept saying that it's hard to clear Mac stuff."

"What does that mean? I have no idea what you're talking about."

"Cleared at the scene? I don't know, I guess I don't really know," I said.

"You said this was temporary," Holly said.

"When did I say that?"

"When we came to see the place. You were like, 'We can look for other places.' You didn't like this house."

"You liked it, I moved in because you liked it." My voice went high. "I don't think anything happened here. And it's probably like identity theft or stolen credit card numbers or something."

"Or selling stuff on the dark web like guns or just like illegal swords, like throwing stars or whatever," Dave said.

"They said an image," Holly said. "Did they leave a phone number?"

"Who?" I said.

"The cops?" Dave asked in a quiet voice.

"I was here alone when they showed up. It was scary, like after the Snelgrove stuff. I was thinking about that the whole time. I nearly brought it up but I just wanted them to get the fuck out of the house, I didn't want to drag it out."

"I'm not trying to be mean," Holly said coldly.

"There was a whole swarm of them. All those people who smoke on the corner were watching. You know the woman who coughs in the night? And that man who's sometimes with her — they were watching. Because the cops were like 'We have a warrant, get out of the way' and I just kept being like, 'Why? Why? Why?' in the doorway."

"Jesus," Dave said.

"It was so over the top," I said.

"This situation is just —" Holly said. "Why didn't you tell me yesterday? When it happened, right away?"

"They took my phone," I said.

"My name's not on the lease," Holly said. "I didn't sign anything."

"You're moving out now?"

"I'm not staying here."

"I can't find someone for January. No one moves in January."

Dave was flipping the beer cap again, not looking at either of us.

"We said temporary."

"The most fucking frigid month of year and everyone is broke," I said.

"You're being really unreasonable, I agreed to temporary. Now I have to call the cops about child pornography, now my name is tangled up in that."

"It's not my fault. It doesn't have anything to do with me," I said.

"I don't want to know," Holly said.

"What?"

"If you're involved in this, in any way," Holly said, "I don't want to know about it."

I wiped my hands on my pants, I couldn't believe I'd been washing her dishes.

"I don't know you that well." Holly stood up.

"I don't know anything except what's in the warrant," I told her.

"I'm going to bed." Holly took the warrant and left the room.

"I might be able to help you find someone for January," Dave said, trailing behind Holly. "I can ask, I think some people at my work were talking about moving, they have a shitty landlord, so."

"I'll find someone." I don't want to live with one of your loser friends, I thought to myself.

I turned the hot water back on and moved the tap back and forth, slicing through the gooey lines of dish soap. If Holly had never shown up, Viv, Mike and I would still be padding around our drafty old house on Patrick Street with the wide halls and big windows. I turned the tap off and left the dishes in the sink with suds dissolving all over them.

I went to the bathroom, picked Holly's glasses off the edge of the sink and dropped them on the floor. When the lenses hit the tiles there was a clink like wine glasses meeting across a table. I was going to leave them on the floor for someone else to accidentally crush, but then I brought my foot down on them. I felt the arms snap out of place and a metal hinge dig into my instep. The glass scratched across the grouting and cracked.

I listened to Holly and Dave moving overhead. Her bedroom door was open. The conversation had gone so differently than I'd anticipated. I lifted my foot and pressed the tender spot where the hinge had dug in. I couldn't hear what Holly was saying; even her tone was difficult to make out. I heard footsteps on the landing, she was coming down.

I darted into the living room and grabbed my coat out from under theirs on the couch. In the porch I stepped in a pool of melted slush and then stuck my wet feet into my sneakers. I could hear her on the stairs, I left with my coat unzipped, pulling the door quietly shut behind me. I had tears in my eyes, maybe from my stinging instep.

The coughing woman gave me a slow nod and I returned it. The sidewalk was covered in thick ice sprinkled with grey salt. I checked the parking lot for cop cars. I walked as quickly as I could on the slippery ground in my sneakers. Holly would cross the living room to see if I was still in the kitchen. She might open the front door.

Outside Needs I stopped and took out my wallet. No quarters. But I had a blue five-dollar bill. Inside the store was warm and bright; there was reggae playing. I took a bruised banana from a wicker basket by the checkout. The cashier had an Iron Maiden T-shirt on with a name tag pinned to it. Mary-Anne. She was baby-faced but the week before I'd seen her calmly lead an old drunk man out of the store by the elbow. The man was yelling, "He's a cunt, he fucked me, fucked me over," and the cashier was saying, "C'mon now, you know you can't be yelling in here."

"Just that?" she asked when I laid the banana on the counter. The countertop was see-through and in the compartment beneath the glass lotto tickets were fanned out in a colourful display. On one ticket a happy couple in white wool sweaters waved from the lawn of an enormous new house.

"Can I get some quarters in the change?" I asked.

My mother's landline is the only phone number I know by heart. I put a quarter in the phone and listened to it drop into the guts of the machine. I pictured the coin landing on a pile of quarters, all dropped down there by desperate people.

My grandmother used to take me to the fountain in the middle of the Village Mall to toss a penny in. The fountain smelled of chlorine, spurts of water on a timer shot up at the ceiling, making the air around the fountain misty. I would climb up on the ledge and look down into the pool with a penny in my fist. Yellow lights shone up through the undulating surface: the tiled bottom was always almost completely covered in change. Some coins winked under the fluorescent lights; others had gone a dull, oxidized green. I wanted to stick my hands in and swish them around. I wasn't allowed, even though it was only about a foot of water. No one was allowed to disturb the tossed coins. I would wind up my arm and fling my penny at the middle of the fountain. It would splish through the surface, then tumble in slow motion towards the bottom. The smell of copper would stay on my sweaty palm, wish residue.

I pressed the buttons on the phone. It rang three times. A young woman left the store with a six-pack, straight blond hair sticking out of either side of her hood. She smiled at me and I nodded, ashamed of what it meant to be on a pay phone, then ashamed of being ashamed. The space between rings stretched out and I worried it was going to voicemail but then the line engaged.

"WHAT IF IT'S in the news?" my mom asked.

"I don't think —" I started.

"It could be," she said. "Just keep that in mind, be prepared. They'll show the house and say the address."

"Do they say the address? Really? They're allowed?"

"They say the area at least."

"I haven't seen anyone out there. Like CBC or VOCM."

"They might not come today. They'll come when it's a slow news day. Do you need me to come get you?"

I thought how nice it would be to sit in the warm car and be coddled, but my mom had a bad back. It was an old injury from being rear-ended in the mall parking lot two years ago. A week ago she'd bent to pick something off the floor, a sheet of paper that had shot out of the printer and glided across the floor of her cramped in-house office, and the old pain had reared up. My dad had to carry her out of the basement with her arms around his neck. For the past week she'd been lying on the couch, her feet propped on the armrest. Every few hours my dad microwaved a Magic Bag and she slowly wedged it under her hips.

"I'm going to the restaurant to see Viv now," I told her.

"Come for dinner, your father will pick you up," she said.

"I'm fine, I just wanted you to know I don't have my phone."

"You can help cook. Your father will come by at five. Don't keep him waiting, have your coat on."

When I hung up I peeled the banana. It was stiff and mealy with a couple of sickeningly soft spots where it'd been banged around. I walked down the street holding the empty skin by the stalk, the leathery strips of peel dancing in the air and slapping against each other. Halfway down Pilot's Hill I dropped the skin in a slush puddle between the tire of a parked car and the curb.

⌒

AT THE RESTAURANT I stepped around a family gathered around the wobbly "Please Wait To Be Seated" sign. Viv was walking through the restaurant with three oval dinner plates, one in each hand and another balanced on her forearm. There were a couple of empty deuces by the bathroom door. I edged back behind the family, letting them know I understood they were ahead of me. I watched Viv unload at a table of middle-aged men, confidently laying each plate in front of the person who'd ordered it.

When I'd worked at the restaurant, I'd been terrified every time I had to carry more than two large plates at once. And I always had to ask, "The turkey sandwich? And you had the club?" as I put the meals down. Viv had gotten me the job and every time I made a mistake, I felt like I was letting her down.

Once, I'd dropped a stack of cleared plates in the dining room. Nothing broke, but there was a loud crash, gravy splattered the floor, cutlery bounced under people's tables. Everyone in the restaurant froze and some asshole called out, "You're no ballerina, are ya?" I had to crouch to pick it all up with the whole room staring at me. Another waitress had rushed off to get a mop for the gravy.

A new server, maybe the girl they'd hired to replace me, led the family to a booth in the front and waved me towards the two-seater in the back. Table twelve. Viv was in the kitchen and didn't know I was there yet.

"I'll be right back to wipe this down for you," the new

server said. She had a tattoo on her neck of a disembodied hand holding a bouquet of wildflowers.

"It's fine, I'm here to see Viv, can you tell her I'm here? I'm just going to have a coffee."

"Vivian just started her break," the girl said.

"Can you tell her I'm here?"

"When she gets back from her break." The girl shifted her body so I could take in the busy dining room she'd been left to tend alone.

When she walked away I reached in my pocket for my phone. I thought for a second I'd lost it, then I remembered the cops still had it. The table was covered in spongy pancake crumbs and drips of maple syrup.

They'd done renovations since I worked there. They'd installed a propane fireplace and put in two new windows so they could advertise a harbour view. In the summer they put a wipeable sandwich board out front with "Harbour View" on one side and lunch specials on the other. Spelled out in swoopy letters with neon marker.

It was hard to judge how long I'd been sitting there because I didn't have my phone to check the time. The new server came back with a slim mug of coffee and a tiny stainless-steel jug of milk. She pulled a cloth out of her apron and swept the crumbs on my table to the floor.

"Thank you."

"She'll be out in a minute."

Just as she said it Viv emerged from the basement steps and came around the counter. Her orange hair glowed in the end-of-day light streaming through the new windows. Her golden eyelashes were lit up. She was wearing a long-sleeved black spandex dress that showed off her big breasts and wide hips. She swept through the middle of the restaurant with a pot of coffee, smiling and refilling people's mugs as she went. I felt proud that she was my friend, that when she got to my table she would have a genuine smile for me, that she would shit-talk all these customers who thought she liked them to me later. There were two sharp rings of a bell and the other server took off towards the kitchen. When Viv got to my table I inhaled the smell of cigarettes on her.

"Are you okay?" she asked.

"They still have my phone." I bent my head to suck up some of the coffee and make room for milk. Tears were welling up in my eyes again. "Holly is acting like this thing with the cops is my fault."

"I can't really talk now. I'm sorry."

"When are you off?" I dribbled milk into my mug.

"I'm closing."

An older lady eating a club sandwich raised two fingers at Viv from across the room.

"Can you come over after?"

"Probably, I'll text you."

"I don't have a phone," I reminded her.

"Fuck."

"Ketchup?" the woman called.

"Come by," I said as Viv walked away.

I finished my coffee and lifted my coat off the back of my chair. It was early afternoon but it would be dark soon, the days were so short this time of year. I could see a car on the other side of the harbour, winding its way up Southside Road. Bright lights on the dock made rippling, cone-shaped reflections on the water. I arrived at the counter at the same time as Viv finished her coffee run.

"Just the coffee?" She set the empty pot on the counter.

"Yeah."

"Don't worry about it."

I pulled out my wallet and started flipping through receipts and movie tickets, looking for my bank card. It reminded me of shuffling through all these bits of paper and plastic the day before, when the cop had asked for my ID in my bedroom. My fingers had been stiff with panic then.

"Seriously, don't worry about it," Viv said.

"I want to pay — I don't have cash, though."

The coffee had made my saliva taste metallic and I was still shaky from the hangover and not sleeping. I took everything out of my wallet and tried sorting it in my hands, laying things on the counter.

"It's fine." Viv slid the coffee pot back into a machine beside the cash and flicked the illuminated switch. "Oh my god, put that away."

"I broke Holly's glasses." I stuffed everything back into the leather pouch.

"On purpose?" Viv asked. "Oh, Stacey. That was stupid. Really fucking stupid. Glasses are expensive."

The bell in the kitchen dinged twice.

"When are you off?" I asked.

"Around eleven, I have to get that."

"Okay, will you come by?"

"Yeah, I'll come by on my way home."

"I can meet you here."

The bell dinged again, three times. The other server was coming back down the centre aisle.

"No, just wait for me. If it's dead I might get off early." Viv pushed the swinging kitchen doors open. The other server rounded the counter. She pulled the half-filled coffee pot out of its slot and replaced it with an empty one. I walked out the steamed-up door into the empty street.

I took a left and walked up to the Battery to kill time; I didn't want to go back to the house. I'd left without my gloves and scarf, the wind was cold on my throat and hands. As I passed the tower of condos alongside the restaurant I remembered a regular who lived there. An elderly man who came in most nights and ordered the Liver and Onions Platter. He always had gluey mashed potatoes instead of fries for his side. He would try to keep me at his table as long as possible, starting with questions about the menu and easing into questions about my life. I could feel the loneliness emanating from him. When it was slow I humoured him; I told him that the cod cakes came frozen in sacks of fifty, that Viv and I lived together, that I didn't have a boyfriend. He said his son had moved to the mainland, his granddaughter was three and he'd never met her. Sometimes the old man would stuff a twenty-dollar bill into the front of my apron and say, "That's just for you." His fingers would go deep into that front pocket. I kept the money, I didn't put it in the tip jar to be split with the other servers and kitchen staff at the end of the week.

Then he stopped showing up. When I realized it'd been two weeks since I last saw him I asked Viv, "You know the old man who orders the liver? He hasn't been in."

"I know," she said.

"Do you think he died?"

She nodded. "Or maybe he got put in a home."

"It's so weird how people can just disappear out of your life," I said.

On my way up to the Battery I looked into the lit-up windows of the condo building. I wondered if his son had come home from the mainland to clean out his apartment.

WHEN I GOT back to the house Holly's boots were gone from the porch. Her glasses weren't on the bathroom floor. I flicked the light off and shut the door so the cats wouldn't rip apart the garbage. Her guitar wasn't leaning against the sofa anymore. I went into the kitchen to check the time on the oven: it was just before five, Dad would be by for me soon. I ran upstairs; Holly's door was open. The blankets and sheets were still on the floor where the cops had left them. She had closed Natalie Swanson's heavy curtains.

There was jewellery spread over the top of her dresser. There were chokers and enamel pins, a brooch with dried flowers caught in resin. There was the choker I'd seen her wear at shows and parties, white leather with two long tails that hung into her cleavage.

The bottom drawer was hauled almost all the way out of the dresser and emptied. I peeked into the closet and saw all her fancy, big-city dresses were still hung up in there. The suitcases she'd moved in with were slouched against each other beneath the dresses. The biggest suitcase was open; there were a few pieces of clothing and a U-lock in the bottom.

I heard a horn outside and lifted the curtain. My parents' car was idling beside the dumpster. From Holly's room you could see into the windows of the apartments on the top floor of the church. Most people had their blinds drawn but I could see a woman standing with her back to the window, shifting a frying pan back and forth over a bright red burner. In another room a young man sat in a recliner bent over a clunky grey laptop. I patted my coat pockets, feeling for my phone, wallet, keys. Then remembered about my phone again. I left Holly's room slowly, making sure not to disrupt anything.

My father pressed the horn as I was coming down over the stairs. I stomped into my sneakers and left the house with the backs of my shoes flattened under my heels. In the car, heat was pumping out of the dashboard.

"Thank you for coming to get me."

"Your mother said there was an incident with the police."

"Yeah, I'm okay." I reached down to fix my shoes.

"You don't have any boots?"

I looked up at Holly's dark window, making sure I'd put the curtain back the way she'd had it. I felt tears burning in my eyes. In the side mirror, I noticed that Fatima's boyfriend's station wagon was behind us. He was patiently waiting to pull into the spot in front of her house.

"We have to go, we're blocking the way."

Dad pulled out. I saw the older kid climbing out of

the back seat in her snowsuit as we rounded the corner by the nurses' union.

Both my parents are retired schoolteachers who make money tutoring in an office in their basement. The walls of the office are lined with shelves of textbooks and binders filled with three-hole punched worksheets and sample tests. A row of spider plants is arranged on the sill of a window set high in the wall. There is a long desk my father built for the room with drawers full of calculators and geometry sets and mechanical pencils.

My parents are beloved. At Christmas, cards from their students are staggered on the mantel and the tree is crowded with decorations picked out by the kids' parents. Two kitchen cupboards are filled with mugs covered in apples and A+ symbols, mugs designed to be gifted to teachers.

Whenever I arrive at my parents' house unannounced I check the front porch for sneakers or jackets to see if there's a tutoring session happening. Even without seeing the sneakers or a coat, I can usually sense if there's a session in progress. When my parents are working with someone a feeling of quiet concentration permeates the house.

It's not uncommon for a kid to emerge from the basement—a math book against their chest, a knapsack slung over one shoulder—with a face that has recently been crying. It's frustrating not being able to do math. Some students get angry.

Once, a boy in grade seven hit my dad in the face with a hardcover textbook. The corner dug into his face below his glasses and immediately left a pinprick bruise that spread throughout the week. His mother apologized profusely in the front porch. After she left there was a long debate about whether they should let the boy come back. My mom didn't want him in the house.

In the end he was allowed back, and the following Tuesday my father tutored him with the bruise on his face. They sat side by side at the desk my father had built, working on long division. The boy had to look up from the lined paper and see the bruise he'd made on my father's cheek.

There were also nights when kids finished a session feeling triumphant, like they had conquered something. Or sessions where they showed up with a test they'd done well on, eager to show one of my parents the smiley their teacher had drawn next to their grade.

Tonight there were no students. In the car my dad explained how that morning my mom thought she would be well enough to sit in the basement and tutor by 3:30, but she had to cancel all her appointments at the last minute. She couldn't get up off the couch because of her back pain. When we arrived she was reading an Agatha Christie novel, a library book with a yellowed sheet of cracked plastic protecting the dust jacket.

"Your aunt Jackie dropped this off for me with the muscle relaxants earlier," she said, putting the book down on her legs. "I'm going stir-crazy just lying here."

She tried to push herself up on the couch cushions and winced. For the first time, I recognized that my mother was getting older and more fragile.

"Did they help?"

"Who?"

"The muscle relaxants."

My father was in the kitchen; I heard beeps as he defrosted fish in the microwave.

"I suppose."

"They're making you loopy?" I asked her.

"Who? Jackie? No, she was fine."

"The muscle relaxants."

"Listen, what did Vivian say about the cops?"

"I didn't really get to talk to her. She was at work."

"I thought you were going down to see her."

"She was at work."

"Does she think it's that girl?"

"What?"

"Your roommate."

"God, Mom, no. It's a mistake. It's just a mistake. The cops make mistakes. That's pretty much all they do." It came out snarly and self-righteous.

"Stacey, can you come in here?" my father called from the kitchen. He'd overheard.

"Viv is coming over to my place later," I told Mom, getting up to leave the room.

My father was grating cheese into a dented steel mixing bowl. I started chopping potatoes. Big fat snowflakes were melting on the window. I preheated the oven. I thought about how nice it was to walk around the kitchen in socks without feeling cold. We ate dinner in the living room with the plates on our laps and watched the NTV news. After eating, I rinsed the plates and fit them into the dishwasher.

Before Dad drove me home, I checked my email on the desktop computer in my parents' bedroom. It took me a moment to remember the password—it was saved in my phone and computer so I almost never had to type it in. *!Snot&Courtney!* There were no new emails, I refreshed my inbox twice and checked the junk. Still nothing from the fancy Toronto casting director about the joint production. I scrolled through my old emails. Mostly it was just stuff from the theatre—the order from Labatt came in, no more comps for this or that show. Pay stubs from Standardized Patient Testing. Would the cops read all that? How far back would they go?

I signed out. Maybe they would think I was a degenerate loser because I was twenty-six and scrambling a living together from all these low-paying, short-term jobs without any plan for a more stable future. I thought about checking Facebook to see if anyone was trying to get in touch but I didn't want to remind myself of all the more personal messages in that inbox. Presumably the cops were rooting around in there too.

When we pulled up in front of my house around 9:30 all the lights were off. So Holly was staying at Dave's. Fuck her anyway.

"Are you sure you're going to be okay in there? You could stay at our house," my dad said.

"Thank you, I think I want to sleep in my own bed."

THE COUGHING WOMAN was wearing a pair of headphones and tapping her foot on the fire escape steps. I locked the door behind me. The floors were still covered in salty footsteps from when the cops came. Normally I would watch something in bed until Viv arrived but I didn't have a computer or phone. Tomorrow the schedule for the theatre would be emailed out and I wouldn't have any way to check it. Plus other people might be trying to reach me. Like that casting director.

There was a new collection of beer bottles on the kitchen table. Holly and Dave must have come back and sat around drinking, probably talking about me, before she went to stay at his place. There was a beer box under the table with three full bottles in it. I put the beer in the crisper and shovelled the empties into the box. I flipped the chairs up onto the table.

I swept, then squirted half a bottle of Pine-Sol into the mop bucket and filled it with hot water from the bathtub tap. I wore rubber gloves and scrubbed the floor on my hands and knees. I used a dishcloth that had been sitting in the sink too long and gone slimy.

I wiped at the grimy footprints and wrung the square of lime-green fabric out over the bucket. I crossed the living room and moved into the kitchen, pushing the bucket along with me, erasing the cops' winding tracks.

The Pine-Sol burned my nostrils and cleared my sinuses. Snot appeared, sniffing the air. He crossed the room, shaking each paw before laying it back down on the wet floor. After the kitchen I cleaned the bathroom. Then I threw the cushions off the living room couch and stuck the vacuum nozzle deep into its crevices, sucking up ancient crumbs.

When the doorbell finally rang I was kneeling on the kitchen counter, emptying the cabinets so I could scrub the peeling wallpaper pasted inside. I hopped down. Viv was standing on the doorstep with her apron in her fist. It was mild out and the snowbanks on either side of her were steaming. Her bangs were in clumps on her forehead, from the damp night or from mopping the restaurant and racing up the hill.

"Come in, I'm cleaning."

I led her through the dark living room to the kitchen.

"Do you want a beer?" I opened the fridge and took out two of Holly's beer. "They're not very cold. I could stick them in the freezer?"

"Let me see." Viv took a beer and pressed it against her cheek. "No, they're fine."

She twisted the cap off and tossed it at the counter, but it bounced and landed on the floor. I picked it up and put it in the open garbage can. Viv dropped her apron on a stack of dinner plates.

"Where's Holly?" she asked.

"She's staying at Dave's, did she message you?"

I put my beer in the freezer.

"No, I haven't heard from her in a while," Viv said.

That made a happy feeling bubble up in my chest; I tried to keep it off my face.

"She's always hanging out with those folk dudes, like Michael Murray and Dave King and them," I said.

"Is she sleeping with Dave?" Viv asked.

"I don't know, probably."

"Can we sit down? I want to look at my blood blister, did I tell you about it? It's huge."

I turned on the floor lamp in the living room. The cats were curled up on the vacuumed couch. I sat beside them and ran a hand over the lines the vacuum nozzle had left on the cushions. Viv put her beer on the coffee table, hiked up her skirt and hauled her tights down to her knees. She shuffled over to the couch with the waistband of the tights holding her legs together and sat beside me. She rolled the stocking off one curled foot and then the other.

"Sorry, my feet stink."

"I don't smell anything." I looked out the window; the fire escape was empty. The streetlight shone on the dumpster.

"Kris was flirting with you at Pleasant Street, she was following you around all night." Viv lifted her left ankle onto the opposite knee and showed me her foot. There was a wobbly burgundy circle the size of a toonie on the bottom of her heel. The blister was surrounded by a yellow bruise.

"Holy fuck, Viv. You need to go to the doctor."

"It's worse than earlier." She tilted her bottle and let beer glug into her mouth. She pressed her thumb down on the centre of the blister and the outside edges bulged with black blood. "Are you into her?"

"Don't!" I stood up. "Oh my god, don't do that. I'm going to get my beer."

When I stepped into the kitchen something moved in the glass of the patio door. I couldn't get a breath. It was the shape of a person. It felt like I was swimming up from the bottom of a pool, my lungs were too big for my chest. I could feel blood rushing through the skinny vessels in the front of my brain. Everything inside me was swelling up, trying to burst out.

"It feels good to take my tights off, let the air at it," Viv called from the living room.

The figure's bottom half was in the same lilac purple as my leggings. I shifted my hips from side to side and watched the blurry figure move with me. I breathed in and my ribs made room for my lungs. Bright white specks danced over everything in the kitchen.

I swung my head back and forth and shook the glowing dust motes out of existence. I went over to the door and tested the handle. The doorknob was made out of cheap gold-coloured metal and had a dent in it. The lock was a tab in the centre of the knob that you twisted with pinched fingers. The door was locked but the handle rocked in my hand. Two of the four screws that held the knob in place waggled in their holes.

"Do you think I should pop it?" Viv called.

"Gross," I yelled back, impressed by how steady my voice sounded.

I turned my back to the door and got my beer out of the freezer. There should be a deadbolt, I thought. I pressed the cool bottle against my cheek like Viv had done. I held it there until it stung and then pressed it into the opposite cheek. I pulled down the neck of my shirt and rolled the beer across my chest. The glowing red numbers on the stove clock changed, it was after midnight. I opened the beer and took it into the living room.

Viv had her feet up on the coffee table and Snot was sitting in her lap, rubbing his head against the bottom of her chin.

"What happened with Holly?" Viv asked when I sat beside her.

"She said, 'If you know anything don't tell me.'"

"What does that mean?" Viv was almost done her beer.

I took my first sip; a cool relief spread through me. It felt good to be on the couch next to Viv, it felt like Patrick Street.

"I guess she was implying that I might have something to do with the incident." I pulled my legs up into my chest and dug my heels into the edge of the cushion.

"That's fucked up."

"There's more beer. Do you want another beer?" I didn't want her to leave.

"I'd have another beer."

"I'll get it, your foot."

I braced myself for my reflection when I stepped into the kitchen. There it was. Snot had followed me in; a blurry version of his tail twitched in the glass. I got Viv's beer and then I flicked the kitchen light off. I waited for my eyes to adjust and looked out at the patio. There was the familiar outline of my bike and the barbeque beneath the snow. I could see the path the cops had made in the snow when they'd come up to the back door. In some places I could make out individual shoe prints, the size and shape and all the ridges. At the door the narrow path widened—they must have gathered together and peered in, waiting for the bald asshole to beckon them. Sergeant Hamlyn. I heard the gentle sound of Snot lapping water out of his dish.

"Do you think it's possible there is something on Holly's hard drive?" I handed Viv the last beer.

"Stacey." She sounded disappointed in me.

"I'm just trying to understand."

"You can't think like that, it makes me worried about you."

"Worried?"

"It's paranoid."

"Another possibility is, what if Dave did something on our internet? Or someone else she had over here?"

Viv took a sip of her new beer. The lamp lit her hair from the back, making it almost translucent blond in some places and coppery red in others.

"The cops said to think about who has been using the internet. People surprise you—remember Jordan Nolan," I tried.

"Stacey, you're going to make yourself crazy."

"Okay," I said. "Don't say crazy though, it's ableist."

"Okay, I know," Viv said.

"Anyway it was probably the previous tenants, did I tell you how they made us take over their internet account?"

"I don't know." Viv shook her head. "You might not know, like ever. Chances are they're not going to tell you."

Then we talked about her sister Jenn who was living in Alberta and working as a receptionist at a dental office. She was coming home to get married. Viv showed me a picture of the bridesmaid dress her sister wanted her to order. A silky purple tube dress with a wide skirt. The screen seemed very bright, it made my eyeballs ache.

"My head hurts, maybe it's the cleaning products." I passed her phone back.

"You know, there's something weird about the air in here," Viv said.

"It's the Pine-Sol."

"No, it's something else."

"It's the Pine-Sol."

"You're probably exhausted." She set her empty beer bottle on the table. "From all this hoopla."

I followed Viv to the porch, with the crochet blanket from the couch wrapped around my shoulders. She bent to tie her shoes. She cringed when she put weight on the blood-blister foot. I shut the door behind her and climbed the steps to bed in the empty house.

EIGHT

A few months before all of this, I'd tried to download *Carol*. When I opened the file I saw something that might have been a snuff film. For a moment I was looking at footage of a naked woman in a bathtub with a curling iron bobbing beside her. The cord stretched out of the frame. What the fuck is this? Is this how it begins? Shaky, handheld footage in a too-bright room. This isn't what it seemed like from the trailer. Is this the backstory? The camera starts moving towards the bathtub. Click the "X." Ick. Fuck. Gross. What the fuck was that? The woman was still and limp but the curling iron was see-sawing in the water like it had just been tossed in. The silver tip sinking and surfacing, the red light on the handle bright beneath the surface. That was fake. I hope it was fake. How long was I looking at it? Five seconds probably. Maybe less.

⌒

IN JUNIOR HIGH I was known for having big breasts. Kyle Patterson was known for being a mild-mannered boy. People thought he was handsome, he had dark hair that he wore gelled up into hard curls. He never got in trouble, he even had a reputation for being a goody two-shoes, tattletale kind of boy — but he was well liked. He started this thing of walking up to girls, sticking a finger in their breast and saying "ding-dong." Maybe he didn't start it but he made it popular.

There's a photo of me when I'm fourteen and my breasts are enormous. I have a kid's frame with my grandmother's heavy breasts hanging off it. My nan gave me some hand-me-down bras around that time. They were white or champagne coloured with thick, padded straps. She told me they were a model called "the minimizer." She said the name like I would find it reassuring.

Kyle Patterson came up to me in the hall and drove a finger into my breast. There was a knot of what felt like inflamed veins in each of my breasts that ached all the time. In bed at night I squeezed my breasts and it was sort of like poking a blister — it was a relief because it was a different kind of pain. Even through the firm cup of the minimizer Kyle Patterson's finger managed to make contact with the aching knot. The hallway was crowded and loud, it was the end of the day on a Friday and people were throwing books and boots and jackets in the air.

He lost steam when it was time to say "ding-dong." He could tell by my face that he'd hurt me, like caused me physical pain, but he had to say "ding-dong," otherwise it would be weird. Otherwise it might mean that he liked the poking, that it wasn't purely a joke for other people's benefit, and that would be uncomfortable for both of us. After he said it I shrieked indignantly and swung my knapsack at his stomach, but my heart wasn't in it, it was a performance to save him from the embarrassment of what he'd done to me.

That night after Kyle Patterson poked me and embarrassed us both, I had a dream. I was watching two or three boys in a field. They had cut off my breasts and wrapped them in cellophane. They were tossing the package back and forth between them. Blood pooled in the places where the plastic wrap rippled. They were laughing and saying mean things, calling me fat, squishing the package in their hands. I was lying on my stomach in some tall grass watching. My chest stung. I didn't want them to find me but I needed to hear all the nasty things they were saying about me. When I woke up I was relieved the dream wasn't real but also disgusted that my brain came up with the scene. That's the same feeling I got when I saw that woman in the bath with the curling iron. It felt like the scene came from inside me. It was conjured up because there are people in the world who would click on it, and I had. I didn't mean to but I'd clicked it.

A COUPLE OF DAYS after the search I realized I hadn't cooked since the cops had come, not even eggs. I didn't like being in the kitchen. The big window in the back door made me nervous. I'd been eating toast with peanut butter for most meals and I was almost out of peanut butter.

The only food I had in the fridge was a handful of carrots whose tips had gone limp and a two-litre of milk I'd picked up at Needs. Holly rarely bought groceries and she hadn't been back since our fight anyway. The only things in the fridge belonging to her were a takeout box from Venice Pizza and a Tupperware of orange-coloured soup with islands of white mould in it.

The theatre had deposited my pay the day before, so I threw away the sad vegetables and went to the supermarket. Snot and Courtney watched in the window as I locked the front door.

I crossed Military Road and walked through the park, taking the long way to kill time and avoid being alone in the house. People were skating the loop at Bannerman Park, disco music was playing through the speakers that surround the rink. Children dragged each other around the shiny ice, tipping over in their heavy gear and scrambling back up, clutching each other's coats. The neighbour kids were with them; I smiled and the brother waved. A woman was skating smooth, steady strokes around the loop. Fatima. I waited for her to look my way and waved. She smiled, surprised to see me at the edge of the rink.

Walking through the quieter part of the park I noticed the stars were out. From a distance I saw a figure playing catch with a big dog in the baseball diamond. Some anxiety shook loose in my chest, tumbled through my body, splattered into my sneakers and seeped out into the snow. I felt light on the way to the supermarket. I caught myself humming "Born to Be Alive," the song from the skating loop.

But then the automatic doors at the Sobeys glided open on a sad scene in the supermarket's porch. A security guard was wrestling a man in a windbreaker too thin for the cold.

"Call the cops," the security guard called into the supermarket, holding fistfuls of the man's jacket. The man dropped to the floor and wriggled like a fish. The security guard planted a foot on either side of his writhing body and bent down, grabbing at the man's coat. I stood limply outside the glass doors. The man in the windbreaker was trying to roll onto his stomach. The doors shut in front of me and opened again.

"I'll have you charged, you'll be charged for this," the security guard was saying. He had managed to tug the man's coat open. Three bright red steaks in white Styrofoam trays, a box of Uncle Ben's Mexican-Style Rice, and a block of cheese spilled onto the grey, slush-covered carpet. People were bottlenecked behind the gliding doors on the supermarket side of the porch, their carts heaped with plastic bags stuffed with groceries.

"Get up, get up," the security guard said, his voice full of disgust.

The man stood slowly, putting a hand on his bent knee to help himself up. Then he bolted—the doors stuttered open and he ran out into the starry night, sprinting across the parking lot. The security guard cursed and started picking the food off the floor.

"No-chase policy," he explained as I passed him, sounding sorry for himself.

I went to the produce section, I wanted to make a stir-fry—something fast but hot with vegetables in it. I picked up mushrooms and an orange pepper; I put back a bag of snap peas because I realized they were almost seven dollars and already speckled with black spots. The sprinklers above the broccoli were sending down a shower of mist. I hesitated before reaching for a head of broccoli, I didn't want to get my sleeve wet.

I felt eyes on me and looked around. A woman in a black pea coat with short grey hair was standing behind me. I grabbed a head of broccoli and turned it in my hand; when I looked back the woman was still there. A spike of fear shot up from my feet and hardened like a stalagmite in my chest.

She wasn't the plainclothes security guard who wandered the aisles, loading and unloading her cart, watching for shoplifters. That woman was in her thirties and had bright blue hair. I often wondered if they hired her because of her edgy look or if she transformed herself to go undercover. I liked picturing her at home in her bathroom with a towel over her shoulders, reading the side of a tub of Manic Panic Blue Steel dye. Then sighing as she untwisted the top and scooped a glob out with three fingers.

The broccoli I'd picked was old: the stalk was rubbery and the flowers on top were open and yellowing. I put it back and chose another. My sleeve got covered in tiny beads of water. I could feel the woman behind me. She looked like a cop—just the way she held herself, there was a macho confidence about her posture. I imagined her trailing me on foot through the park. The thought of her seeing me wave to Fatima and her kids made my stomach turn over. But no, she'd probably followed me in a car and drove around the park.

I picked a stiffer head of broccoli, still covered in the crystals of ice, and added it to the vegetables I was squishing against my coat. I veered away from the produce section and into the bakery area. I stood beside a table of white cakes with red poinsettias piped on them. I picked up a cake with my free hand, turning it like I was inspecting it through the clear plastic lid. There was a tremor in my hand.

I watched her choose her own broccoli and add it to the mound of bagged fruits and vegetables in her cart. I was waiting for her to look my way again. Then I would know. But she swung her cart around and headed towards the pharmacy.

I wandered through the freezer section, the thud of panic dying down in my chest. The store was closing soon and the lines were long. I joined the shortest one. The woman was in line at the opposite end of the store. I couldn't stop staring at her. She was typing on her phone, one finger hovering over the screen before plunking down again and again.

The man behind me in line made a noise to let me know it was time to move ahead. I dropped my things onto the conveyor belt. I had to ask the cashier to repeat what she'd said about the weather because I was distracted by watching the woman leave the store with bunches of plastic shopping bags.

I walked through the park on the way home but the skating loop had cleared out and the music was shut off for the night. The emptiness of the park felt menacing. I started rushing across the snow, slipped and banged my knee on the ice beneath it. The orange pepper rolled out of my shopping bag; I wiped the snow off it on my jeans and dropped it back in the bag.

When I got home the thought of chopping up the vegetables with my back to the door was so unpleasant that I left the groceries on the counter and went to bed without eating.

I HAD TROUBLE falling asleep because I was hungry. When I'd tripped in the park I'd landed on my hand in a weird way, the hand I thought of as my bitten hand. Now it was aching. The day of the bite I'd gone for a walk in the Battery. This was last spring, when I was still living on Patrick Street with Viv and Mike. I liked to go up there early in the morning. I'd pet the pack of cats that loll on their bellies under cars up there. They're marmalades with white splotches, skinny with matted hair and black crust in their eyes. I'd climb up the wooden platform beneath the cannon that points at the harbour and make a wish on the ocean, touching the cool metal for good luck. I always go up there when I need to make a wish. Usually I wish for acting work or for some unexpected money to show up in the mail—almost always selfish wishes.

On my way down the hill that morning I ran into an old co-worker, a server at the restaurant. Madonna. She

was about my mom's age and when we'd worked together
her daughter had just moved home from Alberta with a
two-year-old son. Madonna had a German shepherd. The
leash was wrapped around her fist three times and the dog
was dragging her.

"Who's walking who?" I said as we approached one
another on the narrow road.

"Sit," Madonna said and the dog obeyed.

I had been hoping I wouldn't have to stop.

"Where are you working now?" Madonna asked.
"They're hiring for summer at the restaurant."

"Oh, I have a job," I said.

"Where? They'd hire you back. You know everything
already."

"How's your daughter?" I asked. The wind was blowing
right through my sweatshirt.

"Oh wonderful, she just got Tyler into daycare, the
place had a three-month wait-list."

"Great, well nice to see you," I said.

"Give me a hug," Madonna said. "Don't mind the dog,
he might bark but he's harmless."

I stepped in and put an arm around Madonna's shoulder. Madonna was taller than me and thin. I felt teeth
meet in my hand. Teeth brushing against each other
inside me. I held up my hand and two bright streams of
blood ran into my sweatshirt and all the way down to my
elbow. There were drips of blood on the sidewalk around
us, there was blood on my jeans and on my sneakers.
Madonna pulled the dog away and stood in the ditch with
the ocean behind her.

"I have to go," I said.

"Oh fuck, can you move it? Can you move your fingers?"

"I don't know." I was afraid I might faint.

"I'm sorry, he doesn't usually, let me give you my phone number." Madonna tried to get at her phone in the zippered pocket of her windbreaker.

"I think I'm going to go." I turned and started down the hill. I was nauseous with the pain. It was a hot, throbbing pain. I breathed through my nose. I wanted to get away from Madonna.

A silver car pulled up next to me. Kyle Patterson put down the window. Ding-dong.

"Stacey? Are you okay?"

I could imagine how absurd I looked, speed-walking past a garden full of purple tulips and fat-breasted hens with blood dripping out of my sleeve.

"I got bit by a dog, a German shepherd."

"Do you want a ride?" he said. And then, with urgency, "You need to sit down."

Kyle opened the driver's-side door and got out, the car still running. He put his hands on my shoulders and steered me around the front of the car. A jeep pulled up behind us and rolled to a stop; I saw the driver looking at my hand. I felt tears on my cheeks. The kind of tears that come when you're trying not to cough while someone else is doing public speaking.

"Do you want me to call someone?" Kyle Patterson opened the passenger door and gave the jeep the "one minute" signal. I sat down, keeping my feet on the pavement and my thighs together to catch the blood and keep it off Kyle's seats.

"No, I don't know." I knew Viv was at work and my parents were an hour outside of town, visiting relatives. I felt something rumbling up my throat with the force of projectile vomit. A dramatic, childish noise bleached out of me. A sob. Kyle Patterson was looking me right in the eyes when it happened and he didn't flinch. I could tell he'd cared for people, he'd been subjected to wailing in the past. He touched the side of my knee, directing me to put my feet in the car, a touch devoid of sleaziness.

"Okay, okay," he said. I wasn't sure if he was talking to me or the jeep. He shut my door and walked around the front.

"I'm on my way to work at Caines," Kyle said. "You can come in and clean up in the bathroom and we'll get you a cab to the hospital." He did up his seat belt and we rolled out of the Battery, the sun catching on waves in the harbour, sending up searing white flashes.

"Sometimes stuff bleeds a lot and it's not that serious," Kyle said. There was congestion downtown, a warm Sunday morning. I whined about the pain as we crawled along Water Street. We passed groups of people carrying ice creams and takeout coffees.

"I would take you right to the hospital but I'm already late and we're short on staff, I know it'll be busy today," Kyle said.

We parked around the corner and walked down the street to his work, leaving drips of blood behind us. People moved to the edges of the sidewalk to let us pass. Most of my arm was covered in blood; in some places it had gone black and crusty, in other places it was gooey. In Caines' I dripped blood on the floor. Kyle waved to his co-worker, an old lady with a gold cross hanging in her wrinkled cleavage. He led me up a set of stairs in the back.

"Just get cleaned up, I'll call you a cab." Kyle closed the bathroom door and I heard him jog down the stairs.

In the square mirror above the sink I saw palettes of canned goods stacked behind me. Mix-and-matched rows of bright labels, tinned peas and meatballs and chopped-up carrots. I could see my face was pale, even my lips looked pale. I bent over to unroll some toilet paper and when I stood up the room dipped. I held onto the edge of the sink with my good hand; everything was black but I could feel the cool lip of the sink in my hand, I was thinking "Just hold on tight." Then I was on my knees, the bloody hand was coated in grime from the floor, grey scuzz and rocks and some long hairs. My head was pounding. My good hand was above my head, still holding the edge of the sink.

"Stacey?" Kyle Patterson said from outside the door. "Stacey? Cab's here."

I realized he was knocking. I'd heard him knocking but at first I hadn't been able to differentiate it from the pulsing in my head and hand.

"Come in," I said.

"Whoa." Kyle put his hands in my damp armpits and lifted me off the floor. It was brotherly, the way he held me. He helped me wrap rough paper towel around my hand. Blood soaked through it almost immediately. Kyle paid for a can of Pepsi and ran out to speak to the cab driver.

"The sugar might help," he said. "Might wake you up a bit."

I sat on the steps leading up to the storage room/bathroom, a few feet from where I'd passed out. The woman behind the counter was dealing with a steady stream of customers. I was trembly and cold. The pain in my hand felt like a bouquet of needles driving deep into the hollow between my last two knuckles and pulling out slowly, over and over.

"You don't have anyone to call?" Kyle Patterson asked.

"I'm okay. Get the cab to swing by my house, I'll get my wallet."

"I'll pay for it, just worried about you getting home."

"You don't have to pay, you already got me this," I held up the can. "Thank you, for everything."

"It's no problem," Kyle said. "It's nothing, I can pay."

The woman at the counter was looking at him, the line at the cash had swelled and lost its shape.

"No." I stood up, I was unsteady but determined to make it to the cab. I pushed the heavy door with my good hand and the bells tied to the door frame bounced against each other in the breeze.

At the hospital, the nurse disinfected the wound and put three neat stitches on the back of my hand and another four on my palm. The doctor gave me a sheet of paper with illustrations depicting the stretches I would need to do to stop the bite from diminishing my mobility. The nurse wrapped my hand in gauze while the doctor demonstrated each of the manoeuvres.

"You're lucky, he went right through you but he missed all the important stuff," she told me.

I started walking home, passing the duck pond with the gazebo where hospital staff and university students gathered to smoke. A horn honked and a car slowed beside me. My grandmother was driving. I climbed into her pristine car. Rescued for a second time that day.

"I was in talking to the specialist about my knee," she said. "Oh no, what's wrong with your hand?"

I explained about the bite, I stressed how the doctor said the teeth hadn't snagged on any nerves or veins. That everything would go back to normal. When we pulled up in front of the house on Patrick Street my grandmother told me, "I'm going to say a prayer for you tonight, Stacey, a prayer for your hand. I'm going to ask for you to heal up properly."

"Thank you," I said, my good hand on the door handle.

"You know what?" my grandmother said. "I think you're ready for your spoon. I'm going to give it to you next time I see you."

"Thank you, Nanny," I said, opening the car door.

Eventually the tunnel the dog's teeth made in my hand closed up, and the stitches fell out. My fingers wiggle a little looser on the other hand and probably I'll have early-onset arthritis, but basically it's fine. Before the bite I would stick my hand out and pet any dog I saw in the street. Now I never pet a dog I don't know.

WHEN I WOKE UP, my T-shirt was damp with sweat. It was cold in my room and I'd slept with the electric blanket on the highest setting. I'd wriggled out of my underwear and socks in the night.

The blanket gave me strange dreams. My grandmother had warned me that electric blankets cause brain damage. I had been trying to reassure her that I wasn't too cold in my drafty downtown house: I had slippers, a space heater, the electric blanket. But my grandmother had heard a program on the radio, those blankets send waves of electricity through your body. There was frost on the inside of the window. Snot and Courtney were curled together under the covers, down by my hip. The air I breathed in was cold in my nostrils and on the back of my throat. The sun streaming in was pissy yellow.

"Don't have it on all night, Stacey, it'll fry your brain. You don't leave it on all night, do you?"

"No, no, not all night." But I kept it on all night. I'd have wild dreams and wake up every morning soaked in sweat.

I couldn't check the time because I didn't have my phone. The reality of the situation with the cops came back each morning a few moments after I woke up.

This morning the electric blanket had pulled a memory up to the surface of my brain like a poultice. A music video I made for a friend's band when I was in university. I took the opening shot. It's my feet walking through hundreds of squirming tadpoles at Massey Drive. The bottom of the pond is yellow sand, there are legions of tadpoles, their plump, gyrating bodies fill the screen. I shuffle forward, moving to avoid a smashed beer bottle, the water laps against my hairy, muscled calves. My toes are painted baby pink.

We filmed it in a day. The tadpole shot was spliced together with video of me and another girl making out in an inflatable chair covered in glow-in-the-dark polka dots. Sweating beneath the electric blanket, I tried to fish her name out of my memory but it was lost.

We were wearing candy necklaces and matching fluorescent bikinis we'd picked out at Wal-Mart. Mine was neon green and the other girl's was electric pink. The chair was off Amazon. It was a new version of the inflatable furniture and backpacks that were popular when I was in elementary school. The photo on the front of the box was a teenage boy in cargo pants, slouched in an inflatable chair that was covered in pentagrams.

The camera was set up on a tripod in the corner of the room. The other girl was a good kisser and I liked the way her body felt against me but I couldn't quite lose myself in it. I wasn't sure how much we were supposed to be faking for the camera. How real did it feel for her? I didn't want to give over completely if she wasn't.

After a while it became tedious. The plastic chair got sticky and made farting noises when we moved.

Someone I knew had a short film about BDSM in a porn film festival in Germany and she suggested we enter the music video. But I thought it was too tame to count as porn or even be of interest to anyone. It was still buried somewhere in my computer, though. And maybe the cops would spin it into something to justify storming through my house at seven in the morning. I tried to remember

what the file was called. It might have had some preten-
tious title but hopefully it was something innocuous like
"video2223." There were probably countless other things
I'd forgotten about buried in there. I threw the hot blanket off.

I pulled on my fleece-lined leggings and put my blue
bathrobe with the burnt sleeve over my sweaty T-shirt.
The cats crawled out from under the covers and stretched.
Usually they stalked around the room in the morning
mewling for breakfast, but the electric blanket did strange
things to them too. The second they touched it they went
limp. Under the blanket they let me haul them into my
body and cuddle them in a way they'd normally refuse by
swatting at my face. My grandmother had also warned,
"That thing could burn down the house." I yanked the
cord out of the wall.

Once, I came home and realized I'd left the blanket
on all day. Snot and Courtney were deep asleep under the
covers, dreaming vivid cat dreams—heaps of wet food,
backyards full of fat baby birds learning to fly. I'd rubbed
my palm across the mattress and felt the S-shape of all the
springs burning beneath the padded top.

I went to the kitchen to check the time on the stove.
Eleven-thirty. I never slept that late. I felt like I'd woken
up in a different time zone. I shook kibble into Snot and
Courtney's bowls. There were still stacks of clean plates
lined up on the counter from my cleaning spree before
Viv's visit. How long ago was that? I lifted them back into
the dirty cabinets and put my groceries away. I was losing
track of the days. The only way to tell time was by the

clock on the stove. I hadn't seen Holly since our conversation about her staying with Dave. Without a phone or a computer no one could reach me. If I wanted to talk to someone I had to correctly guess where they were and engineer a meeting or find their phone number somehow and a phone to use.

I needed to shower and go to the theatre and find out when I was working. Snot sauntered over to his food dish; the blanket had gone cold and he'd managed to shake himself out of the special stupor it put him in.

There was a knock. Snot lifted his head and looked at the door. My arms quivered with the weight of the plates as I lowered them back to the counter. First I looked out the back door; I couldn't see anyone on the deck. A second, more urgent knock. I wrapped the housecoat tight around me and walked to the porch. I could see a tall figure on the step through the three frosted glass panels in the door. I saw the person lift their fist to knock again and I pulled the door open quickly.

"Somebody here order Mary Brown's?" the man asked. He had a big, black delivery bag, the kind with a silver lining designed to keep takeout hot. I could tell the bag was heavy from the way he was standing.

"No."

The man looked about fifty, he had close-cropped grey hair and a brown leather bomber jacket.

"This is 2 Clarke Avenue?" He was looking at the gold number 2 screwed onto the siding next to our mailbox. I could see in his face that he knew something wasn't right. I smelled warm grease.

"This is 2 Clarke Avenue but no one ordered Mary Brown's." I was sure he was just a lost delivery man but adrenaline was coursing through my body. I looked behind me to make sure Snot wasn't trying to get out.

"Sorry, the cat," I said, easing the door closed, so we were speaking through a smaller opening and I was mostly concealed.

He took a bulky device out of his pocket; it looked like a walkie-talkie. "What this says is 2 Clarke Avenue, for the Bright Horizons Youth Group, contact person Tammy. Definitely says 2 Clarke Avenue."

"It must be the church," I said. "They've got all kinds of groups over there."

I stuck my arm out the door and pointed at the side entrance of the church.

"Oh yeah, just in there? In those doors there?" he asked.

"I think so, yeah. In the basement." The coughing woman was out on the steps with her headphones around her neck, watching our interaction. For a moment I thought about asking her advice, was that the best entrance? But the delivery man was already walking away.

"Thanks my love," he called over his shoulder.

At least there was the coughing woman, I thought as I closed the door — if there was an emergency or something.

I MADE THE water in the shower hot. Snot sat on the toilet tank and watched me shampoo my hair; Courtney curled up in the sink, licking the bottom of the faucet. I tried to work out which day of the week it was: the Pleasant party was a Friday night, then Viv had visited, and last night I'd been alone. Monday?

I walked over to the theatre; Joanna was working box office. She was watching a muted episode of *Grey's Anatomy* with the subtitles on and drinking a Diet Coke. She tapped the space bar to pause the episode when I walked in. The Rolodex we used for organizing purchased tickets was out on the counter. I flipped through it, recognizing almost all of the names. Actors, directors, playwrights and regulars. It was opening night of a comedy about the cod moratorium. The play was backed by an anonymous investor, it had a huge budget. The production company had hoodies and other merch on display, underwear with the show's title printed across the butt.

After two nights in St. John's, the show was going on a Canada-wide tour with a long run at the National Arts Centre in Ottawa. The cast would be flown from city to city; the truck would drive to meet them as they slept in their hotel rooms. I'd heard three drivers had been hired so they could switch out when they got tired and the truck would never have to stop. I'd watched it in rehearsal, before the police invasion—it felt like a lifetime ago even though only two days had passed. Or three days?

"Is tonight sold out?" I asked.

"Oh completely, why? You wanted to go?"

The phone rang and Joanna held up a finger to say "one minute." I leaned on the counter as she tried to talk someone through buying a ticket online. A lot of the patrons were elderly and not computer-literate. Eventually Joanna asked for the woman's credit card number and keyed it into the Moneris machine on the counter. She minimized the full-screen image of a doctor with a clipboard held against her chest — the words *I don't want to frighten you but* in chunky white font at the bottom of the screen. She pulled up the program we use to sell tickets. She scrunched the phone between her shoulder and ear as she typed the woman's information into the system.

"It'll be here waiting for you, just tell us your name and we'll grab it for you. Of course, no problem, you as well." Joanna was rolling her eyes.

"Did Claire send out the schedule?" I asked when she finally laid the receiver down.

"Yeah, last night, you didn't get it?"

At first, the thought of telling the story again made me feel tired but once I got going Joanna's reaction brought me to life. She thought the cops' behaviour was despicable. I was getting wound up, a blustery rage filling my chest as I thought about the young cop in my messy bedroom.

"I wasn't even dressed!" I was practically shouting in Joanna's face.

"Fucking assholes," Joanna said. "And I can say that 'cause my dad's a cop."

I paused, taking it in, trying not to let anything show on my face.

"I mean I had a T-shirt and bike shorts on, but I wasn't wearing a bra." I wanted to maintain the same level of outrage so she'd know my opinion of her hadn't changed, but I'd lost momentum.

"Still," Joanna said. "You were in your own home."

"Anyway, I just came down to find out when I'm working."

Joanna put the straw to her lips and sucked up the last drips of her pop.

"I'll look it up."

She printed out the schedule for me. When she handed it to me, I felt disappointed that there was no reason to stick around. Nowhere to go besides my empty house. I wasn't working until the following night. I folded the piece of paper twice and put it in my coat pocket.

"I'm just going to use the phone for a sec, okay?"

"Go for it." Joanna un-paused her show.

I went to dial Viv's number but realized I didn't have it memorized. I should have written it down. I wanted to ask her if she was going to the punk show at The Peter Easton.

"Never mind." I put the receiver back in place.

Joanna gave me a concerned look.

"All good! Thank you!" I left, feeling deeply lonely.

On the way home I saw a woman stopped on the corner near Venice Pizza. She was holding a single-slice box, head tilted back, looking into the sky. The spectacle the woman was making of staring up at the sky annoyed me. I almost didn't ask what she was looking at because she clearly wanted to be asked so badly. But then I felt guilty about being so mean-spirited.

"Something up there?"

"There, straight up above the door," the woman said.

I saw two piercing red lights on the belly of a hovering grey bot, about eight feet above our heads. When I listened for it, I could hear it buzzing, the mechanical equivalent of treading water.

"A drone." I glanced at the woman to see if she knew that already.

"It's creepy." She nodded.

"They're cheap now," I said. "It's probably a kid."

"This is the second time I've seen it in this neighbourhood." The woman swooped her finger around, a gesture that seemed to include my street.

"My little cousin got one for his birthday, he flew it up too high the first time he had it out and it blew away. There are cheap ones now," I said again, "relatively cheap. A couple hundred bucks."

The woman nodded but looked unconvinced. I walked on. I glanced over my shoulder, some part of me was worried the whirring machine was following me, but the drone was just hovering above the door to the pizza shop.

WHEN I GOT home there was a cruiser pulled up in front of the house and a cop on the step. He was tall, with thick, fluffy hair. From the top of the street I couldn't tell his age. I watched him turn on the step and walk towards the car.

"Excuse me." My voice came out quiet at first but I rushed down the street towards him and that caught his attention. As I got closer I saw he was mid-thirties-ish with a square face and big, pond-green eyes below blond eyebrows. I resented that—I would have preferred to talk to some dumpy older man. This guy had all the arrogance of a young cop mixed with the added smugness of knowing he was conventionally handsome.

"Excuse me," I said, more firmly this time.

"Yeah?"

"I live here," I said over the top of his car.

A window was open in the big industrial kitchen on the first floor of the church. Shaggy's "Angel" was blasting inside and the smell of baking cinnamon buns was pouring into the parking lot.

"What's your name?" he asked.

"Stacey Power."

He came around the front of the car and stood over me. "Can I see some ID?"

"I don't have any ID." I looked into his movie-star face. His uniform was snug around his broad shoulders. I hated him.

"Not in the house?" he asked.

Maybe he was going to arrest me. Maybe I had horribly underestimated the situation. I looked to the fire escape but no one was there. I was all on my own.

"What is this concerning?" I said finally.

He looked me up and down, annoyed by my tone. "I have a document for you but I need to confirm your identity first. That's all."

I saw he had two envelopes in his hand—normal-sized envelopes with a coat of arms printed in the top corner of each. My name was handwritten in pen on the front in scratchy letters.

"What is it?" I asked. When he didn't answer I added, "concerning?"

"I'm going to need to see ID. You can come down to the station at your own convenience if you'd rather, but you'll have to bring ID down there too."

I breathed in the cold, yeasty air. "Angel" ended and Shakira's "Whenever, Wherever" started. Someone's '90s playlist. A band of dark clouds was gathering over the church, they were grey at the top and bruise-blue on the bottom.

"I'll run in and get it."

"Okay." He rested an elbow on the roof of the car, like he was bragging about his height.

I shut the door behind me and left him on the sidewalk. Once I found my ID I brought it outside and closed the door behind me again. Pinpricks of icy rain were falling. He looked at the ID and handed it back to me with one of the envelopes.

"Is there a letter for Holly Deveraux too? She's my roommate, I can give it to her."

"I can't give you that information. If you want to read your letter now I can answer any questions you have about your letter."

I tore the envelope open and scanned the page. I couldn't take in full sentences, only certain words and phrases. *Available for pickup. Signature required. Investigation ongoing.*

"I can get my things?" I asked.

"Yeah," he answered. "Bring down your ID."

He walked around the car.

"Anything else?" he asked, opening the car door.

"Does this mean they're done with me?"

Standing in the open door he shifted his hips.

"I'm not a suspect?"

"I don't have that information. I can tell you the investigation is ongoing."

"But this is good. Right?" It felt like grovelling.

"The investigation is ongoing." He pursed his lips.

I tried to think of another way to phrase the question; sometimes if you find the right way to ask they have to answer. Or they're supposed to, anyway.

"Okay?" He said it in a way that meant goodbye.

"When should I come to the station?"

"Anytime after three p.m. tomorrow." He slapped the top of the car and swung down into the seat.

I went into the house, balling the letter and envelope up with both hands. The stiff corners dug into my palms. I threw it across the room—it hit the wall and dropped to the floor, almost landing in Snot and Courtney's water dish. After a moment I picked up my crumpled letter and brought it upstairs. I might need it to get my things back.

I smoothed the letter out on the vinyl seat of the kitchen chair I kept in my room. I took a plastic file folder out of my closet, a cheap thing made of hot-pink plastic. I stored all my important bits of paper in it: my birth certificate, my high school and university diplomas, my T4s. Proof that I was born and educated and worked. I slid the letter into the back of the folder. Proof of what?

I WENT DOWN to the restaurant to tell Viv about the letter. It was steamy inside and smelled like pea soup. The owner

was in with his family, so Viv could only talk for a moment
in the porch by the "Please Wait To Be Seated" sign.

"Are you okay?" she asked.

"Yeah, I'm fine, I think it's good, they're giving my stuff
back. That seems good, right?"

"He's looking at me, I literally just brought their order
to the kitchen. Like two minutes ago. I have to go. Unless
you want a table?"

I thought about staying and drinking a skinny mug
of coffee but I hated being around the owner, especially
since he fired me. I took a step back towards the door so
he wouldn't see me.

"Can you come over later?" I asked.

"We're going to Mike's parents' for supper, his sister is
in town with his niece," she said.

"When will you be home?"

"I think it might be kind of late. His sister's in town."

"I could meet you when you get off and walk you
home."

"Mike is picking me up, we're going straight to dinner.
Do you want to come see Mike's band tomorrow night?"

"I'm working."

"I'll meet you at the theatre when I get off." Viv turned
towards the owner's table; I saw her face transform into
her serving smile. It was a very convincing smile — if I
hadn't known what her real smile looked like I would've
believed it. I was always telling Viv she should be an actress.

THE NEXT DAY I walked through drizzle to the station with the letter folded in the pocket of my rain jacket. There was about two feet of dirty snow on the unplowed sidewalk. I walked a path flattened by people on their way to work that morning.

It was the first time I'd been inside the cop shop. The doors were two heavy sheets of tinted glass. There were smudges left by people's palms on the tube-shaped metal handles.

The lobby was lined with back-lit display cases filled with Royal Newfoundland Constabulary propaganda. In one case a huge, broad-shouldered mannequin wore a black cape with a gold clasp, black pants, and shiny black shoes with thick rubber heels. A black helmet rested above the mannequin's smooth, featureless face. White letters on the wall behind the mannequin spelled OBSERVANT, and a little further down, above a smattering of black-and-white photos, BRAVE, and in the bottom corner near the ground, EMPATHETIC.

Near the door, a young couple were taking turns bending to speak into a circular hole cut in the bulletproof Plexiglas that protected a cop doing administrative work.

"He's a Jack Russell terrier," the girl said into the hole. "You can't get them here, my mom had to fly to Nova Scotia and bring him back."

The guy leaned in: "It's a fifteen-hundred-dollar dog."

"Plus the travel expenses," the girl said.

The cop spoke into a microphone on a silver coil. "Someone told you to come down here? On the phone?"

"They said we need a form," the girl said. "I'm worried about Flakey. People are sick."

"You don't know what they'll do," her boyfriend added.

"Give me a minute." The cop stood and walked to a wall of squat filing cabinets. Was he wearing a gun? Yes.

"Check Facebook again," the guy said to his girlfriend, putting a hand on her back.

"I just checked it." But she pulled her phone out of her pocket and checked again.

I looked into the display case to avoid staring. I could have commiserated but the moment had passed and now I needed to pretend I wasn't eavesdropping. I wandered towards a case in the back of the room. WHAT MAKES A CONSTABLE? was printed above a collection of photos of cops on horseback patrolling St. John's back before the streets were paved. Words you might find on the wall of a kindergarten classroom were printed below the question. FAIR and TEAMWORK.

"Lost Pets NL just shared it," she said. "They've got over two thousand followers."

"There you go," the guy said.

The cop came back from the filing cabinet empty-handed and said into the microphone, "Why do you think he's stolen?"

"The leash was clipped to the clothesline," the girl said. "The gate was closed. It's got a latch."

"We told your buddy on the phone this already," the guy said. "It's a fifteen-hundred-dollar dog. You can train them for acting, you see them in commercials all the time."

"People will steal anything," the girl said. "They're sick."

I thought I should make my way around the room and

stand behind them, assert that I was waiting. Someone else might come in and take my place in the line.

"I don't know who told you to come in here. I can't imagine what form they're talking about. I'd say Facebook is your best bet, honestly. People have a lot of luck with that."

"First they sent us up to the other location, in CBS. We were waiting twenty minutes there, they said come down here."

"Must have been a misunderstanding," the cop said.

"This is a fucking joke," the boyfriend said, shaking his head.

His skin was windburned. He looked older than the girlfriend, easily ten years older. His hands made big fists at his sides. The woman looked at me, a look that was part warning, part apology.

"Step away from the counter," the cop said. "I'm going to help this young lady now."

The boyfriend bent and spoke into the hole, "A fucking joke."

"Garry," the girl said quietly.

The cop stood up on the other side of the glass.

"Yeah, I'm going." The guy rolled his shoulders and walked to the entrance, the woman followed behind him. The cop settled back into his wheelie office chair. The heavy door yawned shut behind the couple with the missing dog. By the time the door met the frame they were halfway across the rainy parking lot, the man stomping ahead of his girlfriend.

The cop beckoned me by folding his fingers into his palm.

"Someone delivered this to me," I said into the hole and slid the letter through a narrow slot in the bottom of the glass shield.

The cop opened the letter and read it. I watched his face, it stayed neutral. I had been wrapped up in the drama of Flakey and the poor woman sent out into the rain with her hostile boyfriend, but now that I was alone with the officer, anxiety about my own situation crept up through my chest. He dropped the letter on the counter and looked me in the face; I could tell by the way his chin moved that he was trying to work something out of his back tooth with his tongue. After a moment he picked the letter up again and looked over it.

"Okay, wait here. I'm going to see if Constable Bradley is able to see you." He left the open letter on the counter and disappeared through a door behind the glass.

There was a clock above that door, a white face ringed in black plastic. Just after four. Since they'd taken my phone I was noticing clocks: like phone booths, they are a disappearing blessing when you don't have a phone. Maybe Constable Bradley was going to tell me they'd found something disturbing on my hard drive or in my phone, something they hadn't even been looking for. Texts about buying drugs, PDFs of anti-state literature. I didn't want to meet the man who'd waded through everything inside my computer.

Eventually the cop came back. He folded my letter up, fit it back into its envelope and slid it out through the slot.

"Constable Bradley isn't in right now." The cop sat in his wheelie chair and rolled back and forth until he was at his preferred distance from his computer screen.

"He said to come by any time, the officer who delivered it."

The cop sighed through his nose.

"Normally that would be true, but Constable Bradley had some unexpected medical issues this week."

It was very quiet in the lobby. I picked my letter off the counter.

"I need my things."

"We're hoping Constable Bradley will be back before the end of the week. Call down tomorrow and hopefully I can give you some more information then. It's a medical issue, see."

"I don't have a phone." My voice came out whiney.

"You can find a phone." The cop turned his attention to the computer. "Have a good evening."

NINE

When I got back from the cop station I ate a piece of plain toast so I wouldn't be hungry at work. I whipped the crumbs off my chest and sniffed my armpits. I stank; it was an unfamiliar, metallic stink. I went up to my bedroom and rubbed deodorant into my sweaty armpit hair and found a clean shirt. Then I rushed down the stairs looking for my swipe card for the theatre — sometimes I hung it over the post at the bottom of the stairs. I heard a noise in the bathroom and thought it was the cats. I went to shoo them out; they always tore up the garbage and stole used Q-tips. They ripped the fluff off the tops and left the naked plastic sticks on the couch or on the living room rug.

But it was Holly in the bathroom. She had curled her highlighter-yellow hair into ringlets and pulled her fingers through it, turning the tight curls into loose, billowy waves. I'd watched her do that to her hair before. I used to sit on the edge of the bathtub and we'd share a joint while getting ready to go out. It was a ritual we'd started at Patrick Street with Viv and continued at Clarke Avenue.

I stopped in the doorway. "Hi, I'm just getting ready for work, have you seen my swipe card?" I'd decided to act like our last interaction hadn't been a fight. Like I hadn't crushed her glasses under my bare foot. She was choosing an eyeliner from a pile of makeup on the shelf above the toilet.

"I haven't seen it," she said without looking at me.

I stood in the doorway, watching her make matching wings on her eyelids. As soon as we moved in she'd taken over that whole shelf with her little beige tubs and silver tubes. She didn't even ask. Later more of it started accumulating on the skinny ledge above the mirrored cabinet.

"Maybe I left it at work," I said eventually.

She kept her eyes on the mirror and didn't respond. I slammed the front door when I left. I ended up having to borrow the box office person's swipe card.

THERE'D BEEN A media blitz about the cod moratorium play that morning. NTV and CBC Newfoundland & Labrador had shown up earlier in the week with all their gear to film the rehearsal. They'd interviewed the actors on the wooden stage outside the theatre — the cast wore their costumes under winter coats. A reviewer in the *Telegram* called it "Nouveau Codco."

When the show got out, the cast and their friends

thronged to the bar with an endless supply of drink tickets.

"That little change in the blocking completely trans-formed the scene for me," the lead was saying as I poured a glass of house white for her. I scribbled *house white* in Sharpie on the ticket and dropped it into a mug filled with used drink tickets.

"You could feel it in the audience," her friend answered. "When it lands, it lands."

"I looked over my shoulder and saw the anger on his face and I really felt it, right in my guts. Thank you." She took the glass of wine from me, turned and leaned both elbows on the bar.

"And that's what we need to carry us into the next scene," her friend said, squinting at the menu above my head.

"I never looked back at him before, so I never saw the anger—I was imagining the anger but I wasn't seeing it. Like literally seeing it."

"As an audience, we need to see you see that anger, to justify the next scene," her friend said. "I'm going to have a glass of the Pinot Grigio too, please—actually, two glasses but you can just pour them into the same glass, save me coming back up."

"You felt like it was stronger than Monday night?" the lead asked.

I tipped two pours into one glass and lifted it carefully up onto the bar. The surface of the wine shivered against the rim of the glass.

"Oh my god, yes." The friend slopped some wine on the bar when she picked up the glass. She looked at the puddle and then looked back at the lead, deciding to ignore it. "Wednesday was good but if I'm honest, the transition between those two scenes wasn't there. Tonight it was there and it made a difference. It was an important lesson for me, actually, as a director."

They sauntered back into the crowd. A man in a suit jacket and jeans put a hand on the lead's back. I saw her stiffen then soften, smiling a customer-service smile at him. Probably a funder.

I'd been hoping to get off early but the cast and crew were high on post-media-blitz glee. Plus there'd been a standing ovation. And it was one of the cast members' birthdays. His mother had brought a lemon meringue pie and everyone sang to him. I dug through the catering cupboard and got them plates and plastic forks. I even found a pie server, a flat stainless-steel triangle with an ornate handle.

"Not very environmentally friendly," I heard one of them say once I was back behind the bar. I looked up and saw a tall skinny guy in a salt-and-pepper hat, one of the actors, twirling a filling-streaked plastic fork.

"You kind of expect more from an arts organization, right?" the stage manager said.

That was when the jealousy hit. No one had even offered me any pie. I thought of how satisfying it would be if I landed a part in the joint-production movie. They'd all be up my hole then.

After they left and I'd done the cash and the inventory count, I wiped pie crumbs off the table at the back of the room. There was a jellied lump of bright yellow filling on the table: I scooped it up with my finger and ate it. Much tarter than I'd expected.

Viv was waiting for me outside the theatre when I got off. She was sitting cross-legged on the wooden stage, her bouncy red curls spilling all over the shoulders of her puffy black coat. She was wearing the dark red lipstick she sometimes put on for a night out.

"I've been here for an hour," she said, hopping off the stage. "We have to hurry, they're on next."

"I'm sorry—I would've texted you if I had my phone." I pulled on the door, making double-sure it was locked. I could hear the alarm beeping inside, counting down the ten seconds until it was activated. The transport truck that would carry the set across the country was parked beside the loading door to the theatre. There were two guys inside the truck smoking; I recognized them both from the bar earlier. They'd come down after loading the sets and drunk a quick beer by themselves while the actors and their friends decided where to go next, The Duke or The Rockhouse.

"It's okay," Viv said.

One of the guys in the truck cracked the window as we walked past. He was probably in his mid-thirties and he was wearing a cowboy shirt. His lank hair was down to his jaw.

"Hey," he said.

"Hey." I stopped.

"Want to check out the truck? We have weed." He held up the joint.

I looked at Viv.

"We have to get to the show," she said. "They're on next."

"We're going to a show," I said to the guys in the truck, even though I really wanted to see inside. I was picturing a bunk with a quilt tucked around a thin mattress, a stack of paperback books, a cooler with some sandwiches. Maybe a lamp?

They nodded and put the window up. Viv was a couple of paces ahead of me and I had to rush to catch up to her.

"Have you been talking to Holly? Is she going to the show?" I asked her.

"Yeah."

"She's going?" I asked.

"Yes, why?"

"She's not talking to me."

"It's because of the glasses thing," Viv said.

"It's just really childish. Can we slow down?"

"They're going on now."

"Now?"

Viv looked at her phone. "He said in ten minutes, that was a while ago."

"Like we're living together, don't you think that's childish? Refusing to speak to someone? Someone you're living with?"

Viv can make her blue eyes go completely dead: it's like there's a dimmer switch on her irises. When she's annoyed she cranks the voltage down; she won't be dignifying you with the full intensity of her beautiful eyes.

"I don't want to talk about it," she said. "I can't understand why you did that."

"She has like three pairs of glasses. They're probably

from one of those cheap websites." I'd had the same scratched-up glasses for about five years.

"It's not okay, it's shitty," Viv said.

There was a big group of people smoking outside The Peter Easton when we arrived. I checked the crowd for Holly. It was mostly men, metal guys with long hair and chunky rings on their fingers. When we got inside I ordered me and Viv two double gin and sodas. The bartender poured them into fluted glasses like the ones my grandmother used for Jell-O sundaes. She hooked a wizened lime wedge on each glass.

I paid with my tips from the theatre. Some people with drink tickets don't tip at all, others tip more because they're not paying for drinks. In the end it rounded up to a better than usual night money-wise; I'd left the theatre with four twenties in my pocket. I saw Holly as I was handing the bartender my money. She was coming out of the bathroom, noticed me and looked away.

I found Viv up front, nodding along to Mike's band. The singer took one big step forward, bent at the waist, and started whipping his head around, turning his long brown hair into a tornado. Viv was smiling at Mike, who was playing an elaborate guitar solo on the left side of the stage. I presented her with the drink and she wrapped one arm around me in a hug; she'd forgotten she was annoyed with me. I was leaning into Viv's hug, holding my drink up high to protect it from getting jostled, when I saw Kris over her shoulder.

"I don't really want this," Viv said about the drink I'd bought her. "I'll hold it until you're ready for it."

"Are you mad at me?" I asked her.

"I'm just tired, I'm going to leave after the next band."

I finished my drink in three long slurps on the short straw and took the second glass from Viv.

Halfway through the set there was some technical difficulty—a pedal wasn't working, cords had to be adjusted. Viv ducked through the crowd to say hi to her co-worker, the girl with the neck tattoo. Holly was on the plaid couch in the corner of the room, cozied up to Dave King. I waited for Kris to look my way. When she did, I smiled and she nodded. The band started back up and a mosh pit erupted between us.

"I was about to ask if you wanted a beer but it looks like you're all set." Kris was whisper-yelling in my ear with a hand cupped by her mouth. I hadn't seen her cross the room.

She walked off in the direction of the bar.

"What did she say to you?" Viv screamed in my ear when she reappeared beside me.

"Asked if I wanted a beer," I screamed back.

A COUPLE OF drinks later I kissed Viv goodnight on each cheek in the bathroom. A stall door opened behind her and pushed her into me while my lips were on her face. We fell against the sink. I smeared saliva across her cheek; the back of my shirt got wet from water that had splashed up on the lip of the sink. We both laughed.

"Okay, I'm leaving," Viv said, untangling herself from me. "Are you going to sleep with Kris?"

"I think so, I want to, does it seem like it?"

We both stepped back to let the woman who'd been in the stall get at the sink.

"Yes."

"Either of you girls spare a cigarette?" the woman asked. She looked about sixty; she was wearing a pink top with spaghetti straps and her hair was dyed jet black. The pores on her cheeks were deep and wide. Her eyes were glossy with drunkenness.

"Sorry," Viv and I said together.

We followed the woman out of the bathroom into the bar. Mike was waiting by the door, his guitar case strapped to his back, Viv's coat in his arms. Sometimes I got overwhelmed with affection for Mike, because he loved Viv too. She walked over to him, waving to me as she went. The punk band that'd been playing were tearing down and Blue Öyster Cult came through the bar speakers.

I found Kris in a crowd of people gathered around the break-open dispenser. Holly was in the middle of the semicircle, feeding a five dollar bill into the slot in the front of the machine. The bill shot back out and floated down to the carpet. Kris made room for me to stand beside her but her eyes were on Holly. On either side of the break-open machine there were four VLTs pushed up against the wall, a tall stool set in front of each one. Every one of those stools was filled. The screens flashed bright lights on the faces of the VLT players.

"Put it in the other way," someone said.

Holly smoothed the bill out, flipped it around and fed it into the slot. The machine obediently swallowed it.

Everyone cheered. Kris made a fist by her chest and slowly pulled it down to her hip in celebration. Holly clocked me at Kris's side. In the machine, the metal rings that held a row of break-opens twirled backwards and released two tickets. Holly crouched and fished the tickets out of the bottom.

"Last ones," she said, holding them up.

"(Don't Fear) The Reaper" shifted from the wheedling guitar solo to the pounding finale. I felt Kris's arm around my hips, her small hand squeezing the pudge there. Holly tore open all the tabs on the first ticket. The crowd moaned when she flashed the worthless rows of mismatched symbols that had been hidden under the tabs. Kris stood on tiptoe to whisper in my ear, "What are you doing now?"

"I don't know, why? What are you doing? You're leaving?"

"I'm leaving now soon, yeah."

"I'm probably going to leave soon too," I said.

Everyone around us was heckling Holly to buy another round of break-opens. They were digging through their pockets looking for money to huck in.

"Want to walk together?" Kris asked.

Blue Öyster Cult ended and the joyful acapella opening to "Fat Bottomed Girls" filled the bar. The woman from the bathroom whooped and held an empty shot glass in the air.

"Yeah," I said.

"Okay, I'm going to grab my coat."

We pushed through people smoking outside the front door and walked quickly up the street. It'd been warm that afternoon but the temperature dropped when it got dark and now the sidewalks were slicked with invisible ice. At the top of the street my foot shot out from beneath me; Kris caught and righted me.

"Nearly lost you," she said.

She had a practical coat, puffy pockets of synthetic down sheathed in slick waterproof material. I held tight to her sleeve, both of us skating along the sidewalk to her house. She unlocked her front door and we stumbled up the steps to her third-floor bedroom.

We dropped our wet winter coats on the bedroom floor. I pushed her onto her bed and when she reclined, I undid her pants. She had bike grease caked around her fingernails. She flipped me over and held my hands over my head. We made out and ground our crotches together through our pants for a long time before stripping all our clothes off.

THE NEXT MORNING I woke up hungover in Kris's tidy bedroom. I had a voice acting gig later that day. A thirty-second spot for a mobile home vendor with a big lot on the outskirts of town. I poked Kris in the ribs and felt the muscle stretched around her narrow rib cage.

"Do you have the time?" I asked quietly.

She opened her eyes, skimmed a hand beneath the blankets and shook her phone free from the sheets. It was only eight-thirty in the morning, hours before I had to be at the recording studio to read copy about a blowout sale on units with built-in compost toilets.

"Should I make us coffee?" Kris asked.

When we got downstairs, Frankie was already in the kitchen making themself a smoothie. They were shaking a bag of frozen mango chunks into the blender in pink terry-cloth shorts. They weren't wearing a shirt and I had to stop myself from staring at the triangular patch of thick curly hair on their skinny chest. Frankie's laptop was open on the table. They were streaming CBC's *The Sunday Edition.*

Kris changed the filter in the coffee percolator. She peeled the plastic lid off a big tin of supermarket-brand coffee and shook grinds into the basket without measuring. Viv would not have approved. It was bright in the kitchen. I thought how nice it was not to be waking up alone at Clarke Avenue.

"Sorry," Frankie said and pressed the button on the blender. They pulsed it in a series of short bursts and then opened the lid to pour in more almond milk.

"Oh, this came for you." Kris held up a silver package with a mailing label stuck to the front. "What is it?"

Frankie stared at the package; they lifted the lid off the blender, stuck a finger in and tasted the smoothie.

"Something you ordered online, looks like it's from the States," Kris said, shaking the bag. "Something light."

"Oh!" Frankie snatched it from her.

"What is it?"

They ripped the packing open: "This!"

It was a butt plug with three feet of fake hair hanging off the end. The tail was pastel purple. Frankie dragged their fingers through it, untangling it.

Kris lifted a cast-iron frying pan off the stove and put it in the sink.

"I mean, it's kind of a joke," Frankie said.

"Expensive joke," Kris answered.

"Don't put dish soap on that," Frankie said.

"I wasn't going to."

Frankie stuffed the toy back into the ripped packaging and tossed it on the table.

"It's just really hard to get them seasoned properly."

"I know. I know how to wash it. So it's kind of not a joke?" Kris asked.

"It wasn't that expensive. Do you want some smoothie?"

Kris shook her head.

"Stacey? Do you want some smoothie?" Frankie took down a second glass and held the lip of the blender over it. "Lots here."

"I'm just asking," Kris said. "No judgement."

"You can taste it first if you want, spoons are in there," Frankie said.

I wasn't expecting to be included in the conversation. "It looks good, I don't need to taste it first," I told them.

"Big glass?" they asked.

"Please." I nodded.

After breakfast I went upstairs and collected my coat from Kris's bedroom. When I came down she was waiting in the porch to say goodbye.

"That was fun," she said.

"Yeah." Coats were hung three and four deep on a row of hooks by the front door. When I stood up from tying my shoes, I brushed against a parka and a landslide of coats fell to the floor.

"Don't worry about that." Kris picked the coats up and draped them over her arm. "We should hang out again."

"Yeah." I knew what was coming. Frankie was tidying in the kitchen, the radio show had ended or maybe been turned off and I was sure they could hear everything.

"So maybe I'll message you?" Kris said.

"Well, my phone is kind of broken."

"I think I have you on Facebook, though, right?" she asked.

"Yeah, I just don't have a phone right now." I could see she was trying to work out what I was saying. "So I can't really look at Facebook right now. But I'm going to get another phone, soon. Probably tomorrow, I'm working today and tonight."

"So message you on Facebook?"

"Yeah."

I opened the door and stepped into the street. I wished I'd kissed her before I left.

ON THE DAY of the search, I'd looked over Sergeant Hamlyn's shoulder and seen the young cop kneel in front of the braided rag rug in the living room. Viv had made the rug years before, at an all-day workshop at the Anna Templeton Centre. She gave it to me when I moved into the house by the church because Courtney liked sleeping on it. It was coated in orange fur: when you stepped on it puffs of fur rose up and floated away.

The young cop had laid all our electronics out on the rug. Why there? Everything was cluttered together on the lumpy oval: my laptop, phone, and flash drives; Holly's external hard drive; one small piece of paper—maybe a receipt?

"What do you know about the girls who lived here before?" Sergeant Hamlyn asked.

"Nothing, I don't know them."

Hamlyn was making notes in his coil-bound notebook. He wrapped his hand around the back of the book and tilted it towards himself so I couldn't read what he was writing. The gesture seemed childish to me.

"You know their names," he said.

"Just Natalie Swanson, I don't remember the other one."

The young cop lifted a heavy camera out of a black, soft-sided bag. He took a wide shot of the electronics on the hairy mat and then leaned down for a close-up of each one.

"You met them both?" Hamlyn asked.

"Like, very briefly."

"Where?"

"Here, in this house. When we were moving in."

The young cop collected the flash drives and another cop crossed the room and took them from him. The second cop walked out of view and I heard the front door close.

"Don't worry about him." Hamlyn said. "You stay focused on what we're doing here."

I looked Hamlyn in the face. His skin was dry; the

wrinkles around his mouth were collecting dusty bits of dead skin.

"Why were they still here?" he asked.

I could hear the young cop moving around and tried hard not to look in his direction.

"It was a little bit before, a few days before we moved in. Holly — we bought some furniture off Natalie, a bedroom set."

Hamlyn made a note in his pad, and I took the opportunity to look over his shoulder at the young cop, who was sliding my laptop into a clear plastic bag. He took a stack of multicoloured sticky notes out of his pocket. I could see other uniformed cops walking back and forth outside the living-room windows, squeezing the walkie-talkies on their shoulders and craning their necks to speak into them.

"And the other one?" Hamlyn asked.

The young cop slapped a lime-green sticky note on the bag with my computer in it and wrote on it with a pen. He turned his wrist to look at his watch and made another note.

"I didn't talk to her, she was just on her way out when were moving in."

"What did you talk to Natalie Swanson about?"

"I don't know," I said.

"Think about it." Hamlyn was holding his pen above the notebook.

"The bed, I guess. Holly tested out the bed."

⌐

WHEN WE WERE twelve and thirteen Viv and I spent most weekends at the mall. On this particular Saturday, like most Saturdays at that time, me, Viv and Heather were hoping to run into Christian Sharpe and his friends. The boys were three years older than us, already in high school. We'd met them at an all-ages punk show in the church hall down the street from my house.

They were always mid-scheme when we found them. Once we bought a package of army-man action figures with parachutes from the dollar store and threw them one by one over the railing by Victoria's Secret, aiming for people's heads. The army men had spiralled and then drifted serenely away from their targets, landing on their sides on the tiled floor.

Another time the boys superglued a toonie to the floor in the food court and we watched people trying to pick it up for hours. They would glance around, stoop, and pick at it, becoming more and more confused and frustrated. They'd straighten up, red in the face, and half-heartedly kick at it before walking away.

Next we ripped open a condom package and glued the greasy plastic tube to the floor. We giggled at the people who gave it a wide berth, some shaking their heads with a renewed disdain for the world.

Christian got banned from the mall for two months because he used a screwdriver to undo the top of a bubble gum machine and scooped gum balls into his bookbag. He saw the security guard coming and jogged out of the mall with his knapsack flapping open. We watched it all happen, crowded around a four-seater on the opposite side of the food court. We met him down in the parking garage.

It was dim in the parking garage. The ceiling and walls were made from lumpy concrete that looked like oatmeal, the air smelled of gas. When we found Christian his hands were streaked with rainbow dye. We passed his open bookbag around, everyone taking out a sticky fistful of gum balls. They were coated in grime from the bottom of his knapsack and the dye had worn off in places, leaving them mostly grey. We all stuffed our cheeks with the gum and chewed. The boys let sugary spit dribble down their chins. I saw Christian and Viv looking at each other, their faces distorted by lumps of gum moving in their chipmunk cheeks. Later that summer they made out in *Anger Management* starring Jack Nicholson and were briefly a couple. Viv had lots of boyfriends when we were teenagers; I never dated anyone until university. I was always sitting beside her in the movies, staring straight ahead while she leaned over the opposite armrest, all tangled up with whatever guy she was dating at the time. I'd tell her about the parts she'd missed while we waited in the porch for her mom to pick us up.

We were having a contest to see how far we could spit our stiff hunks of gum across the parking lot when two security guards appeared.

"We've got your picture, you're banned," one of them called. "You with the bookbag, two months' probation. If we see your face in there again, we're calling the cops."

Nicola Stevens had been caught shoplifting once and she'd told us the security guards brought her into a cinderblock office where they watched every corner of the mall on closed-circuit TVs. The walls were plastered with pixelated images of people who were banned from the mall. Now Christian's face would be added to the mosaic.

The two men kept their distance—maybe the parking garage was outside of their jurisdiction. They'd come to hand down Christian's sentence, and when they were done they walked towards the elevator that would carry them back up into the mall. Once the security guards were far enough away, the boys made a show of laughing hysterically, slapping their thighs, yelling, "You're not even real cops!"

"Who cares? Who fucking cares?" Christian was saying. "Banned from the mall? Who cares?"

He kicked the concrete wall with his torn Converse sneaker, then tried to stomp the pain out of his toes. One of his friends wrapped an arm around his shoulder. "Fuck them, man."

On the Saturday I was remembering, two months had passed since the gum day—we'd been counting down. We knew Christian was allowed back at the mall, now with the revered status of the formerly banned. Viv, Heather and I spent the evening wandering around, hoping to run into him and his friends.

We'd already walked through the arcade, checking for spools of red tickets left hanging out of the machines. We put on tester lipsticks in Shoppers. We dribbled basketballs in the sports aisle at Wal-Mart. We walked through the lobby of the movie theatre and fished abandoned bags of popcorn out of the garbage. The whole time we were giddy with hope that we might run into the boys.

After cycling through both levels of the mall, we sat in the food court with our cold popcorn, losing faith. There was only an hour until the mall closed. The three of us pooled our change to take a photo in the booth at the edge of the food court. It cost three-fifty and we paid the last twenty-five cents in nickels. I sat on the circular stool, Heather squeezed in behind me and Viv sat on my lap. Viv pulled the pleated curtain closed. When the first flash filled the booth, Heather wrapped her arms around me and Viv and we all smiled into the glare. In the dark afterwards Viv said, "Lift up your shirt."

She pulled her own shirt and bra up over her face; her bare side brushed against my cheek. Behind me, Heather pulled her shirt up.

"Quick," Viv said.

I lifted my shirt, straightened up and tried to suck my tummy in. Light filled the booth. I wished I wasn't sitting down. I could feel my belly hanging over my pyramid-spike belt. Viv and Heather were both washboard-thin, I would look so stupid beside them. We stayed frozen in the same position as the light went off two more times. The sounds of the food court were loud in the booth; feet walked by the curtain. We waited for a fifth flash but nothing happened.

"I think it's done," Viv said.

We shifted our clothes back into place. Viv pulled the curtain open and we gathered around the front of the machine. The booth hummed loudly. We made a human shield around the slot where the photos were dispensed.

"Is it working?" Heather asked.

"It takes three to five minutes," I said, reading the back-lit poster on the side of the booth.

"Did we pick colour or black and white?" Viv asked.

"Colour," Heather said.

"We should've done black and white, it would've been classier."

The strip of photos slid out of the slot; Viv caught it and pressed it to her chest. She peeled the strip away from her body, looking down her nose at it. She laughed a loud, harsh laugh and pressed the photos back into her T-shirt.

"Let me see," I said.

"Hold it so we can see," Heather said.

"They're hilarious, you guys should see your faces."

"Let me see it." I felt a rush of heat travelling up my neck into my cheeks.

Viv held the strip up over her head and waved it in the air.

"Oh my god! Stop it!" Heather screamed.

A mother eating burgers with her two kids gave us a dirty look.

"Fine." Viv passed the photos to Heather, who held them so I could see.

Heather was right: colour was a mistake. Everything was so garish. I actually didn't mind how my body looked. My boobs were way bigger than Viv' and Heather's — they looked like children next to me. The bottom half of my stomach, the part that hung out over my belt, was out of the frame.

"Stacey looks hot," Viv said, and snatched the photo strip out of Heather's hand. She folded it in two and slid it into her jeans pocket.

"What are you doing with that?" I asked.

"I'm going to put it somewhere safe," Viv said.

"We should rip it up," Heather said.

"No way," Viv said.

I didn't weigh in but I silently hoped Viv wouldn't rip it up. I hoped it hard, directing my wish up through the asbestos-filled ceiling tiles, not to god exactly but into the sky. I'd never liked how I looked in a photo before, especially not when I was beside Viv.

We had forty-five minutes until Viv's mom showed up, so we took a final trip around the mall. We checked for the boys in the skateboarding store where they sometimes leaned on the glass case filled with bearings and wheels and other heavy parts. We checked in the family bathroom where they sometimes hopped up on the change table to roll joints on exercise books in their laps. We pushed open a heavy side door and stuck our heads into the dark wind-tunnel of an alley where they sometimes smoked the joints. Mostly we wanted to brag. The boys hadn't come to the mall that night but in their absence we'd come up with our own scheme, something worse than anything they could ever have dreamed up or executed.

A few days after we took the photos, Viv called. I pulled a chair up to the wall so I could rest my sock feet on the heater and look out the kitchen window while we talked. Viv called every night after supper and I always sat in this spot until it got dark and my reflection showed up in the window. There were two grey smears on the white radiator from me resting my dirty feet there.

"Are you alone?" she asked me.

"What do you mean?"

"Is anyone around you? Like your mom?"

"She's upstairs."

"The police have our photo booth pictures. My mom saw it on the news."

I squeezed a tangle of curly phone cord in my hand and released it.

"Is she going to tell my mom?"

"They don't know it's us, she said the police are looking for three girls who got photo booth pictures at the mall and they're going to arrest them for indecent exposure."

"Viv!"

"I don't know what happened, I must have dropped it. It was an accident."

"Did you tell Heather?"

"No, don't tell Heather, she'll tell her mom."

I was tempted to tell my mom.

That night I dreamed I opened the door to the family bathroom and a wall of water crashed out. I was swept through the mall in a wave filled with scraps of shit-stained toilet paper and used tampons.

The next day Viv was late for homeroom — the teacher was taking attendance when Viv walked in wearing a chopped-up pair of red fishnet stockings on her forearms. The armbands annoyed me. I was annoyed that she'd taken time to get dressed up when we had a serious problem to address. The photos had been her idea; the fact they were discovered was her fault. She had threaded red laces through the holes in her army boots to match the sleeves. Because she was late, all the desks around me were full and she had to sit on the opposite side of the room.

When the loudspeaker crackled to life for morning announcements I was convinced the principal would call us down to the office. But it was just the usual: tickets for the semi-formal were still on sale, smoking on school property was still banned, a piece of jewellery had been found in the third-floor girls' bathroom.

Viv and I met in the hallway when homeroom got out.

"Mom was lying," she said.

Viv had put her jeans in the washer with the folded photo strip in the pocket. Her mother found the damp string of images when she changed the clothes over later that afternoon.

"Is she mad?" I asked.

"Yeah."

"Is she going to tell my mom?"

The crowd in the hallway was thinning out; I had to get to biology on the third floor. Hannah Reese was standing at her open locker, clearly listening to our conversation.

"I don't know, I guess not." Viv shrugged dramatically, Hannah Reese slammed her locker shut. It was like someone had shaken up a two-litre of pop and unscrewed the cap inside my chest. A carbonated spray of relief.

HOLLY WASN'T AROUND when I got home from my first sleepover at Kris's, but Snot and Courtney raced down the stairs to greet me. They screeched angry meows about being made to wait for their breakfast. I had planned to go to the cop station again to try to pick up my things but because I'd spent the morning lounging around Kris's drinking mango smoothie, there wasn't time before my radio gig.

There was nothing to eat in the house, so I made a tray of muffins from an old bag of mix in the cupboard. Just add water. It wasn't mine and I couldn't picture Holly buying it, so it must have been left by Natalie Swanson or the other one.

I lay in bed staring at the ceiling while the muffins baked, listening for the oven timer. The baseboard heater in my room wasn't working and even under the electric blanket, I was freezing. I missed Viv; she would be getting off the breakfast shift soon. I imagined us still living on Patrick Street and Mike being out somewhere: she would have got in bed with me and told me about all the shitty customers and how rude the owner had been to her. I would have told her about my night with Kris.

I decided to haul my mattress out into the wide hallway, where the heater worked. I flung the blankets and pillows out first. The mattress slumped into an L-shape in the doorway and wouldn't budge; when I tried to push it further I heard the metal springs crunching together. I had to climb over the mattress to get into the hall — passing through the padded doorway, I felt like a surfer emerging from the curl of a wave. In the hall, I tugged the mattress through the door from the other side. I cranked the heat.

I looked into my bedroom: without the mattress the room looked strange, everything pressed against the perimeter to make room for an empty space. My bed frame had been in pieces in the basement since we moved in; I kept meaning to bring it up and assemble it. The oven timer beeped just as I was lying down. I waited another few minutes and a burning smell started drifting up over the stairs.

I got the bus up to Kenmount Road to record the radio ad for Marv's Mobile Home Paradise before an evening shift at the theatre. I'd wrapped two muffins in cellophane and stuck them in the front pouch of my knapsack. I'd planned to save one to eat at the theatre but ate both on the bus, getting crumbs all over my jacket and the floor in front of me.

The first fat drops of a predicted downpour started falling as I crossed the radio station parking lot. I pressed the intercom button and looked into the glossy black bulge of the camera above the speaker.

"Stacey Power, here for the Marv's—" I started.

"You come right in, I remember you." The receptionist's voice rode out of the speaker on a wave of crackling static. A buzzing noise signalled that the door was briefly unlocked. I tugged the handle.

The receptionist's face was powdered with dusty concealer and she had a thick line of wet-looking liner around her eyes. She had on a silky blouse and a pencil skirt. She was what my grandmother would call "put-together."

"Do they really need that whole security setup out there?" I asked as she led me down a carpeted hallway.

"There's a lot of expensive gear in here," the receptionist said, waving a set of pointy nails at the recording booths on either side of us. In one, a bald guy in a paisley dress shirt was laughing into a microphone.

The receptionist stopped at the door of a recording booth. There was a guy in a Gore-Tex jacket with *Marv's Mobile Homes* embroidered on the breast sitting at a round table that had three mics and sets of headphones plugged into it.

"Here's our girl," the receptionist said, patting me on the back. I felt too old for my ripped-up jeans. I noticed how dirty my bookbag looked and hid it under my chair. The man hopped up to shake my hand. Marv had obviously sent his son to deliver the ad copy and supervise the session.

"I'll leave you to it," the receptionist said.

"Thanks, honey," Marv's son said.

He slid the paper across the table at me. "This is pretty fun what we've got here, I think. I actually wrote it myself, usually Dad hires someone but I was like, let me give it go, and I think what I came up with is kind of fun."

I read the copy, Marv's son watching me from the other side of the table.

"At Marv's Mobile Home Paradise we're hosting our annual May two-four big-time blowout sale. Does the freedom of the open road with all the comforts of home sound like paradise to you? On Friday May twenty-third purchase any mobile home with an environmentally friendly and cost-efficient compost toilet for twenty-five percent off. A deal so good, you'll know you're in paradise. Get set for summer at Marv's."

"Fun?" he asked when I looked up from the sheet.

I flipped the page over to see if there was more on the other side. Nothing. The receptionist came back with two plastic glasses of water. She set them down on either side of the table. Marv nodded a thank-you at her but kept talking to me. "You can improvise if you want—you know, play with it."

"Cool," I said.

The receptionist turned to leave and Marv's son said, "Hang on sweetheart, do you mind letting Tony know we're ready to roll in here?"

"Sure." She smiled.

I wondered if being called "sweetheart" pissed her off. If it did, you couldn't tell at all. Maybe she was immune to condescending pet names from working almost exclusively with middle-aged men every day.

Marv's son sat back in the chair, smiled and shook his head. "So you do this for a living? This is your main gig?"

"Sort of." I took a sip of water even though I knew I should save it to drink between takes. I had a feeling Marv's son was going to want a lot of takes.

"Sort of?"

"I bartend too."

"But you're hoping to make this the main gig." He waved his hand at the microphones. "Eventually."

"I guess, sort of." I knew I sounded like a petulant teenager.

"Do what you love and you'll never work a day in your life," he said. "Right?"

Finally, Tony arrived. Tony was probably forty-five, with a greying goatee. He was wearing a T-shirt with Gene Simmons's face on it. Gene Simmons's tongue curved over Tony's beer belly and Tony's nipples were visible on either side of Gene's painted forehead.

"Howdy," he said, shutting the door of the room behind him. Marv's son stood and reached across the table to shake his hand.

"Nice to meet you, man," Tony said. "Let's get our headphones on."

I pushed my hair back and let the padded headphones clamp down over my ears. Marv's son winked at me as he picked up the headphones in front of him.

"Whenever you're ready, Stacey." Tony flicked a switch on the table and slouched down in his chair, wrinkling Gene Simmons's face.

I read the copy in a bright, perky voice, carefully enunciating every syllable. I imagined that I was the receptionist or someone like her. Someone who had their hair and nails done at a salon, someone who commanded a certain respect, who was about being able to play the game instead of trying to circumvent it by going around coated in grime and giving themself a shitty haircut. When I finished, Tony stuck his bottom lip out and nodded thoughtfully before sliding his headphones off.

"Sounded pretty spot on to me," Tony said, looking at Marv's son. "One more for good luck?"

"Sure, whatever you think, you're the expert," Marv's son answered.

I read the copy a second time in the same peppy tone.

"That's it?" Marv's son asked Tony. He slid the sleeve of his jacket up and checked the time on an ostentatious watch with a clunky gold strap.

"Sounded good to me," Tony said and dropped his headphones on the table.

"Well, it was a pleasure to meet you," Marv's son said. It sounded like he'd invited Tony up for a nightcap and been turned down.

Marv's son and I walked down the hallway to the front entrance together. The receptionist was on the phone. Rain was beating against the glass door.

"You have a ride?" Marv's son asked.

I thought about walking along the busy road to the bus station in the rain. There wasn't that much time before I had to be at the theatre.

"I don't."

Marv's son brightened.

"Where do you live? I'll give you a lift." He unlocked the car from inside the lobby with a toggle on his keychain and told me to wait while he pulled around.

"Giving you a lift, is he?" the receptionist asked. "That's sweet."

I turned and nodded at her — she for sure had her own car. Marv's son had a hatchback with decals of his father's business logo on both sides.

"Thank you," I said when I climbed in, holding my filthy bookbag in my lap.

"You know, I take photos," Marv's son said.

"Oh cool, landscapes or?"

"Landscapes, people, you know—portraits," he said. "I'm just saying, I could have pursued that."

"Yeah." I tried to sound encouraging.

"I felt all this pressure to like, get a real job," he said. "I guess I'm saying I find you inspiring, life doesn't have to be about making money."

We came to a long line of traffic waiting on a red light.

"Lunchtime, see," Marv's son said. "People on their lunch break. But like boudoir photography is huge right now."

Traffic was backed up so far it looked like we might have to wait for the light to change twice before we made it through the intersection.

"I could be doing that, I'd be good at it because I make people comfortable. That's one of the things you learn in business school, actually."

"In theatre school too," I said.

"It's not pervy," he said.

"It's empowering? For the subjects?" For some reason I was trying to help him out.

"Yeah, exactly. It's all about making them feel sexy." Marv's son laughed and bounced his fingers on the steering wheel. "That's what you mean by 'empowering'?"

The light turned red again when we were just three car-lengths away from making it through. Rain blurred everything outside the windows.

"Kind of."

~

WHEN I ARRIVED at the theatre for my shift there were
about thirty women in the bar, most of them wearing
bodysuits held together at the crotch by a set of silver
snaps.

They all wore their long hair down. Later I'd realize
hair-tossing, a slowed-down version of a move I'd seen
guys do at metal shows, was a big part of the performance.
They all wore dark eyeliner and a block of red eyeshadow.

Two people were always scheduled to be on bar during
Saucy Soldiers because the audiences were usually big
drinkers and sometimes got rowdy. I was relieved to find
out I was working with Dana. She knew how to void drinks
and how to shimmy the cash drawer when it got stuck. We
restocked the coolers and did inventory and unloaded the
dishwasher. It went quickly because there were two of us
and when it was done there was nothing to do but stare
out into the bar and wait for someone to order.

There wasn't enough room for all the performers in
the dressing room, so until about an hour before the show
started they used the bar as extra changing/warming-up
space. Women were stretching on the floor, legs open in a
V, working their hands down one calf and then the other.
Others were practising a dance—staring into the distance,
twitching a hip and doing a series of wrist flicks.

I'd read in the program that Saucy Soldiers was supposed to be body-positive, all body-types welcome or
something, and some of the girls were bigger but mostly
they were thin and white and very put-together. One

woman whipped off a baggy T-shirt and rummaged through her bookbag in her body stocking.

"I like to think I don't objectify women but I do find this kind of —" Dana paused, looking for the right word, "distracting."

I laughed.

Soon boyfriends and mothers started arriving, ordering beer and white wine respectively. The boyfriends wore striped dress shirts with dark denim and some of them brought bouquets. One asked me if I could stick the flowers in the cooler for him; he leaned in and asked like me and him were in it together. I could feel Dana watching protectively. I eased the flowers into the fridge, squishing the bouquet between the bottom rack and some tins of pop. The boyfriend winked and dropped a toonie in the tip jar.

Eventually an instructor moved through the bar, ushering women into the stairwell that led up into the theatre. Dana left to hand out programs because we were short on volunteers—none of them had wanted to work Saucy Soldiers. The volunteers were mostly in their fifties and sixties; some were married couples who did shifts together. In exchange for taking tickets at the door and leading latecomers to their seats with a small flashlight, volunteers got to see the play for free and received a complimentary beverage of their choice afterwards. Lots of them had been doing it for years. When I'd hand them their flashlight they'd say, "Now, are there fresh batteries in this one?" like I was trying to pull one over on them.

Tonight there was only one volunteer, a woman with purple in her short grey hair. After the first show she came down to collect her free drink; she chose a club soda. Music was pounding through the ceiling and you could hear high heels stamping on the stage.

"A lot of energy goes into these shows," she said.

I flipped up the tab on the mouth of the tin before passing it to the woman. She cheersed the air with it.

"The first time I saw it I was horrified, I thought this is everything we'd fought against," the woman said. I looked around the room — there were a couple of girls who had already danced but none of them were paying attention to the conversation.

"I haven't seen it," I said.

"I mean I guess they enjoy it," the volunteer said. "The women."

The music stopped and there was stomping and applause. Dana appeared and slipped behind the bar.

"They're on their way down," Dana said. "Put the music on."

I flipped the switch on the soundboard and turned on an eighties dance playlist. The opening to "Don't You Want Me" by The Human League pounded out of two speakers in the front of the room. Dana grinned at me.

"I was just saying," the volunteer said, speaking loudly to be heard over my music, "I used to find this show horrifying but I guess the women enjoy themselves."

"I just hate the boyfriends," Dana said.

"What are they thinking? Do they go home with the women after and think, well, she's just the hottest thing?" the volunteer asked.

"They fucking better," Dana said.

⌒

FOR THE NIGHT'S second show, I went upstairs and handed out programs. When the lights went down I sat in an empty seat near the exit. A video advertising Saucy Soldiers dance classes was projected on a screen at the back of the stage. It was a montage of women in skimpy outfits doing complicated routines under stage lights, spliced together with footage of women stretching and laughing in the dance studio. I heard banging on the steel door to the theatre. I thought of my light-catcher bouncing against the window when the cops came. It was my job to open the door. I popped out of my seat. Two big guys were waiting in the bright hallway.

"Is it started?" one of them asked.

"Sort of," I whispered. "Can I see your tickets?"

"I already showed it to the girl downstairs," the same guy answered, lowering his voice. He reeked of cologne. Behind me the video shut off.

"It has your seat on it, I'm supposed to show you to your seat." I pushed the button on the back of the flashlight I'd brought up with me and a beam of weak light hit his shoe. The other guy reached in his pocket and passed me his ticket. He was seated right next to me.

"I don't know what I did with it, I'm next to him," the first guy said.

I showed the latecomers to their seats and sat down beside them. The music started up; the show was billed as a Beyoncé tribute and the first song was "Formation." A line of mostly white women marched on stage.

The guy beside me cupped his hands around his mouth and hollered, "THAT'S MY GIRL!" I jumped in my seat, his elbow was on the armrest and I brushed against it. I pulled my arms in tight, he didn't seem to notice. Stills of Beyoncé and short clips from her music videos played on the screen behind the dancers. The girls turned their backs to the audience and started twerking. The man beside me made a loudspeaker with his hands again and yelled, "YEAH BABY, YEAH KELLY, YEAH THAT'S MY GIRL." His friend contributed a half-hearted "Wooo, yeah."

I tried not to look at them. I tried to stare straight ahead. "Formation" ended and a slower, sexier song came on. A different group of women slinked on stage; the guy beside me relaxed into his seat. These women were wearing sparkly leotards. They split into pairs and rubbed against each other. Some of the girls I recognized from the bar earlier. There was a tall, skinny girl with a thick townie accent who'd asked me to fill her water bottle. She was centre stage, stroking her partner's thigh. Suddenly she flopped into a dramatic backbend and her partner dragged a hand down the middle of her chest. The muscles in my vagina clenched. I felt a jolt of shame. I was turned on. I looked at the man beside me without turning my head. His phone was lit up in his lap, he was scrolling with a finger.

The song changed and he flipped the phone over on his leg, like he was worried he might be caught. A fast number. Two-piece outfits. Kelly was back on stage. The latecomer leaned forward and roared, "THAT'S MY BABY!"

When the whole ensemble came out to bow at the end

and a spray of plastic-wrapped bouquets rained down from the audience, I scuttled downstairs with the box of leftover programs.

"They're on the way," I warned Dana. She plugged the aux cord into her phone and played some radio hit.

"What'd you think?"

"It's a lot," I said.

"In a good or bad way?"

"Do you have Coors Light?" The latecomer saved me.

WHEN I GOT home that night the upstairs hallway was filled with the smell of burning dust because I'd cranked the heat before I left. I climbed into my bed in the hallway with all my clothes on. The view from the hall windows was different from this angle. Normally the windows were filled with the parking lot and the dumpster and the fluttering vhs tape, but from down on the floor I could see a stretch of uninterrupted sky. There were stars that night. A stream of milky light intensified in the corner of the window closest to the door and I thought the moon must be just out of view.

I noticed a pinprick of red light swooping over the roof of my neighbour's house. The light swung to the left, then reappeared in the window on the opposite side of the room. It travelled up, towards the roof of the church, and rounded the corner into the empty lot behind it. I thought of the woman outside Venice Pizza who'd pointed the drone out to me. That was where the light was coming from now, from Venice Pizza.

TEN

For three mornings in a row I went to the pay phone around the corner and called the police station. Each time I brought the letter with me so I could read the number off the bottom as I dialled. On the third morning Constable Bradley had come back to work.

The same cop was on the reception desk when I got to the station. He nodded, letting me know he recognized me.

"Going to need some government-issued photo ID," he told me. "And you don't have a phone on you?"

"No."

"Right, I have to ask."

When I passed my ID through the slot he opened a drawer in his desk and tossed it in. I saw a few cell phones in the drawer—their owners' IDs were strapped to the fronts with varying sizes of elastic bands. The cop got

up and left the room; a door a little further down the hall
opened and he stepped out and walked into the lobby.
It seemed unfair that he could leave the office and enter
the Wild West of the lobby whenever he wanted. I liked
having a thick sheet of cloudy plastic between us.

"Put this on and follow me." He passed me a lamin-
ated visitor's pass on a piece of thin white string with a
messy knot at the top. I hung it around my neck and we
walked down a longer hallway lined with beige doors.
We passed a group of cops in uniform gathered around
a water cooler, drinking from paper cones. One of them
was a woman; she was shorter than the others and had
frizzy hair pinned in a bun at the back of her neck. We
were about the same age. The water cooler cops nodded
hello to us, one raised a paper cone and the front desk
cop nodded back.

He led me into a windowless conference room. There
was a large table surrounded by wheelie chairs and a dry-
erase board on the wall with a rolled-up screen above it;
a projector was mounted on a brace that hung from the
ceiling.

A man in a suit stood up from the head of the table.
He was tall, he had to be more than six feet. He was pale
with dark circles under his eyes. He had thick black hair
that was receding on either side of his forehead.

"Constable Bradley." He held his huge hand out to me
and I shook it.

"You're all good in here?" the front desk cop asked.

There were papers spread out on the table and I saw
my computer and phone inside a sealed plastic bag with

my name on it. Seeing the sticker of a cartoon cat slurping up a spaghetti noodle that I'd stuck on my phone case made me queasy.

"Do you want some water?" Constable Bradley asked me.

"No, thank you."

"We're all good, then."

The front desk cop left and I was alone with Constable Bradley.

"Have a seat," he said. "So first I have to let you know the investigation is ongoing, so I won't be able to answer a lot of questions."

I sat on the side of the table closest to the door and left one seat between us. Even though his frame was huge, Constable Bradley looked slim; his suit was loose on him. He moved some papers around, saying, "I was just reviewing your file this morning. We're just as disappointed as you are that the warrant wasn't executed more quickly."

"More quickly?"

"It's a small unit, so we can't get to things as quickly as we'd like. It's just a few guys with this specialized skill set. Obviously we have to prioritize cases with a live victim. If someone is in danger, we prioritize that. Sometimes things take longer than is ideal—in a case like this, it means the suspects may have moved on."

"So I'm not a suspect? They were looking for someone else?"

"At this point the investigation is still ongoing. I will say we're not feeling hopeful."

"The people who lived there before us? They were women, young women. Well, like my age."

"Looks like there was a boyfriend. Did you meet a boyfriend?"

"You don't know who was living there?"

"These things take time, it's frustrating for everyone. What's really frustrating is it's looking like we lost the suspect this time around."

"Can I have my things back?"

Constable Bradley slid the plastic package with my phone and computer across the table to me. I took it in my lap.

"You can take them out of that. I've got a form here for you to sign, just have a look to make sure nothing's been damaged."

I flipped the package over. The air in the room was dry, the inside of my mouth was sticky. I wished I'd said yes to the glass of water. "They seem fine, I'll sign it."

"Usually people power them up."

I ripped the plastic open with my nails. I opened the computer on the table and pressed the power button; a celebratory blast of music rang out. The wallpaper was a photo of me and Viv holding Snot and Courtney when I first brought them home to Patrick Street. We're sunburned and smiling, I have a bleached chunk in the front of my dark bangs and Viv's red hair is cut into a messy mullet. I closed my computer.

Then I held down the button on top of my phone until the screen illuminated — a photo of Snot and Courtney curled together on the armchair in Viv's old bedroom at Patrick Street. After a moment, red notifications appeared on the screen signalling new texts, emails, Instagram DMs. I pressed the button on top of my phone again and turned it off.

"It seems fine." I lay the phone face down on top of my closed computer. I hated being alone with him. I knew it was unlikely anything would happen to me, because I was white, because I didn't look especially poor or vulnerable. But I was alone in a windowless room with a strange man who had probably seen naked photos of me, who could order me to do whatever he wanted.

"So you'll delete all my information now — the stuff from my hard drive?" I asked.

"So what we've done," Constable Bradley looked me right in the eyes and spoke slowly, "is acquire the entire physical content of your drives, including unused disk space and deleted data. We used algorithms to verify the authenticity of the data. We created a forensic image that is an exact duplicate of the original source data. We've had trained officers search that data and we found nothing incriminating. That said, this case is still under investigation."

The whole time he was talking I was picturing the front desk cop appearing with a jug of cold water and two clean glasses on a tray. Or maybe just some of those paper cones from the water dispenser in the hall.

"It wasn't you?" I asked.

"What?"

"Who looked through my hard drive?"

"Not me — trained officers. Good people who have been doing this work for a long time."

I tried to pull myself back into the room, to focus.

"What makes them good?"

"Pardon?" Constable Bradley asked.

"Nothing. So I'm not a suspect? This is all done now, my name isn't linked to any of this?"

"Unfortunately, I can't say because the investigation is not yet closed; there's a few more avenues to explore," Constable Bradley told me.

I felt very, very thirsty. How had he known I would need a glass of water? Something about the room, about the situation.

"Can I sign the form? I actually have to work this evening."

Constable Bradley pushed the form across the table along with a pen, the kind where you have to twist the top to make the nib emerge. It felt like my throat was swelling shut. I didn't read the form. I printed my name in all caps on one line and signed the line below it.

Constable Bradley led me back to the lobby, saying, "Remember, return your visitor's pass and pick up your ID before you go."

I lined up behind two middle-aged men in baseball caps and Carhartt jackets.

"No, no," one of the men said into the hole; his buddy shook his head in agreement.

"Small game," his buddy said.

"Small game," the first man repeated into the hole.

I didn't have a sleeve for my computer so I worked it back into the torn plastic bag. There was a label with my name and *processed* written on it. Eventually the front desk cop went to the filing cabinet and found some forms for the men to sign. They took turns leaning on the narrow counter to write with a pen attached to the desk by a flimsy chain. When it was my turn at the window, the cop slid my ID across the counter with a smile, like he was a bartender who remembered my favourite drink.

I WAITED UNTIL I was outside to check the messages and emails on my phone. I walked across the parking lot and down the street before I illuminated the screen. The battery was 100 percent charged, I guess the cops had plugged it in.

There was a long string of texts from Viv — she'd kept messaging and then saying, *Shit, forgot you don't have a phone.* Were the cops reading all those messages as they rolled in? Were they recorded somewhere? There was a Facebook message from Kris. She'd sent it two days ago. *We should hang out again sometime.*

I tried phoning Holly but she didn't answer. Maybe she was at work, probably she wasn't taking my calls. I sent her a message: *Call me when you can, I talked to the cops. Have new info.*

I thought about what to say to Kris. She must have thought I'd ignored her. *Hey! Finally got a new phone. I would love to hang out.*

Then I checked my emails. There was an email from the casting director of the joint production. My guts fluttered, a twinge deep down like the warning signs of diarrhea. A reply this late had to be a rejection unless there was some complication, like maybe the person they'd wanted had backed out. Until I opened the email, there was still a chance. A very small chance.

I was standing at the top of Long's Hill in the glow of Long's Hill Convenience. There was a pay phone inside the store, nestled between the counter and a rack of snack-sized bags of chips. The man who worked there always announced how many days there were until Christmas when you got up to the counter, even in the middle of July. They sold individual tea bags and cigarettes. It felt like a good place to open the email, a safe haven.

I pressed on the casting director's name. It was a very short email that began, *Hi Stacey, thank you so much for coming down*... Disappointment mixed with embarrassment spread through me and pushed itself out of my pores: I felt like I needed a shower. I went into the store and walked to the cooler in the back. I got a cold can of Pepsi and a bag of Doritos. At the counter the old man told me there were thirteen days until Christmas.

"How many until the Regatta though, that's what I'd like to know."

"You stay warm now," he told me as he handed over my change.

I cracked the can open as soon as I got outside. I don't drink pop very often, and I could feel the sugar seeping into my blood, turning it syrupy, making it rush through me like an antidote to the disappointment. I stood next to the cement garbage bin by the bus stop on the top of the hill and chugged my Pepsi. A mom and her school-aged daughter watched from inside the plastic walls of the bus shelter. I crumpled the can and dropped it onto the snow-covered garbage that already filled the bin.

I called Viv. It was such a relief to be able to call Viv.

"You have a phone!" Viv said.

"I didn't get the part." I held the phone between my ear and shoulder so I could peel the chip bag open. "Will you come over and smoke a joint with me?"

"Come to my place, I'm making soup."

"They said I could be an extra."

"Assholes," Viv said. "Are you going to do it?"

"Yeah, I need money."

I turned around and started walking back the way I'd come, towards Viv's new house.

ON THE DAY we'd arranged, I stood in the living room window waiting for Kris to pick me up. The coughing woman was out having a smoke. The neighbour kids were racing around the parking lot on their bikes. A young woman with green hair sat at the picnic table watching them, maybe also waiting for a ride.

I heard the music playing in Kris's car when she pulled up outside the house. The girl squeezed her brakes hard and her brother skidded to a stop beside her. They stood with the bike frames between their legs, hard pebbles of snow landing on their curly hair. They were waiting for the car to leave or park so they could get back to careening around. I waved to the kids as I got in the car, they each lifted a gloved hand in response.

Kris was playing Lucinda Williams through the radio,

an album my parents loved. The dashboard heater was twisted to the thickest part of the red stripe.

"Still up for Bell Island?" she asked.

"Yup." I watched the kids kick off in the rear-view, the brother losing ground almost immediately.

"My parents had this on a tape when I was a kid, we used to listen to it in the car. This was side A and Sheryl Crow was on the other side," I told Kris.

"Which Sheryl Crow?"

"The one that goes 'sun coming up over something something something.'"

"'All I Wanna Do.'" Kris picked her phone up from beside the gear shift, shuffling through the songs as she drove down Military Road. We stopped at the lights by the restaurant. There were seasonal decals on the window, snowflakes and Christmas bulbs. I was hoping to catch a glimpse of Viv. The new server was wiping a table in the front window. She had a spray bottle of electric-blue cleaning fluid in one hand and a microfibre cloth in the other. I remembered the prickly feel of those cloths. My hands had always been dry from fishing mugs out of a sink filled with diluted bleach and the cloths chafed them. Kris turned on the Sheryl Crow song.

"I used to work there," I said.

"Want to stop and get something to eat?"

"No. Maybe if Viv was there, I don't think she's on today."

On the ferry we left the car and climbed the narrow metal steps up to the deck. I liked the feeling of the water shifting the floor beneath me. For a while we leaned against a big vent that poured out warm air from the engine room. But even next to the vent the wind was brutal, the snow had turned to freezing rain and it stung my face.

"Do you want to go in?" Kris asked. Kris's haircut left the tips of her ears unprotected and they'd turned bright pink.

"Yeah, in one minute," I said and walked to the back of the boat. I wanted to stand over the propeller and see it ripping the dark waves down the middle. Three thick lines of froth stretched away from the boat, aquamarine water seething in the ruts between them. The wake reached as far back as I could see. But I knew that out of my range of sight the ocean was zipping itself shut, closing over the motor's dissolving white trails.

"Oh man, I can't look at that." Kris had joined me at the rail. "Makes me seasick."

I decided I wasn't going to tell her about the cops and the investigation. Hopefully the situation would just resolve itself and I would never have to tell her.

"Let's go inside," I said.

For the last ten minutes of the ride we sat on a bench seat in the cabin. I watched Bell Island grow bigger and bigger through rain-streaked windows. Kris had her head tilted back against the seat and her eyes closed, fighting off seasickness.

"Look," I said when we got close enough to see the varying shades of rust in the island's cliffs. People around us were gathering their things, getting ready to troop below deck to their cars.

"It's almost like Arizona or Utah, you know those desert-y parts of the States?" Kris said.

When we got off the ferry we went to Dicks' for fish and chips. Kris and I sat in a booth with a view of the dance floor. It was four-thirty in the afternoon; we were the only people on the restaurant side, but the bar was filling up. On the back wall a mural of the town of Wabana was framed by tubes of red and green LED lights. Red and green paper garlands hung from the ceiling and a post in the centre of the room was wrapped in silver and gold tinsel. Trad music was piping out of two PAs up by the stage.

Kris ordered a ginger ale with her meal to try to settle her stomach.

"I'll be fine," she said, cracking her drink open.

"Are you going to be able to eat this?"

"Eating might help," Kris said.

She took out her phone and made a Boomerang of me dripping ketchup over my fries. She turned the screen to show me the video: I smile as a spatter of ketchup sucks itself back into the nozzle of the red squeeze bottle and flies out again. I liked the idea of her posting it. Everyone would know we were out here together.

Kris was still pale after eating; she paused on the way to the car and bent over with her hands on her thighs. I thought she was going to vomit but she straightened up after a moment.

The freezing rain had let up but it was cold enough that a layer of slush stayed on the ground. We drove around the island with the windows down—Kris said the fresh

air was helping so I didn't complain about the cold. The
sun was almost set, a bit of custard yellow streaked the
navy sky.

"Do you know when the last ferry is?" I said.

"I think at eight."

"It's every half hour?"

"We have lots of time." Kris turned her face towards
the window and took a deep breath.

"Did you know there's an abandoned air strip here and
they use it for dirt bike racing?" I asked.

"I think your phone's ringing." Kris said.

I took it out of my pocket. Holly was calling. I stuck it
back in my coat still buzzing.

"You can take it," Kris said.

"It's just my roommate, I'll call her later."

The phone kept buzzing.

"I don't mind. What if she's locked out or something?"

The buzzing continued, she was calling a second time.

"I can't really help her in that case."

"Wow, cold."

Finally my phone went quiet.

We drove past abandoned houses, boarded-up community halls and rusted-out cars. But also houses with
smoke coming out of their chimneys and dogs lounging
in the driveways. Occasionally cars and quads passed us.
We saw a woman driving an electric wheelchair along the
shoulder of the road, the tires flicking up slush. And later
an old man walking two Shih Tzus with brown stains on
the white fur around their eyes. We passed a house with a
cracked boulder on the lawn — someone had painted the

words 'TIS BUT ONE LIFE on one half and 'TWILL SOON BE PAST on the other half.

"Did you see that?" I said. "Go back."

Kris stopped the car, inched backwards along the shoulder and took a photo out the open window.

"Maybe it's a 'live life to its fullest' kind of thing," I said.

"Or maybe it's a 'can't wait to get to heaven' kind of thing," Kris said.

Later, Kris stopped the car in front of a church on an empty stretch of road. It looked deflated—all the walls were concave, buckling towards the centre. We got out and walked through tall yellow grass to look in the windows. The ground was boggy. When we reached the church I stepped on the cracked cement foundation and held onto a window ledge. The wooden ledge had turned soft and silver-grey in the sun; it wobbled in my hands.

"Can you see anything?" Kris asked.

I let go with one hand and reached into my pocket for my phone. I flicked the flashlight on with my thumb and shone the light through the rippled window. The pews were gone and the floorboards were broken in places.

"It's empty."

"Should we go in?" Kris was standing at the bottom of a set of stairs that led to the front doors.

"The floor is rotten." I hopped off the cement ledge, landing on squishy ground.

"I'm just going to see if it's open." Kris walked up the steps and tugged on each handle. There was a new lock on the old wooden doors, they shook in the frame but wouldn't open.

We walked through the graveyard beside the church instead. The grass made my jeans wet. A truck passed on the road; the headlights threw the church's shadow over the graveyard as it drove by. I walked over to where Kris had stopped in front of a headstone. She bent to read the inscription. I leaned in and pressed the back of my hand against hers. She didn't move her hand away. I turned my face to her but she kept looking at the stone.

"Bernadette Murphy, Dearly Departed, Loving Wife and Mother," Kris said.

"'Tis but one life, 'twill soon be past," I said.

Kris drew her hand away. She took her phone out of her pocket and looked at the time.

"We should probably head back to the wharf," she said.

I stopped by a juniper tree with a twisted trunk growing next to a stooped headstone. Its needles were almost lime green; I put one between my front teeth and my mouth filled with the bitter taste. Kris was clomping through the snow ahead of me, almost at the car. I looked up at the stars and took a long breath, trying to suck in the squat trees at the edge of the graveyard, the sunken church, the wet road, the plate of fries, the ocean. Trying to fill up on that and not leave any room for disappointment.

In the car I took my phone out of my pocket. Notifications about the two missed calls from Holly were on the screen.

WHEN WE GOT back to Kris's house, Frankie was blasting "All I Want for Christmas Is You" in their room. The song finished and started over again while we took off our winter gear.

"They're practising a lip-synch," Kris said, closing her bedroom door behind us.

She went over to the computer and put on an Emmylou Harris album from YouTube. I didn't know the songs but I recognized her voice, the way it oscillated between husky and startlingly high and clear. I sat on the bed.

"Well, this is my room," she said.

"I've been here before."

"Oh yeah."

Kris walked over and stood above me. She undid the top button of my jean jacket. The second button was harder, she had to squeeze the sides of the buttonhole to wiggle the silver fastener loose. I didn't help her.

"Do you want this?" she asked.

I nodded.

She undid the rest of the buttons. Then I sat up and tugged at the sleeves to get my arms out. When I found my way out of the jacket she climbed on top of me and kissed me. A sloppy make-out kiss with her hands in my hair and her knee grinding into my crotch. She put her hands under my shirt and grabbed onto my hips.

"You're so cold," I said.

She straightened her back, put her hands together and blew into them. She rubbed them together like someone warming up over a fire, then touched the back of one hand to my belly.

"Better?"

I pressed my crotch into her knee and curled my torso

up to kiss her. I took my shirt off, shimmied back on the bed and undid my jeans. She stood and pulled my pants off by the cuffs, walking backwards and yanking. Then she undressed in front of me. She had on a sports bra and matching boxers, the brand name circling her hips and rib cage.

I felt self-conscious about my faded underwear; loose curls of elastic stuck out of the waistband. The last time I did laundry, Holly pointed at a line of my panties drying on the upstairs rail and said, "Time to throw those out."

We got out of our underwear and rolled around, grinding and shifting our weight until we slid together. I was on top and I found a way to move without losing the warm wet of her crotch against mine. She started bucking into me, my hip joint was aching but I kept up with her. She dug her nails into the fat on my hips and I swatted her hands away with hard slaps. I was sweating but I didn't stop moving until I felt her relax into the mattress beneath me.

"Did you come?" I asked, slowing but still jerking back and forth on top of her.

"Yeah," she sighed.

"Really?"

"Yeah."

"Really?" I said.

She flipped me over and went down on me. I warned her I was about to come—I reached out and tapped her urgently on shoulder, "I'm going to come, is it okay if I come? I'm really going to come"—and she kept flicking her tongue against my clit until it happened. We got under the blankets, both covered in cooling sweat. The Emmylou

Harris album had ended and "All I Want for Christmas" rose through the floor. The first time we'd had sex it was easy and quick because we were drunk. This was more awkward and intimate.

"Had you ever slept with someone who isn't a cis dude before me?" Kris asked.

"Yeah."

"Yeah, you had?"

"Yeah, I had." I hated that I was blushing.

Kris rolled over to get a water bottle that was wedged between the wall and the side of the bed. She scooched up on the pillows and pulled the nozzle open with her front teeth.

"Why?" I asked.

"Just wondering." Kris squeezed the bottle and shot a stream of water into her open mouth. The bottle was see-through purple with WATER IS A HUMAN RIGHT in bold print on it. There was a scummy square of dirt where a sticker had worn off.

"Have you done it with a strap-on?" she asked.

I thought about lying.

"No," I said. "Do you have one?"

"Not anymore, I threw it out when me and my ex broke up."

We lay there quietly, my cheek resting just above her breast.

"What time is it? My phone's in my coat," I said eventually.

Kris dug around in the blankets.

"It's eight o'clock," she said. "I'm starved."

We dressed and Kris drove us to the mall. She plugged in her phone and Lucinda's voice filled the car again, backed by twangy guitar. One of the breakup songs.

"I love the part about them listening to ZZ Top real loud," I said. "Do you find it weird that she likes ZZ Top? Like kind of surprising?" Partly I was just showing off that I knew the words, trying to impress her.

Kris nodded. "You just get so much about their relationship from that line though, right? This whole album is about intense, destructive love."

"I mean, 'Drunken Angel' obviously, yeah," I said.

"Yeah but even like 'Car Wheels,'" Kris said.

When the chorus came around again we sang it together, imitating Lucinda's Louisiana accent. I stared straight through the windshield during the "forever and *all* time" part, afraid of what my face might be revealing.

We ate in the food court. My underwear was still damp. I felt like I was in a sex-hormone-induced daze. I ate an enormous pile of fried noodles, and dipped golden chicken balls in cherry sauce so bright it glowed in the Styrofoam tub.

I'd never been with a woman publicly. Dan, who I'd lived with above the laundromat before Viv and I moved in together, was the only real relationship I'd ever had. When Kris dropped me home, I wandered around the house thinking about the feel of the upholstery on her car seats, the way her body jerked against mine when she came, how good it felt to sit across from each other in the food court for everyone to see. I thought about how downcast she became at 'Tis But One Life, 'Twill Soon Be Past.

MY GRANDMOTHER BAPTIZED me herself because my parents refused to do it. She shook a bottle of holy water over me in the front seat of her car. When I slept over at her house as a kid she knelt by the side of the bed in the spare room and we recited "Now I Lay Me Down to Sleep." It was the only prayer I knew by heart. We prayed before eating but it was a silent prayer.

One night I found a bottle of holy water under the pillow in the spare room where I slept when I stayed at her house. It was a white plastic vial with an ornate gold cross in raised plastic on the front. It was dark in the bedroom but the streetlight outside the window made the reflective crucifix gleam. It scared me. I called my grandmother in and she took the bottle and put it on the dresser next to her satin jewellery box.

"I don't know how that got there," she said. My grandmother never misplaced things. She scrubbed the silverware with a toothbrush every Sunday and ironed T-shirts. My grandmother thought I needed protection.

She believed in signs from the universe, she had premonitory dreams and saw ghosts. She hated cats because her mother warned her cats would try to curl up on sleeping babies' chests and suck their souls out through their lips. She threw extra salt over her shoulder into the devil's eyes.

Even though my mom rejected the church, she would sometimes ask me, "She's catholic?" or say, "That's a protestant name," when I mentioned a new friend. Mostly it was about figuring out if she knew their family, I think. Names don't have that meaning for me.

I've never been to mass in my entire life. Most of what I know about the Bible I learned from *Jesus Christ Superstar*, starring Ted Neeley. From the time we were seven until we were about ten, Viv and I rented that movie over and over again. That one and *Titanic*. We would rewind and fast-forward *Jesus Christ Superstar* to find our favourite songs. On the screen, Jesus and his disciples walked backwards through the desert, chopped up by two thick lines of static.

We loved the high priests. We wrapped ourselves in navy sheets and stalked back and forth across the coffee table singing along, each of us taking a specific role. Viv hated Jesus, she hated his lank blond hair and she thought his voice was whiny. When he stormed through the temple and smashed a slowly rotating rack of mirrors she sighed. "What a drama queen."

Our elementary school, Bishop Field, had once been an all-boys catholic school. Religion was officially stripped out of the school system the year I started kindergarten, but there was still a small wooden cross with a tortured brass Jesus hung up by the loudspeaker in every classroom.

There was a single bowling lane locked behind a door in the basement of the school. I'd only ever heard rumours about it until a volunteer after-school drama teacher accidentally unlocked the door in front of us one afternoon when she was looking for the multi-purpose room. Beams of light poured down on the bowling lane from three huge windows. The shellacked wood gleamed; a row of dusty pins was lined up at the bottom of the lane. Black balls, smaller than the ones at Holiday Lanes, sat in a rack up against the wall.

"Oops," the volunteer had said, shutting the door quickly. "Must be down the hall."

I knew the bowling lane was a relic from Bishop Field's catholic days and as a kid I had assumed it had to do with some religious ceremony. We whined for her to let us bowl or even just stand in the room for a minute but she shook the bag of papier mâché mask-making supplies at us.

In music class we still sang "The Battle Hymn of the Republic." The lyrics of hymns were organized in a stack of red Duo-Tangs, their covers worn soft by generations of tiny hands. We stood shoulder to shoulder on the risers, facing a new poster about respecting differences as we bellowed, "He hath loosed the fateful lightning of His terrible, swift sword / His truth is marching on." We loved the violence of it. Some of us swung our fists at our sides as we sang and even lifted our feet, marching in place.

WHEN KRIS DROPPED me home after the mall, I plugged my phone in by the side of the couch and returned Holly's calls. I was looking out the window at the parking lot, tethered to the wall by the charger. I hoped she wouldn't pick up: I wanted to enjoy my post-date euphoria for as long as possible. But the line engaged on the third ring.

"Hey," I said. "What are you doing? Are you busy?"

"Did you break my glasses?"

"No."

There was silence on Holly's end.

"Have you been talking to the cops?" I asked.

"Yeah."

"They gave you your stuff back?"

"I know you broke my glasses."

"I'll pay for them."

"It's fucked up that you did that."

"It was stupid, I'm sorry, I'm really sorry. Honestly. Did they tell you they were looking for those girls, Natalie Swanson and the other one. It was one of their boyfriends."

"I don't want to talk about any of that."

"Did you sign a form? When they gave you your stuff back? I didn't even read it."

"I signed the form. Listen, the thing about my glasses, it was aggressive."

"Holly. I'm sorry, it was an accident."

"It wasn't an accident."

"It wasn't an accident but I didn't mean it, I didn't plan it."

"See, I can't trust anything you say. I don't feel safe in that house," she said.

"I don't think anything happened in the house, they said the investigation took so long because they prioritize cases where someone is in danger. So I guess no one was in danger? Which is good—obviously."

Holly didn't say anything.

"Did they tell you what they were looking for? Maybe it was some kind of credit card theft thing. Were you talking to the really tall guy? Constable Bradley?"

"I mean with you," Holly said.

"What?"

"I don't feel safe living with you."

"Oh."

"I'm going to go now. I'm jamming."

"You're not coming back to the house?"

"I'm coming back to the house, I don't have anywhere else to go."

"I didn't plan that, I was just really frustrated and upset. I was hurt that you thought—"

"I'm late for jamming."

"Okay."

"They cost three hundred dollars."

"Okay."

"You can e-transfer me."

"Okay."

"Okay, bye," Holly said and hung up.

I didn't have three hundred dollars to e-transfer Holly for the stupid glasses. Maybe I could send twenty, like a down payment, to show I was taking it seriously. I had a new text from Kris: *There's a Drag Race screening at the print shop tonight you should come down.* The queasy feeling that had welled up during the conversation with Holly evaporated. Kris wanted to see me again, a second time in the same day. I called Viv to see if she would go with me.

WHEN WE ARRIVED most of the chairs were already full. There was some kind of printmaking machine in the centre of the room that was about the size of a photo-copier and looked like it weighed hundreds of pounds. Two banks of fold-out chairs were arranged on either side of the machine. A white bedsheet was thumbtacked to the back wall between two floor-to-ceiling windows that looked out on the harbour. The other walls were covered in prints of varying sizes, some framed, some mounted on poster board, most with a thematic link to Newfoundland—smeary reliefs of cod and puffins and dories and row houses.

A woman with waist-length red ringlets and a sequined bra was bent over an Acer laptop plugged into a set of computer speakers. A thick blue extension cord snaked across the hardwood floor between the chairs and around the printmaking machine to an outlet on the other side of the room.

"We're starting in ten minutes," the woman with the ringlets called. "So do your pee, grab a beer, sit down and shut up.'

The sheet behind her lit up with a projection of a desktop screen. The background photo was a selfie of two young men standing under the dangling flowers of a golden chain tree in a fenced-in backyard. The one taking the photo was holding a scruffy dog with a diamond-studded collar; the other guy was resting his chin on the photographer's shoulder. The image was covered with folders and thumbnails of photographs. The woman with the ringlets was also the man curled around his boyfriend in the photo.

I undid the line of snaps down the front of my jacket, scanning the room for Kris. There were only a handful of people in drag; the audience was mostly men around our age in snug sweaters and jeans. Kris was in the front row, sitting next to Frankie. She was talking close to their face, waving her hands in the air. Frankie was nodding and wincing: it looked like it was a story about bodily injury or maybe about an intensely uncomfortable social situation. I unwound my scarf and took my mitts off, stuffing it all down into my bookbag.

"Should we get a beer?" Viv asked.

A guy in the back of the room was selling India out of a case on the floor. He had a see-through fanny pack clipped around his hips with some crumpled bills and change in it.

"Sure," I said, I took a ten out of my jeans pocket and handed it to Viv. "Can you get it? I'm going to find us some seats."

I didn't want to look like I was rushing towards the open chairs behind Kris—I felt like a kid trying not to get caught running on the pool deck. But I knocked into the back of Frankie's chair making my way down the aisle. Frankie and Kris both turned around in their seats and looked at me.

"Viv is here too," I said.

"Everyone kindly shut the fuck up," the host said.

The screen lit up with a pixelated live stream of the opening of *RuPaul's Drag Race*. Viv jostled down the narrow aisle with two beers. I lifted my coat off the seat I'd saved for her. Kris turned around and gave Viv a friendly wave. Usually it was me and Viv at a thing hoping to run into the person she was seeing. Or me and Viv at a thing with the person she was seeing. I held my beer up to Viv for a little cheers.

"Thank you for coming with me," I said into her ear.

"Did you talk to Holly?" she asked me.

"No." I turned back to the screen.

The show started with a recap from last week; a communal moan flooded out of the people around us when footage of the most recent elimination played. Viv and I looked around, surprised. Kris leaned back in her chair, making it balance on two legs, and grinned at us. She'd caught our tourist-y surprise.

"I know, right?" the host said into the microphone. She was slumped in a plastic chair next to her laptop.

During the first commercial break, the host muted the stream and called Tiffany Trash to the front of the room. A tall, thin woman in a short shift dress made from strung-together toilet paper rolls and a stole made of layer upon layer of bunched-up toilet paper strode up to the stage. She lip-synched to "Downtown," flicking the stole around as she danced. When Tiffany finished, the audience whooped and she curtsied, lifting her toilet-paper-roll dress as she bent her knees. The host pulled the live stream up on the screen as Tiffany made her way to her seat.

"Silence you saucy friggers!" the host roared into the mic, swishing her ringlets around.

When the screening finished, Viv and Kris and Frankie and I stood together getting our coats on.

"What're you guys doing now?" Kris asked.

"I'm going home, I have to work in the morning," Viv said.

People were folding up the chairs around us and stacking them against the wall.

"You want to come over, Stacey?" Kris asked. "One more beer?"

We all trooped down the steep steps to the street together.

"Well, I guess I'm going this way," Viv said when we got outside. "Goodnight."

The three of us murmured goodnight and Viv started walking towards her new house. I watched her back as she pulled a mitt out of each pocket. It was strange for the night to end without us debriefing about what had happened. Part of me wanted to chase after her. Instead I took my phone out and sent her a smiley emoji with heart eyes.

ELEVEN

A couple of days later, I asked Kris if she wanted to go to the Santa Claus parade. I had to stop by the theatre to pick up my tips, so I told her to meet me there.

There was a rehearsal of *Scrooge: The Musical* happening upstairs. The night before I'd done box office for a poorly attended stand-up-comedy open mic in the bar. After every show the bartender splits the tips with the person on box office and leaves the money in a sealed envelope in the staff mailbox. I felt a cold lump of change through the paper. I ripped it open — three toonies and a quarter. I put the change in my pocket and dropped the envelope in the recycling bin.

When I stepped out of the office I saw Kris waiting outside the theatre through the floor-to-ceiling glass of the lobby. She was wearing a black bomber jacket and had a big purple scarf swirled around her neck.

"Come in, I'm going to make us some hot chocolate."

Kris leaned on the bar and I plugged in the kettle. An actress in an ankle-length dress and a frilly apron rushed through on her way to the dressing room. When she came back she held up a round, poufy hat. "Forgot this!"

Kris raised her eyebrows at me as the woman left the room.

"It's always like this," I told her.

"Like what?" she asked.

"I don't know."

"You're an actor, right?" Kris said.

"I went to school for it. I'm not really doing it right now." I ripped open a hot chocolate packet and split it between our two cups.

"Why?"

"I did go to an audition recently."

"You're waiting to hear."

"I didn't get it."

"Oh."

I dropped one of my tip toonies into the register and we left, walking along Gower Street holding the hot chocolates. There were big flakes of wet snow coming down—normally the parade would be cancelled, but it had already been postponed three or four times due to bad weather. We stopped halfway up Prescott, above the crush of families who were filling the sidewalk and spilling into the road. Kris took my hand and I leaned into her and put my cheek on her shoulder.

A pack of teenagers in big sweatshirts and shiny tan-coloured tights were doing a dance routine. A girl in the back carried a boom box with an iPod stuck into the dock on top of it. The rest of the group kicked their legs together, did a twirl and wiggled their fingers in the air before taking a few steps forward and doing it all again. Some of their faces were slack with boredom and others had tetanus-stiff smiles. Kris loved the dog groups: the owners chatted amongst themselves and the dogs trotted obediently ahead in a pack, leashes crisscrossed behind them. Heavenly Creatures, Beagle Paws, Greyhound Rescue. After a half hour we got cold and I invited Kris back to my house. We climbed the hill with empty Styrofoam cups in our hands. When we got to the front door I remembered about my mattress being out in the hallway.

"The heater is broken in my room," I said, pushing my shoulder into the door.

"Okay," Kris said.

"So I brought my bed into the hall."

"Like you would," Kris said.

She helped me wrestle the mattress back into my room. We stopped for a moment with the bed in the doorway. Kris touched her toes and reached for the ceiling.

"How did you do this by yourself?" she said.

"It was kind of nice to look out these windows from a different perspective, you know what I mean? Different vantage point, different view."

"Never do this again, you fucking weirdo," Kris said, laughing. "Get your heater fixed."

⌒

THE NEXT MORNING I got up long before Kris and made myself a coffee. I was waiting on an English muffin I had in the toaster, leaning on the counter scrolling through Kris's Instagram. I had gone far enough back that she looked younger, maybe three years back.

There was a knock on the door and, like every knock since the cops had stormed in, it tightened my chest. But it was a gentle, patient knock. I opened the door to two old women in blazers and matching skirts. One was dressed completely in lavender, the other in dusty pink. They each had felt hats with felt flowers on the brim. One was wearing white gloves with pearl buttons on the wrists.

"Good morning," the woman in lavender said.

"Do you have a moment?" the other woman asked.

The neighbour kids were playing with a basketball in the plowed parking lot. The older one was throwing the ball high into the sky with both hands and then rushing backwards, letting it crash back down and bounce until it stilled on its own and started rolling away.

"Sort of," I said, still waiting for them to ask for directions.

"Have you accepted Jesus Christ into your heart?"

I hesitated.

"Let me just give you this, it's free." She held a magazine out to me and I took it. "There's a lot of interesting information in there. You know there are a lot of things that were predicted in the Bible and later confirmed by science. For example, Jesus knew we should wash our hands to prevent getting sick long before science confirmed it."

The cover of the magazine was an illustration of an empty highway stretching into a broody sky. It looked like the cover of a science fiction novel or a heavy metal album. White font in the bottom corner read, *What Does the Future Hold?*

"I don't think we can take the Bible literally, though." What I meant to say was I'm gay, my girlfriend's upstairs in bed.

"It's about the message," the woman in lavender said. "It's about Jesus Christ's message."

In the doorway I towered over the women, they were old and frail.

"I'm actually getting ready for work," I said.

"We'll come back to talk more another time. When would be good?" the woman in lavender asked.

"I'm not sure," I said.

"We'll come by and hope to catch you."

I watched them walk very slowly across the parking lot to their car. The woman in pink held her partner's elbow. When they got to the car they tried to unlock it with the remote car starter and accidentally popped the trunk. The woman in pink helped her friend into the front seat, then went around to close the trunk. I could see it was hard for her to reach up enough to get her fingers on the lip of the trunk. Then she didn't bring it down hard enough and it bounced open. She had to press down with both hands; her elbows came up around her neck and the back of her blazer wrinkled. Finally it stayed down.

That night Kris and I went to a movie. We'd barely spent a minute apart since the parade. Kris had gone home to shower and change her clothes but that was it. I'd been ignoring Viv's texts, she even called and I didn't pick up. I knew she wanted to talk about Holly and the situation with the cops.

When we arrived, the mall was packed with people doing Christmas shopping. There was a long line of children waiting to be photographed with Santa. A girl with a big plaid bow pinned to the top of her head was howling. Her mother knelt beside her, cajoling. There were about fifteen sets of parents and children ahead of them in line. The girl threw her head back and wailed; the sound ricocheted off the mall's domed ceiling. Shoppers around the photo area turned to look at the girl and her kneeling mother.

I saw a grandmother holding a small boy's hand look Kris up and down. It was a slow, deliberate scan. Short hair and men's clothes. She stretched her mouth into a thin mean line and turned away.

"God," I said indignantly.

"What?"

"That old lady gave you a dirty look."

"Did she? I don't even notice that anymore. Fuck 'em." But she didn't say it with her usual conviction.

The mall was closed when we left the movie. Everyone who'd been in the theatre with us walked in a staggered procession to the escalator. A girl with a plush unicorn backpack and her older boyfriend were ahead of us. The girl leaned in and nuzzled his shoulder and then they started making out on the escalator. A steel ball in the girl's cheek caught the light and shone up at me. Kris was looking at a display of Christmas decorations hung from the ceiling with see-through thread. I poked her in the side and pointed with my chin at the couple on the step below us. Kris nodded like "Oh, I know." I tried to keep from laughing and ended up snorting.

At the bottom of the escalator the couple separated. After a few steps, the girl leaned her head against her boy-friend's shoulder again and they slowed to a shuffle. We passed them.

"Gross," Kris said when we were out of earshot.

"'Cause he's older?" I said.

"Yeah, but also just PDA in general, it's obnoxious. Especially when straight people do it."

I thought of earlier when I'd taken Kris's hand while we waited in line for a cup of pretzel bites. She'd let me hold it for a moment but then she shook me off to adjust the strap of her messenger bag, and when she'd dropped her hand again she didn't reach for me. I felt a lick of shame whip through me.

"I don't find it obnoxious."

"Making out on the escalator is pretty obnoxious."

"You said PDA in general."

"You laughed at them too," Kris said. "I can't believe we spent like thirty bucks on that movie."

Freezing rain was pelting the sliding glass doors at the entrance to the mall. There was a layer of grey slush the texture of mashed potatoes on the ground. It splashed up on my jeans when we ran through the parking lot. All the cars that had been surrounding Kris's were gone. I stood in the driving rain while Kris dug through her pockets for the keys. As soon as she got in the car she dove across the seats to unlock my door but I kept tugging the handle right at the moment that she was pulling up on the lock. Eventually we were able to co-ordinate, making eye contact through the slush on the window. I let go, she pulled the lock up, I squeezed the handle—it felt like we'd executed a complicated dance move.

We had to wait a long time for the car to warm up. Kris's cheeks glowed pink from the cold rain; I leaned over and kissed her. She turned her head and caught my bottom lip between her teeth.

On the drive home Kris said, "Something feels weird."

Kris was always turning down the radio to listen to the car or sniffing the air and asking, "Do you smell something burning?" We drove slowly for a while. I could tell by her face that she was trying to diagnose the problem. I stayed quiet.

"I think we have a flat, does it feel like we have a flat?" Kris asked.

As soon as she said it, I felt it: the equilibrium was off, like being in a listing boat. We pulled into the Mary Brown's parking lot. Kris got out and walked around the car. She paused by the back tire on my side, then walked up to my window and tapped it with a knuckle. I rolled the window down.

"It's flat," she said.

I nodded grimly. Kris stood by the window, a mush of freezing rain sliding down her chest, while I stared up at her from the warmth of the car.

"What should we do?" I said eventually.

"I'm going to put on the spare," Kris said. "Pop the trunk."

I'd never dated anyone who knew how to change a tire and had everything they needed to do it on hand. I offered to help but Kris sent me into the Mary Brown's.

"Go warm up," she said.

The restaurant closed in a half hour and the kid at the register seemed to be the only one working. I saw his face fall when I pushed the door open. Probably he had prematurely cleaned the kitchen equipment.

"We got a flat," I told him.

He looked pointedly at the illuminated menu above his head.

"Just a small taters, please."

I was the only person in the restaurant. "Last Christmas" by Wham! was playing and the air smelled of grease. I watched Kris through the window. She took a stack of flyers sealed in white plastic bags out of the trunk and dropped them into the slush. She knelt on the papers and turned her body towards the tire. I saw her bent arm rise and fall as she worked the nuts on the hubcap. Eventually she stood and bounced on the wrench with one foot.

When the fries were ready I pumped ketchup into a white paper cup and took my tray to a booth. After the first bite of taters my mouth was coated in slippery, stale grease. I felt it on the back of my teeth.

I watched Kris get a spare tire out of the trunk. "The donut." Who taught me that? Probably my grandfather. When she'd lowered the car back into the slush and all her tools were loaded in the trunk, Kris came to get me. I had half a box of cold taters in front of me. She stood at the edge of the table, took three taters at once and plunged them into the ketchup cup, making the sauce pour over the rim like a science-project volcano. She had black grease on her hands.

"Help yourself," I said.

"Oh, I will."

"Do you want anything? They close in five minutes."

"No." She took three more taters and swabbed the ketchup cup with them.

Kris was completely drenched, her clothes hanging heavy from all the rain they'd absorbed. I could feel the boy at the counter watching us.

"Finish those, I'm done with them."

"Yeah?" She sat in the seat across from me.

"You must be freezing."

"Not really, I'm warm from doing the tire."

"You will be, though," I said.

"Probably." She picked the last crispy bits of batter out of the cardboard box.

I said "Thank you" to the kid at the counter as Kris shook the tray against the flap in the garbage receptacle. He followed us to the door and locked it behind us.

It had been two weeks since the police had come to the house but when we pulled up at home I still found myself checking the parking lot for cop cars. First for unmarked cop cars and then, wondering if Holly was home, for Dave King's brand-new silver Yaris. Neither were there.

All the lights were off downstairs and Holly's shoes weren't in the porch. I put all our clothes in the dryer, underwear and dirty socks and winter coats in one big snarl. The zipper from one of our coats made a ticking sound as it tumbled around in the dryer. We got straight in the shower. I knelt in the hard tub and kissed up and down the insides of Kris's thighs while she ran her nails over my scalp. The parts of me that were outside the circumference of warm dripping water got cold and goose-pimpled but I didn't care. I heard the front door and sat back on my heels. "Holly's home."

"Okay," Kris said, looking down at me.

I put my face against her warm thigh again but dread was sliding through me. I hadn't seen Holly since we talked about her glasses on the phone. I hadn't sent any money. Maybe she was just here to pick up some things and go on back to Dave's. I moved my face into Kris's crotch, spread it with my fingers and started sucking but I was listening for Dave's voice, straining to hear Holly's footsteps. Kris reached outside the shower and braced herself with a hand on the edge of the sink. She bent her knees and back a little to make the angle easier on my neck, then she pushed her crotch into my face. I saw her eyes were closed and her bottom lip was moving. I focused on her exhales and tried to match them with my tongue. Eventually she pushed my forehead away gently and straightened up.

"You're done?"

She nodded, but I couldn't tell from her face if she'd come.

It was hard to stand up, my knees ached. Kris stretched the arm that'd been outside the shower across her chest, twirling her wrist. I heard the drawer in the bottom of the oven screech open.

"I can't believe the water's still warm," she said.

"We have oil heat," I told her. "The water never gets cold."

When I shut the shower off I heard a man's voice, followed by Holly's. I couldn't make out the words but it sounded like they might be arguing. I lifted folded towels off the tarnished gold rack that'd been in the bathroom when we moved in. The towels were white and stained with bright pink splotches from when I washed them with red dish towels.

"Holly's got someone over," I said.

Kris wrapped the towel around herself and tucked a corner in by her armpit. I opened the door to the bathroom and cold air flooded in. We walked down the strange, windowless hallway between the bathroom and kitchen. I opened the second door; Holly was ripping open a bag of frozen fries with a big knife. Dave was standing in the centre of the kitchen. I thought, they must be sleeping together.

"Just tell me how to help," he was saying.

Holly whirled around. She'd dyed her hair washed-out pink.

"You changed your hair," I said.

"Yeah," Holly said.

Dave looked at the floor, to avoid looking at Kris and me in our towels.

"This is Kris," I said.

"Hi," Kris said.

"Hi," Holly said.

Dave looked up and nodded.

"I think we've met, maybe at Pleasant Street," he said to Kris.

"Nice to meet you again, then," Kris said.

Holly didn't say anything. She stood with the bag of fries in her hand and the knife pointed at the ceiling.

"Okay, well," I said and walked towards the stairs, Kris following me. When we stepped onto the dark staircase, the cooking noises resumed. I wondered if Holly was surprised that I was with a woman—we'd never talked about relationships. Maybe Viv had told her about Kris. The thought of them hanging out together without me made my lungs sting.

In my bedroom I flicked on the light, revealing the mess of dirty laundry spread around the floor. I hadn't been watering the geraniums, lots of the flowers had dried out on their stalks and lost petals. The broad, velvety leaves had patches of yellow.

"That was awkward," Kris said as soon as I closed the bedroom door.

"Yeah."

"What's her problem?"

"Maybe she was tired from work." As I said it I felt hot guilt spreading through my chest.

"Our clothes are still in the dryer," Kris said.

"Fuck."

I opened my closet and took out my lime-green bathrobe.

"Wait here," I told Kris.

"Obviously." She sat on the bed, wrapped in the splotchy towel.

"I'm sorry, it's so cold in here," I told her. "There's wool socks in the top drawer, if you want to borrow a pair."

I had to walk through the kitchen again to get to the laundry area. The light was on in the oven, illuminating a tray of fries. Holly and Dave were sitting side by side at the table, reading something on Holly's phone. Dave looked up and nodded at me as I walked by. Holly ignored me, lazily stroking the phone with one finger. She tugged Dave's sleeve to draw his attention back to the screen.

When I walked past again with an unruly mound of clothes pressed into my belly, they both ignored me. A sweater sleeve flopped around my thighs, a hot zipper pressed its teeth into my neck.

"'Night guys." I tried to make my voice friendly. I should be grateful she hadn't said anything in front of Kris.

Upstairs, I dropped the laundry on the bed and Kris picked her hoodie out of the pile. She zipped it shut around her, then shimmied the towel out from underneath. Her legs were thin but muscular and covered in dark, curly hair.

I dropped my towel on the floor and climbed into the bed. I wormed my legs around under the blankets, knocking warm laundry onto the floor. Kris picked her underwear up and stepped into them.

"Are you leaving?" I asked.

"I don't have to," she said.

I lifted the covers and she climbed in.

One of the cats was scratching at my bedroom door but I left him in the hallway. I heard Holly and Dave on the stairs, then their voices mumbled past the door. I could hear them more clearly through the bedroom wall. Sometimes an individual word was audible but not enough to give a sense of what they were talking about. I pressed my face into Kris's neck, flattening my nose against her skin.

I heard my phone vibrate on the floor; I must have dropped it down the side of the bed. There were three separate sets of twin vibrations. Three new texts. Most likely Viv. I left my phone down in the crack amongst dust-covered socks and books I'd never finished. I wanted to concentrate on how good it felt to have Kris's small, strong body in my arms.

The bare bulb dangling from the ceiling was bright. I tried to tune Holly and Dave out but it was impossible to stop straining to understand. Kris laid one of her legs on my belly, pinning me to the mattress. I closed my eyes but the light burned on the other side of my lids.

"Are you sleeping over?" I asked.

"I find it hard to breathe here," Kris said.

"So you're leaving?"

"No, I'll stay, go turn off the light."

I got out from under the warm covers. I turned off the light but the room stayed bright because of the street-light in the parking lot. I heard the coughing woman's deep, body-rattling hacking coming from the fire escape. I walked naked across the room and tugged the cord that lowered the blind. The bottom of the blind smacked the window ledge, shaking loose a shower of brittle geranium petals. I got back in bed and rubbed my cold feet on Kris's calves.

"I have to tell you something weird," I said, curling in tighter, pressing my face into the stretch of skin between her breast and collarbone. Her breathing was shallow and scratchy. "Don't be freaked out, it's just some kind of misunderstanding."

I started telling her about the search. Kris sat up—then we were both sitting in the dark. I was cross-legged with the blankets around me.

"You should go to the media," she said.

"And say what?"

"That they searched your house for no reason. All the stuff you told me," she said.

"I don't really understand the situation. I should have asked more questions," I said.

"What does 'illegal digital material' mean?" Kris said.

"I don't know."

"Well that's another thing, they didn't explain anything to you."

"I just want it to go away, I don't want anything to do with it."

"Call VOCM first thing tomorrow morning," Kris said. "Then file an official complaint. Or do the complaint first, whatever."

"Holly is moving out," I said, lowering my voice. "She hasn't been here in days, she blames me. She basically, she insinuated that I did something." I didn't mention about the glasses, about the money I still owed her.

"You need to file a complaint, Stacey. Are you going to?"

"Yeah maybe. I'm tired." I reclined into the pillow and

tugged on her arm but Kris wouldn't lie down. She looked at me like someone scolding a child.

"They're probably watching everything I do on the internet," I said. "They might be watching the house." I wanted to say about how the woman at the supermarket had frightened me. And the drone. That I wasn't eating properly because I didn't like standing with my back to the door to cook. And not eating was making it all worse.

"Don't you think that's wrong?" Kris said.

"Yeah, but it's probably not illegal. You know what I mean? It doesn't matter how I feel."

I stretched my legs out and reached for my toes. I regretted telling her.

"Go to the media then," Kris said.

"Anyway, I just really don't want to think about it right now, come down here," I said.

I wrapped my arms around her waist. She lay down next to me and I put a leg across her hips. I closed my eyes, thinking how good it felt to be close to another person's warm body. After a moment she said, "You kind of have a responsibility."

"What?"

"To file a complaint."

I rolled off her. "Oh my god, people have way worse experiences with the cops. Did you read about the violent arrests of peaceful protestors at Muskrat Falls? It's in the news, all kinds of stories like that. Endless stories that are far, far worse."

"Yeah, exactly, you're in a good position to say

something about this particular thing. The thing that happened to you. Let this be one thing they don't get away with, so they think twice in the future. About all the ways they abuse their power."

We both lay on our backs in the dark.

"It's my choice," I told her.

"Yeah, I know."

"So respect my choice."

"Okay."

And then after a moment, "Anyway, I'll think about it. I am thinking about it."

"I really find it hard to breathe in here." Kris rubbed her chest below her throat.

TWELVE

In the morning, Kris had to go out to Stavanger Drive to pick up a package from the UPS depot, a special bike part. There was a big sale on at Mark's Work Wearhouse and she dropped me off there while she went to collect her mail. The store was packed with people trying to finish their Christmas shopping.

A woman in a blue hijab took a rubber boot off the shelf and stepped into it. A mother held up a black hiking boot with bright purple laces for her teenage daughter to see, nearly whacking me in the face with it.

"It's waterproof," the mother said, turning the boot from side to side in the air.

The girl was stone-faced. The mother put the boot back on the shelf. There was a red circle on the ankle. Fifty percent off.

"You can save up and buy boots with a heel later. That's

not what we're here for," the mother said. "We're here to find practical, warm, dry winter boots."

The boot was perfect. Butchy but with girly purple laces. I waited for the mother and daughter to move on so I could see the price marked below it on the shelf. More than I'd planned to spend. I crouched and leaned in to read the sizes on the boxes stacked beneath the display boot.

I found a bench with a puffy leather seat and laced the boots. I stuck my legs straight out in front of me and admired them. They felt good, a warm, fleece lining. I threaded the laces through the two top holes and tightened them around my ankles. I dug my heels into the carpet and swayed the boots from side to side. Soft butch.

I took the boots off; they fit into the box like puzzle pieces. Toe to neck and neck to toe. I carried the box to the front of the store. There was a long line of people shaped by a maze of hip-height elastic belts stretched between plastic posts. I stood behind the mother who had been advocating for my boots. Her daughter was carrying a pair of flat-soled nude boots with fake sheep's-wool lining. Compromise boots.

I took my phone out and started calculating how much my boots would be with the discount. A young guy with an iPad was pacing back and forth outside the elastic belts.

"Excuse me?" He stopped beside me.

"Hi," I said.

The daughter with the nude boots turned to watch our interaction.

"Would you like a thirty-percent discount on your purchase today?" the guy asked me. He wasn't handsome but he was clean-cut and you could see muscles under his checkered dress shirt.

"I just need some information, no payment at all," he said.

"Can I still get the storewide discount?" I asked.

"No problem at all," the guy said.

The line had grown behind me.

"I can have both discounts?"

"Shouldn't be a problem," he said. "Zero fees to register." His finger hovered over the screen.

"Okay."

"You want to do it?" His blond hair was gelled into business-school spikes.

"Yeah," I said.

"You'll have to step out of the line," he said.

I was so warm in my coat and there were only three people ahead of me now.

"Hang on," he said quietly to me and then hollered at the girl on cash: "She's just stepping out of the line to sign up, can she head straight to the checkout after?"

People turned to look at me. I felt ashamed. Now everyone knew I was giving away all my personal information, offering myself up for identity theft. I should have gone to the Army-Navy store.

The sales guy unclipped the elastic belt between us from its post. I stepped out of the line.

"I'm going to need a picture ID, do you have a driver's licence on you? Something like that?"

I got my wallet out. What if Kris came in and saw me talking to this guy like a little old lady buying fistfuls of iTunes cards for phone scammers. When I handed him my licence, he surprised me by taking a picture of it. The iPad was on full volume and the picture-taking sound rang out.

"What's that for?" I asked.

He handed me back the card.

"Just part of the process. What do you do?" He looked me up and down.

"I work at a theatre."

"Movie theatre?"

"No, like for plays, I bartend and do box office." I thought about adding "I also act" or "sometimes I act" but it seemed pathetic.

"Oh okay, that's pretty cool, I think you're my first theatre person, showbiz." He was scrolling through a drop-down list of possible professions. "Let's say 'enter-tainment industry.'"

I resented his attitude.

"Okay, so how much do you make a year? Just roughly, an estimate?" He was scrolling through another drop-down menu.

"That seems like a lot of information," My voice came out in a croak. I was so deep in it already.

"You know what, it doesn't really matter, let's just go with this." He pressed $50,000.

"Well —"

"Almost done, it'll just take fifteen to twenty minutes to be approved. Do you want to wait or is it okay if the card is mailed to you?"

"I get the discount either way?" I felt stomach-sick.

"Absolutely, if it's approved."

"Okay."

"Okay, mail it?"

"Yeah, and I can just go straight to the counter?"

"She's okay to come up to the counter?" he yelled at the woman on cash, who nodded.

I stepped in front of the person at the head of the line without making eye contact. I put the box on the counter.

"So you get the discount?" the cashier said.

"Yeah," I said.

The guy with the iPad was pacing the line again. The cashier waved him over. "She gets the discount?"

"It's not approved, you're getting the approval by mail, you chose approval by mail," he said.

"It's not a credit card though, right?" I said to the cashier.

"It's definitely a credit card, he wasn't clear?"

"No."

She grimaced and nodded.

"Can you cancel that? I want to cancel that," I said to the guy.

"I can't cancel it, I'm not authorized to do that."

He shrugged and started walking away. I accidentally met eyes with the man whose place I'd taken in the line.

"Call and cancel it as soon as you get home." She shone the barcode reader at the side of the box. "You can find the number online."

She passed me the debit machine and I tapped my card against it. Anxiety cycloned in my chest as the receipt started working itself out of the printer. Probably it wouldn't be approved, but what about the $50,000 lie?

Could I be charged with fraud? And what about my photographed ID card? I thought of the cops storming through the house, and I wanted to get home to Snot and Courtney.

"Just call as soon as you leave here," the girl told me as she slid the box into an enormous plastic bag. She could feel the panic radiating off me.

I waited outside the store for Kris. I held the box between my knees so I could unzip my coat. It hurt to breathe because the air was cold but my body was sweaty.

"You got boots!" she said.

"Want to see?" I started pulling off the crinkly bag.

"I do but I'm just going to run in there for a second, is that okay? They have these gloves, I want to get them while the sale is on." She cut the engine.

"Yeah, of course." I sank back into my seat, pulling the box into my gut. I could see two possible futures stretching out in front of me — one where I phoned Mark's Work Wearhouse immediately and possibly resolved the situation, and another where I let myself forget about it until it inevitably came back to haunt me, months or maybe years later.

Kris opened her door. "You're not coming in? Come in with me."

I climbed out and laid the box on the seat. The sun was setting, all the stores across the road were lit from behind with popsicle-pink light.

I stood beside Kris at the glove display. I could see the guy with the iPad making his way down the line. Every so often he stopped beside someone and launched into his pitch. From where I stood at the sock rack he looked younger and less confident. A man in a Gore-Tex jacket shook his head no and stared straight ahead when the boy started his spiel. That was the appropriate response.

"That guy tricked me into applying for a credit card." I had decided not to tell Kris about it but it slid out of me.

"Who?" She was holding a pair of neoprene gloves.

"When I was buying my boots, I thought it was some kind of discount thing, a loyalty card." I pointed. "I said I wanted to cancel the application and he wouldn't let me."

"What a smarmy little prick." At first her outrage was satisfying. "Go talk to him again."

She slid her hand into a glove and made a fist. The other glove hung limply from her wrist.

"He said he's not authorized to cancel it."

"No fucking way he's not authorized."

"I'm just going to call when I get home, the girl at the counter said I could cancel it over the phone."

"You let people push you around. Go over there." Kris took the gloves off and returned them to their hook. She picked up a fleece-lined pair. "Go, go on."

"I already talked to him."

"You're being ridiculous, you'll never get through on the phone." Kris held up the fleece-lined gloves and walked away from me. "I'm getting in line now, go talk to him."

The guy was near the cash, talking to a woman with three of the same polar-fleece vest in her arms. I stood beside them waiting for a break in the conversation. Kris watched from the back of the line. I resented the feeling of her eyes on me.

"What do you do?" the guy was asking.

"I'm a psychologist, I have my own practice," she told him.

"Wow, cool, you're my first psychologist."

The woman smiled; I wondered if she found him attractive.

"Excuse me," I said.

"I'll be with you in a minute," he said, keeping his face turned away from me. "Okay, and roughly how much do you make in a year?"

The psychologist looked at me. "You can help this young lady."

"I need you to cancel that, you didn't make it clear that it was a credit card, I don't want it. And you made up my income, you said I make way more than I do." It came out in a rush, all my syllables sliding together.

The sales guy stepped away from the line and started walking backwards into the store, forcing me to follow him away from the psychologist.

"There's nothing I can do, you have to phone them."

"Who do I call? Do you have a number?"

"Here, I'll put it in your phone."

I checked to see if Kris was watching as I handed him my phone. He held the iPad in his armpit and typed the phone number in.

"Okay, thank you," I said.

I found Kris in line.

"Can I have the keys? I'm going to wait in the car, I'm too warm," I said to her from the other side of the elastic belt.

"Did you get it taken care of?"

"Yes."

Kris reached into the breast pocket of her padded vest and dangled the keys in front of me. I expected her to snatch them back when I reached for them but she let me close my fist around them. Outside, the sky was inky blue, all the pink had bled out of it.

I sat with the shoebox in my lap and turned the ignition. The radio came on, epic orchestral music flooded out of the dashboard. I breathed through my nose, inhaling and exhaling on the beat.

Kris got in the car with a smile on her face. She tossed the plastic bag with her new gloves in it at me.

"Ten bucks! That's an amazing deal on those gloves."

I didn't answer but she didn't notice. She turned the radio off.

"Aren't you glad you got that taken care of? That would've been a nightmare."

"Yeah," I said as flatly as possible.

"Should we get McDonald's? I'm kind of craving a chicken wrap. Are you hungry?"

"I guess."

Once we were in line for the drive-through window she said, "Why don't you show me the boots?"

"I'll show you later, I don't want to get them out now."

"You can just open the lid — you don't have to take them out."

I shimmied the box out of the crinkly bag and opened the top. Kris inched the car forward. She glanced at the boots.

"Oh, those are great." She sounded genuinely impressed.

I felt the anger shrinking in my chest. I admired the bright purple laces.

"They're my style."

Kris reached over and felt the lining.

"They're going to be very warm. Are they waterproof?"

"Yeah, I think, I'm pretty sure it said that on the box. Maybe just water-resistant."

The car in front of us turned the corner and we pulled up to the speaker. I shut the lid.

"What do you want?" Kris asked as she put her window down.

"Chicken wrap, I guess. And a medium Coke."

I twisted around and laid the shoebox in the back seat. I put my window down and emptied the half-full drinks sitting in the cup holder out the window. I would call first thing in the morning.

EVERY YEAR MY parents host a Christmas party. They invite family and friends and also students and students' parents. My mom makes punch in a cut-glass bowl my nan gave her and my dad bakes a ham with cloves stuck in it and a brown sugar glaze. I come over in the afternoon to vacuum and clean the bathroom. I spread out poinsettia napkins on the table where people lay the cookies they've brought. Viv and her mom always come to the party with homemade hummus and mini pita breads.

This year I invited Kris, sort of impulsively.

"I told them you're coming," I said.

"Do they know we're seeing each other, though?" she asked.

"My dad's best friend is gay," I said. "There's a picture of my dad at Pride in Toronto in the eighties. Him and Clive are sitting on the curb with their arms on each other's shoulders, it's really sweet."

"Oh god," she said.

"My aunt is gay."

"Stop," she said.

MY MOM PICKED me up after a matinee shift to go Christmas shopping. There was a film crew making a documentary about Mary Walsh at the theatre that afternoon. They were filming her doing a stand-up set with a live audience, then they were going to boot it to Signal Hill to get a shot of Mary up there before the daylight faded.

I served a lot of coffee and tea, the occasional glass of red wine. The crew told me to help myself to the granola bars and two-bite brownies they'd set out. I had a Mary Oliver book Kris lent me open on the counter and got a splash of red wine on a poem about the ocean. I tried dabbing the page with a wet paper towel but the stain smeared and spread.

I heard the theatre door creak open and the thundering of an audience pouring down over the stairs. I didn't know Kris well enough yet to know whether she would be upset by a stain in a book. The camera crew hustled Mary Walsh out of the building, shouting, "We've got a half hour of light, twenty minutes of light." Only a couple of audience members lingered and ordered a second glass of wine. I texted my mom to let her know I'd be done soon.

After locking up, I climbed into the front seat of my parents' car and swung my bookbag into my lap. Mom had the heat on high and CBC Radio on. There was a scientist on, talking about the likelihood that flooding the dam at Muskrat Falls would cause the North Spur to collapse, flooding surrounding communities.

"It's evil what's going on up there," my mom said, tapping the dial to turn the radio off.

"I know."

"They don't even have an escape plan for people, they're saying—this guy is saying they need an escape plan, the government won't make one."

"So Kris, who I'm bringing to the party —" I'd decided to have the conversation, so I began it.

"This is your new friend, Kris?"

"Yeah."

"The bike mechanic?"

"We're seeing each other."

"What do you mean?"

"Like, romantically."

"Sexually?"

"Yes."

"You've had sex?"

"Yes."

"And you enjoyed it?"

"You've never asked me that about a boyfriend," I said, even though I'd only ever had one real boyfriend.

"I'm asking because, if this woman is really a lesbian, you can't mess around with her feelings. She might be really invested in this."

"I'm not messing around with her feelings."

"You're serious about it? How long has it been going on?"

"Going on?"

"How long have you been seeing her? That's a normal question."

"Anyway I'm just telling you because she asked me to, because she's coming to the party."

The wipers dragged back and forth on the slowest setting, making arcs of slush on the windshield and erasing them.

"You're saying you're a lesbian?"

"I don't know."

"Okay, this is what I'm talking about."

"What?"

"At your age you can't be reckless with other people's feelings," she said.

"Stop saying that! I just mean I don't know about lesbian, the word 'lesbian.'"

"You're not attracted to men? You never were? What about Dan?"

"I don't know."

"You're bisexual?"

"No, I hate that."

"What? You hate what?"

"Let's talk about something else," I said.

"I don't understand your attitude."

"I want to get Angela's kid a lava lamp, I saw them on sale at The Source," I said.

We passed the high school, where a handful of students were crossing the parking lot with instruments in brown leather cases.

"I'm just telling you because she was worried about the party," I said.

"Well she's obviously welcome at the party, obviously."

"Okay, great. Well, that's all. The lava lamps are two-for-one."

I turned on the radio and switched the station to VOWR. They were playing "Frosty the Snowman."

"The only thing is," Mom turned down the radio. "Your grandmother."

We were passing the junior high now — some kids were standing in groups talking, others were tossing balls of icy snow into the road.

"You think she'll be at the party?" I asked.

"If she's well enough."

"She won't know," I said.

"She might not," my mom said. "She's a pretty smart woman."

Traffic had slowed in front of the school; parents waited for their kids to jog across the road and climb into their cars, then pulled ahead.

"Don't worry, we'll figure it out," Mom said eventually. "A lava lamp is a great idea. Maybe I'll get one for Rory too."

ON THE AFTERNOON of the party, Kris called me for the first time ever to ask if she should wear a button-down shirt or something more casual.

"Is it a formal thing? What are you wearing?"

"Just wear whatever you're comfortable in, no one will care," I said.

"What would make me comfortable is to be dressed appropriately." I was surprised by the edge in her voice.

"Wear the button-up, I guess."

Kris brought my parents a bottle of wine with a red velvet bow tied around the neck. Her shirt was buttoned all the way up and tucked into her pants. I leaned in and gave her a kiss on the cheek in the porch and she stiffened.

"Don't," she said.

"What?"

The door opened behind us, more people were trying to come in, we had to make room for a woman with a big stew pot in her arms. Kris reached down and squeezed my hand.

We were pushed into the kitchen by the wave of people squishing themselves into the porch behind us. My mom was microwaving rum sauce for fruitcake. She was rubbing the small of her back, she'd been on her feet but she told me the pain never completely subsided.

"Kris brought you this." I handed my mom the bottle.

"Thank you, Kris, so nice to meet you," my mom said.

A student walked up to us, presenting a sloppy yule log he'd made, and my mom started fawning over the boy. I turned to lead Kris to the food table and Mom put a hand on my arm. She pulled me close to whisper, "Your grandmother is over there. Go say hello."

My grandmother was in an armchair by the Christmas tree with her purse in her lap. She was wearing a pink dress shirt with tan pants that had a crease ironed in them and a pair of electric-blue running sneakers. I leaned over her to say hello and she laid her shaking hands on my shoulders and kissed each of my cheeks. Kris hung back, her hands clasped in front of her like a hostess at a fancy restaurant. It was some other persona, not her usual cowboy swagger. Normally Kris was always leaning an elbow on the counter and flirting with the barista or stomping into the gas station and asking the guy behind the counter if he was "Busy 'er what?"

"This is Kris," I said, straightening up.

"Nice to meet you, Kris," my grandmother said, her eyes drifting over Kris, taking in the short hair and men's pants.

"Nice to meet you," Kris said. "It's a beautiful party."

"What's that?" My grandmother leaned over her purse.

"A lovely party," Kris said louder.

"We're going to get some food, would you like anything?" I asked.

"Wait now, I've got something for you," my grandmother said.

She took something wrapped in a piece of quilted paper towel out of her purse. She pressed it into the palm of my hand. Kris watched over my shoulder as I opened the parcel. The Pope spoon.

"Your great-aunt wanted you to have that." My grandmother took my free hand in hers.

"I remember," I said.

"Take good care of it," she said to me, and then to Kris, "that's a real keepsake from the Pope's visit."

"Thank you." I kissed my nan on the cheek and put the spoon in the pocket of my cardigan.

I brought Kris to the food table and made her a plate with thick slices of ham, a bun and three shortbread cookies. I handed her utensils from a wicker basket I'd lined with a green cloth napkin. I looked at my grandmother, alone on the other side of the room with the party swirling around her. It hurt her to stand up too long.

"See, that wasn't so bad," I said to Kris and started making up my own plate.

"I want to meet your dad, where is he?"

"Gone to get ice."

Kris and I sat on the sofa and tried to cut the ham into bite-size pieces without ripping through our paper plates. Kids were tearing around the room, drips of sauce down the front of their shirts and icing ground into their corduroys. A group of older people drifted towards the couch, the backs of their legs and butts blocking our view of the room. Bits of their conversation tumbled down — they were talking about the public inquiry into the financing of Muskrat Falls. The general sentiment seemed to be "about time."

The five-disc CD changer my parents still used clunked to the next CD. In the pause between the final notes of "Tickle Cove Pond" and the beginning of some medieval choral music someone said, "I mean, if the CEO of the company is calling it a boondoggle." A skinny teenager sat on the arm of the couch, absorbed in a hand-held video game.

"Should we go look for Dad?" I asked Kris.

Right at that moment Viv and Mike broke through the people in front of us and sat on the couch. Viv wrapped her arms tight around me. The hug felt good.

"Hey," Mike said.

Kris nodded to him from the opposite end of the couch, like they had something in common. As partners of me and Viv.

"Here we are, another Christmas party." Viv smiled, she was stoned. "Where the fuck have you been?"

"Let's get some punch, I haven't had any yet," Mike said.

Viv, Mike and I stood up. I waved Kris off the sofa and she followed. I couldn't tell if Viv was actually mad at me.

"Is your mom here?" I asked her as we made our way through the stuffy room. "I want to say hi."

Viv pointed across the room to where her mom was talking to my uncle. She was holding the hummus and pita dish on an upturned palm, plastic wrap still stretched over the top of it.

My dad was at the food table taking up a plate for himself. He hugged Viv and Mike.

"This is Kris," I said.

"Very nice to meet you, will I hug you too?"

"Sure." Kris submitted to the hug.

I set four plastic glasses on the edge of the table and dunked the ladle in the punch.

"None for me," Viv said.

"What? Really?"

"I'm just not feeling great," she said. "My stomach."

"Did you want some, Dad?" I asked.

"Why not?"

I handed Dad the glass I'd filled for Viv; Mike passed Kris a cup before picking up his own. I was touched by the small gesture, he was making an effort to include her.

"What's happening with the cops?" Viv asked.

"What?" I said.

"I haven't seen you in ages."

"I think she should file a complaint," Kris said.

"Against the cops?" Viv said. "Yes! Definitely."

Mike was nodding, impressed by Kris's suggestion.

"You should do it now, there could be a time limit. It might even be too late," Viv said.

"I looked it up, you have up to six months after the incident," Kris said. I noticed that her wide-legged, swash-buckler stance was back.

"I don't know if I want to." I looked at my dad.

"Sounds like something to consider," Dad said. He took a butter knife from the wicker basket and sawed into the melting yule log. "What are you doing for work now, Viv? Are you still at the restaurant?"

Kris helped herself to a second glass of punch. My dad slapped a slice of yule log onto a poinsettia napkin.

"And I think she should go to the media," Kris said.

"Holy shit, yeah," Mike said.

"The investigation is ongoing," I said, reaching into my pocket to rub my thumb over the curved back of the Pope spoon.

A mother tapped my dad on the shoulder, she and

her son were leaving, they wanted to say thank you and goodbye. My dad followed them to the door.

"I think Kris is right, Stace," Viv said, blasting me with the full intensity of her eyes.

"Don't let them get away with it," Kris said.

"Nail those fuckers," Viv said.

THE MORNING AFTER the Christmas party, I woke up and found my phone beneath my pillow. It was dark in my bedroom because I'd been sleeping with the curtains closed since the incident, in case there were cops out in the parking lot. I turned towards the wall to keep the light from the screen out of Kris's face. First I checked my email, then Instagram, and finally Facebook.

I scrolled past a CTV article with the headline "Cost of Muskrat Falls Hydro Project Rises by Another Billion, CEO says" above a photo of two figures in orange jumpsuits hanging off the side of a rock wall in a massive, blasted-out pit. Then a picture of a child's birthday party — a group of kids gathered around a bowl of Cheezies, the elastic chin-straps of their party hats digging into their necks. Then I came to a block of text Viv had posted. It already had over a hundred likes.

> A good friend of mine had her home and privacy invaded
> by a group of Royal Newfoundland Constabulary (Viv
> had tagged the RNC) officers recently. She was alone
> when several cops, all big men, stormed into her house
> to search for "illegal digital material," which they told

her was transmitted from her address months before she
moved in. They confiscated her electronics and are cur-
rently searching them for evidence of illegal activity—no
doubt hoping to find something that would retroactively
justify their actions. Yet another example of the RNC's
dangerous incompetence and lack of accountability.

When had she done this? I looked at Kris's sleeping
face beside me. I checked the timestamp: late last night.
I wished I could rewind to a moment before, to slide back
between Kris's sleep-heavy limbs and lie there a little
longer without knowing this was out in the world.

I went downstairs and turned on the shower. I sat
naked on the toilet seat, still looking at Viv's post while the
bathroom mirror steamed up. There were thirteen comments. I stared at the pattern of mildew on the bottom of
the clear plastic shower curtain for a long moment before
opening the comments. Mostly people I didn't know.
"Holy shit, so fucked up." "Your friend should contact a
lawyer." Strings of sparkling hearts and angry-face emojis.
I dropped my phone in the porcelain basin of the sink.

After I showered, I climbed the stairs in a towel.
I leaned over Kris and let my wet hair drip on her face
and the bed around her.

"Kris."

"What are you doing? You're wet, get away."

I held my phone in her face, showing her the post. She
wasn't fully awake, there were bags tinged with purple
under her brown eyes.

"You're upset?"

"Why would she do that?"

"Nobody knows it's about you."

"Why wouldn't she tell me first?" I said.

"It's not about you. It doesn't say your name. It's about the RNC fucking up." Kris was starting to wake up.

I stood up and screeched open the top drawer of my dresser.

I wanted her to agree with me so we could snuggle and maybe have sex before I had to leave for work. She was lying down scrolling through her phone. I let my towel fall on the ground and stood naked, sorting through my T-shirts. My phone buzzed on my dresser. Viv had sent me a screenshot. And then another.

"What the fuck is this?" I said.

"What?" Kris asked.

"'A message request from Constable Joe Michaels.'" I threw the phone at the bed next to Kris. It bounced on the mattress and landed on her chest.

"Hey!" Kris said. "That's not okay."

"It was an accident." I wished it was an accident. "It slid out of my hand, I'm sorry."

Kris picked up my phone and looked at the message. I watched her eyes flick back and forth across the screen.

YEARS AFTER JORDAN NOLAN there was Keith Pike. I knew Keith Pike from shows too—I started going to all-ages shows when I was thirteen and he'd always been in the most popular bands. He was straight-edge and had three Xs tattooed on the back of his bicep to show he didn't

drink or do drugs. At shows, his friends sold zines about
Anti-O organizing and DIY home repair and queer sex.
Sometimes he brought a lime-green hard-shell suitcase
of tapes recorded by bands from outside of the province.
The tapes were tossed haphazardly in the curved bottom
of the suitcase and the bands' pins and patches were
attached to the polyester lining inside the suitcase's lid.

Between bands Viv and I would wander along the
tables, flipping through zines, opening tape cases to look
at the photocopied inserts. We blushed and mumbled
when the people manning the tables offered bits of information like, "They're from Vancouver" or "That's their
first demo." Keith Pike was the oldest of the older people.

He screamed the lyrics in all of his bands; Flock to
the Fight and Scab Drummer and later Death on the Ice.
When he screamed his face went red. All the frontmen
yelled that way (they were all frontmen), letting cords of
saliva loose on the audience and making the veins in their
necks stand out, but Keith Pike was more of a performer
than the others. He stormed back and forth in front of the
drum kit, whipping the mic cord like a lasso. He punched
and high-kicked the air in front of him. Between songs
he bantered, throwing his head back to laugh at his own
jokes. He barked at the audience to "fucking mosh" and
they hopped on one another's backs. The air would be so
full of everyone's swirled-together body odour and damp-
sneaker stink that it sank into our hair and clothes the way
cigarette smoke does and we took it home with us.

The first night we slept together I'd been standing on a
table in a crowded bar watching a band from out of town.

Below me, guys were circling, pumping their fists in the air, warming up to mosh. I was twenty-one and he was thirty-two. He had some kind of social work/homecare job, he helped people do their taxes and go grocery shopping. I had seen him lifting an older woman's walker onto the bus while they talked about the difference between Tide and no-name-brand laundry detergent.

I had just moved back to St. John's after finishing my degree. Viv was still in Montreal, she would come home later that summer. She arrived in August with Mike, both of them tanned and muscular from riding bikes all over the city. They found a two-bedroom on Boggan Street and invited me to move in with them.

The night I first slept with Keith Pike, Viv was hanging out by the canal in Montreal. She texted me a photo of a dead dove one of her new friends had fished out of the water with a hanger tied to a piece of string. The stiff bird was a smear of white in the middle of a dark photo. I squinted at the screen of my flip phone, the table rocking beneath me, trying to understand the photo. I sent a string of question marks and she responded with a typo-filled explanation. She was drunk. I folded the phone and slid it into my bra.

It was a hot night in St. John's, there were blotches of sweat on everyone's clothes. I was pulling my dress off my back, arching away from the damp fabric, when I felt someone staring at me. I caught Keith Pike's eyes moving over me, resting on my stuck-out chest. There was a screech of feedback, someone smacked into the corner of my table and I had to brace myself against the sweating cinder-block wall. He smiled, letting me know that he knew that I knew he was looking. It was so brazenly sleazy.

Later we walked up from downtown together. I was still living above the laundromat with Dan, smoking the skaters' weed and masturbating on webcam. We stopped at a bench outside Moo Moo's Ice Cream and I said, "I don't know if we should do this, I have a partner and I'm kind of a bit drunk."

"How drunk are you? Are you too drunk?" He did ask those questions.

We were standing under the light that Moo Moo's kept on outside their front entrance even when they were closed.

"I don't think so," I said. "I'm nervous."

"Why are you nervous?"

"I'm afraid I won't be good at it."

"But you've slept with other people?" he asked.

"I've slept with people."

"How many people?"

"Two," I said.

"Oh, it's fine then. You'll be great, I know you will."

"Really?" The way he said it was like there was some empirical evidence.

"Yeah, I can just tell." He raked his chin-length hair out of his face; there were the beginnings of crow's feet around his eyes.

"Maybe we should wait, until next weekend," I said.

"If you want to it has to be tonight."

"Okay."

We didn't talk on the walk to his house but he held my hand. It was strange to hold the hand of someone so tall—he had to bend his elbow for my arm to hang at a natural height. I thought about Dan at home asleep. I thought about how Dan edited all my university papers for me, pointing out run-on sentences and confusing transitions but also good points I'd made. The fitted sheet we had always came loose and I pictured him drooling on the shiny polyester mattress.

Keith Pike lived with a bunch of guys who were closer to my age and also played in punk bands. I left my sneakers in the pile of dirty, worn-out Vans in the porch. His bedroom was lined with bookshelves filled with records. There was a record player with a cracked plastic cover at the end of the bed. A piece of clear packing tape was pasted over the crack.

"I probably have as many books as you have records," I said.

"I own a lot of books too," he said.

"I'm not on birth control."

"Okay."

"So we need to use a condom."

"Yeah, definitely," he said.

He went down on me and I came. When we had sex he put his hands around my neck and squeezed hard. I felt everything closing in. I thought, this must be the way people have sex. I got a panicky feeling from not being able to breathe but I thought, he'll know when it gets too dangerous. When he let go, he said, "Was that okay?" And I worried he knew I was scared.

When we finished, I sat up and said, "I feel dizzy."

I expected him to say, you should stay here, do you

want some water? but he said, "I'll call you a cab."

When I got to the apartment the sun was coming up. I stood at the foot of the bed and put a hand on Dan's calf.

When he opened his eyes I said, "I had sex with someone else."

Dan went to stay with his parents and moved his things out while I was at work. We exchanged cold but respectful emails about cancelling the electricity and divvying up the damage deposit. I couldn't eat for three days. Food seemed disgusting to me. On the third night I woke up at four in the morning and devoured a package of stale Fig Newtons. It felt like swallowing lumps of dust; I let the tap run and swallowed big mouthfuls of cold water to unstick the cookies from the roof of my mouth and the sides of my throat. I let the water splash over my cheeks and neck.

I went out a lot. I drank straight liquor and blacked out. That summer my body spent hours on the patio between Distortion and CBTG's without me. At the end of the night Keith Pike would find me. We would go home and have sex. He praised my body and my flexibility and my endurance, I responded with slurred nonsense. In the morning there were yellow bruises on my thighs and chest. The outline of three long fingers and a thumb wrapped around each of my upper arms.

One night I said, "You can do whatever you want to me, I don't care." I did say that. I said it to a sober man a decade older than me, after slumping against the wall in the hallway and then walking into the door frame in the bedroom—but I said it.

Later he woke me up and said, "We didn't use a condom that time."

In my dream, I'd felt a weight moving on top of me, pinning me to the mattress. My grandmother told me about the old hag—an old woman who visits you in your sleep, sits on you, paralyzes your limbs, howls in your face. Bad things to come. To ward off the old hag you hammer a single rusty nail through a board and sleep with it balanced on your chest, the sharp tip of the nail pointed at the ceiling, ready to impale.

"Yes we did, we used a condom. You walked over to the shelf, you got it off the shelf, remember?" I said, the ceiling swooping back and forth above me.

"Never mind, go back to sleep," he said.

In the morning I walked to my apartment above the laundromat, still queasily drunk. I felt something soupy slide out of me. In the apartment my books were slumped on the shelves because Dan had come by to pick up his books while I was out. The sofa was gone. I took my underwear off in the living room and saw a thick white smear on the crotch. There was something cracked and shiny, like dried egg whites, on the inside of my thighs. It took me a moment to understand. No one had ever come inside me before. Thankfully I started my period later that day, a spot of red-brown luck.

HI VIVIAN,

Constable Joe Michaels here. I work in the com-munications department at the Royal Newfoundland Constabulary. I saw the post you tagged our department in last night and wanted to reach out. I wanted to say that I would be happy to chat with your friend about her experience. At this juncture, I'm reaching out not as a member of the RNC *but as just another human being. Please tell your friend she is welcome to message me here.*

"She needs to delete that post, fucking immediately," I said. I pulled a T-shirt over my head.

"If he's communications he should contact you on behalf of the RNC. What's this touchy-feely 'fellow human being' bullshit? Where was that when they searched your house?" Kris said.

"Give me my phone, I'm going to call Viv and tell her to delete it."

"Okay." Kris put the phone down beside her. "Just think about what you want before you do it. Like, you should definitely keep the screenshot of that message he sent, just in case things escalate. You can use it in your complaint if you decide you want to do one. There's no way he's allowed to do that."

"I'll keep the screenshot but I want the post deleted."

"Okay, here's the thing," Kris said. "I'm worried delet-ing it could make you look bad, guilty. You really need to talk to a lawyer, this whole situation is so fucked up."

She held the phone out to me.

"I have to get ready for work," I said.

"Don't let him get away with this," Kris said, kicking the covers off. "Nail that fucker."

I left the room. My body was vibrating with anger. I wasn't ready to speak to Viv. I didn't want to hear her justification for it.

I was doing box office for a matinee performance of a children's puppet show. I went up the steep stairs to flick on the lights in the theatre, willing my great-great-grandfather to protect me from the nastier ghosts that might be lurking up there. The marionettes were laid out on the stage, the strings that controlled them stretched in straight lines from the crossed pieces of wood above their heads to their limbs.

There were six farm animals, and a human farm girl in a gingham dress with a white apron and a white bonnet. The faces and hands were made of hand-carved, painted wood. There was a rooster with hundreds of rust-coloured feathers sewn to its body and a sheep covered in tufts of unprocessed wool.

The farm girl had strips of lashes stuck above and below her big blue eyes. She had two braids with a stiff gingham bow at the bottom of each one. The braids looked like they were made of real hair—I knew I shouldn't touch them but I picked a braid off her chest and rubbed it between my fingers. It didn't feel like plastic. Maybe horse hair. At that moment the side door of the theatre banged open, letting in a blast of sunlight. I dropped the braid and the bow untied. The puppeteer walked in with a fat tote bag under each arm and a knapsack on her back.

"I was just up here turning on the lights for you," I said, stepping away from the puppets.

"Thanks." She dropped her bags on the stage and wiped sweat off her forehead.

"I should get back to the box office," I said, fleeing the loose bow.

On the way down the stairs I heard the phone ringing. I raced to the box office and pulled the receiver from its cradle.

"The Theatre on Victoria," I huffed into the phone.

"Hi there, this is Constable Joe Michaels from the RNC. I'm looking for Stacey Power."

Outside, an elderly woman was walking towards the entrance, reaching for the button that made the automated door open. I hung up the phone and went to hold the door for her.

"Have you still got tickets to the matinee? I'm taking my granddaughter this afternoon, she's four, is it appropriate for a four-year-old? Could a four-year-old enjoy it?"

"Let me see what's left." I slid behind the desk, my hands were shaking.

I tried not to look at the phone. I took the woman's payment for one senior and one child. How did they know where I worked? From reading my emails. Or maybe I'd said when they interviewed me on the day they searched the house. I felt a rush like tipping backwards on the swings: they knew everything about me. Maybe he'd even checked my work schedule.

I took my phone out and found Constable Joe Michaels's

Facebook profile. I tried to remember if he had been there the day of the search but I couldn't picture any of their faces besides Hamlyn's. This guy looked about thirty-five, his teeth were crowded together, the two front ones overlapping. There was acne around his temples, bright red welts with dark yellow pinpricks at their apex. I clicked through photos of him at some cop barbeque.

He didn't call back. Every time the phone rang my stomach cramped, but he didn't call back all afternoon.

Kris and I had planned to go to a movie when I got off. She parked outside and waited while I did off the cash and locked the float in the closet. When I got in the car she passed me a Tupperware of the fancy boxed macaroni we liked, mixed with kale and frozen peas.

"There's a clean fork in the cup holder," she said, putting the car in reverse. "I think we can make it, we might miss the previews."

I peeled the lid off the plastic container, steam rising off the gluey meal. This was her apology and it worked. I was starving and the noodles were creamy and salty.

"How was your day?" she asked.

For a moment I considered not telling her. It seemed like the sort of thing that could maybe be undone if you never ever mentioned it to another person.

"He called me."

"Who?"

"The cop, the communications guy. On the work phone."

"What? What the fuck? Are they allowed to do that?"

"I don't know what they're allowed to do, whatever

the fuck they want I guess," I said through a lump of masticated macaroni.

"What did he say?"

"Just that he was looking for me, and I hung up."

"Imagine if someone else answered—that could get you fired."

"He knows everything about me, where I work, where I live. He's probably seen naked photos of me."

"Stacey, you have to do a complaint."

I put another forkful of food in my mouth.

"Stacey? Are you going to do it?"

"Yes."

"Yes?"

"I'm going to do it."

My phone buzzed with a message from Viv: *Did you get that screenshot??* I put my phone in my knapsack without answering.

I TYPED THE complaint on the theatre computer during my box office shift the following night. I was expected to wait a half hour after the show started to do off the cash, in case of latecomers. The person on bar was supposed to stay for the length of the show to serve drinks afterwards.

I downloaded the form from an incredibly shitty-looking website and printed it in the office. It was one page: at the top you filled in your information and the date of the incident, the names of the officer(s) involved. I didn't know the names of the officers involved. There were about five empty lines in the middle of the page for you to fill with a description of what happened. Then a space for your signature. I decided to type my description up on a separate sheet and staple it to the back of the form.

I struggled with the tone. I wanted to sound formal but also capture how disturbing the morning had been. I wrote "I was wearing pyjamas." It's hard to feel credible in your pyjamas, especially when the people condemning you are wearing matching uniforms. I wanted to write "I wasn't wearing a bra" but that felt too informal. Even though I'd hated that they could see my nipples through my shirt. It was like the nightmare of finding yourself naked in front of the class. I deleted "I was wearing pyjamas" and wrote "I didn't have a chance to get dressed."

Joanna was on bar that night. She wandered over to the box office and peeled open a Tupperware of squares. Beads of condensation sat on the cookies' smooth chocolate top layer.

"Nanaimo bars, do you want one? What are you working on? I didn't know you write."

I took a square from the container, a mess of golden crumbs fell on the counter. I wanted to finish the complaint so I could print it off and take it home with me.

"Did you make these?" I said.

"Is that a script?"

"No."

"Are you back in school?" Joanna asked.

"No. It's kind of a personal account." I minimized the document.

"Like creative non-fiction?" Joanna Spencer's hair was in a big bun on top of her head. She laid the open Tupperware on the counter and started eating a square. "I'm thinking of writing a play about my open relationship."

"Cool."

"Non-monogamy is all about respect, you just have to be honest and open with each other."

I finished the cookie and sucked the creamy chocolate off my fingers. Joanna was eating hers in small bites, leaving impressions of her front teeth in the chocolate.

"Anyway, I think I told you this before but there's a role in my new film I think you'd be perfect for. I'm going to ask you to read the script if you have time."

"I'd love that." For the past month I'd been trying to think of a way to bring the film up to Joanna every time I saw her, but I was so close to finishing the complaint.

Joanna leaned over and looked at my screen. "Oh, eight-thirty, you're done. I'll let you get to the cash."

I realized she wanted to use the box office computer.

"There's actually a lot of tickets that haven't been picked up, I might wait a bit." I looked purposefully at the computer screen until she took her container back to the bar.

I stood in front of the printer as it pushed my account out line by line—a single, double-sided sheet. I didn't want to have to sit with Constable Bradley in the windowless conference room again. I didn't want there to be another reason for my name to pop up in the cop database when they did searches for files on child porn or credit card theft or whatever "illegal digital material" meant. A part of me even felt guilty that someone might get a talking-to from

their boss—when I get the wrong dish in a restaurant I
don't send it back for the same reason. Probably a moot
concern, though—probably they all agree everyone was
just doing their job. So they were a little overzealous.
Mistakes happen. When cops make a mistake, suddenly
mistakes are allowed to happen. Suddenly we're all just
humans doing our best to make a go of it. I put the complaint inside a magazine to keep it from wrinkling. I'd
packed the magazine in my bookbag for that purpose
before leaving the house. I leaned into the bar and waved
goodbye to Joanna.

Then I walked to the Battery to make a wish. The
whole way up there I recited the complaint in my head,
thinking about my word choice.

A couple were smoking in their station wagon with
the nose pointed at the harbour. A hand reached out the
passenger window and ashed into the snow. I stood on
the thigh-high rock wall that surrounds the cannon; on
the other side of the ledge, a steep hill and then ocean.
Fleetwood Mac was playing in the car behind me. I hoped
the couple didn't think I was going to kill myself—people
went up there to do that. The radio announcer's voice cut
in. Sometimes tourists walked towards the lip of the cliff
with their cameras out and were lifted over the edge by
the wind.

My plan had been to wish that nothing bad came of the
complaint but instead I found myself wishing for a part
in Joanna's film. Then wishing away the awful hope that
there was still time to get a role good enough to change
the direction of my life. Hope, I knew, should be dwindling

every day but was actually getting more and more acute. Every time I got a phone call or an email, hope and dread rushed through me. When it was just a mailing list I'd signed up for or a late notice from the library a swill of disappointment mixed with relief sloshed around inside me because it wasn't an opportunity or a rejection.

I hopped off the wall and started walking home through wet snow in my new boots. Relishing the dryness of my socks. I took out my phone and called Viv.

"What are you doing?" I asked when she picked up.

"You're upset with me."

"Yeah," I said.

"I'm sorry."

"Why would you post that?"

"I don't know. I wasn't thinking. Do you want me to delete it?"

"Kris said deleting it now would make me look guilty or something. You see how fucked up and complicated this is? It's my private business."

"Stacey, I'm really sorry. It was stupid of me."

I kicked a boulder of hard snow the plow had made.

"Are you outside? I hear the wind," Viv said.

"I'm walking in the Battery."

"I miss you."

"I know, I miss you too," I told her.

IT TOOK TWO weeks for the cops to respond to my complaint. I got a call from Constable Michelle Pike. "The first step in the complaint process is that we'll try to resolve things verbally, by having you come in and speak with Constable Bradley," she said.

"What if things aren't resolved verbally?"

"There'll be further review. Would Thursday next week work for you? In the afternoon?"

On Thursday afternoon, I walked to the police station. There was a different front desk cop this time. A young guy with a thick seventies moustache; if I'd seen him out of uniform I would have assumed the moustache was ironic. Maybe he thought his whole career was ironic. I handed him my ID and he led me through the hallway to the same boardroom I'd been in before. This time it was empty.

"Constable Bradley is running late, he'll be right with you." The front desk cop closed the door. I wanted to check to see if he'd locked me in but I resisted the impulse. I sat in the same chair as last time, two down from the head of the table, and waited.

Constable Bradley arrived with sweat on his forehead and above his lip. Again I was struck by how tall he was. I wondered if he'd been bullied about it when he was a kid.

He had on the same kind of pale suit he'd been wearing the first time we met and a messenger bag over one shoulder. He pulled out the wheelie chair at the head of the table.

"Okay, thank you for coming in, I just need a moment to get situated."

I didn't say anything. He started taking piles of paper out of the bag and laying them on the table. A photocopy of my complaint form sat on top of one pile; I recognized my own signature at the bottom of the page.

He patted the three stacks of paperwork and then looked up at me. "So today we're here to try and resolve things verbally. I've reviewed your file and first of all I just want to say, I understand why you were upset. You know I have a mother, a wife and a daughter. I don't like the idea of this happening to them—I can see why you would be scared. It's unpleasant, right?"

He waited for me to answer but I didn't say anything.

"You know what, the other night my son came home from hockey early, I wasn't expecting it, I was alone in the house and it really gave me a fright—me, a big man, a police officer. It's unpleasant to be startled. Nobody likes that."

Again he paused and waited for me to say something.

"Do you want some water?" he asked.

"No thanks." I was thirsty but I didn't want to slow things down.

"I listened to the recording of the incident and you sounded very distraught. So I want to acknowledge this was an unpleasant experience for you."

"Recording?"

"One of the officers was wearing an audio recorder, that's normal."

"No one told me that."

The second wave of cops coming through the back door, being told to sit on the couch, going upstairs to look for the lease, the young cop taking in the mess of tissues around my bed, being read the warrant, the questioning, the small talk as they left. He'd heard all of it. I couldn't look at him.

"They didn't have to go through my computer." My voice came out quiet. "It's a violation of my privacy."

"The officers who reviewed your hard drive are trained professionals. They're looking for evidence of illegal activity. Believe me, they're not interested in your private life. You know what's most disappointing about this case? The bad guy got away. We hate that. You went through all this unpleasantness and we didn't get the bad guy."

"What do you mean?"

"The suspect left the province. We've had to close the case: there's no new evidence, it's a small unit, they have to move on to more pressing concerns."

"So it's done? I'm not connected to this anymore?"

"Absolutely not. Do you have any other questions?"

"What were they looking for?"

"Unfortunately, I can't disclose that."

"That guy shouldn't have called my work."

"Do you feel like we've resolved things verbally?" he asked.

"No."

He nodded.

"Will I see you out?" he asked.

"Okay."

"What happens now?" I asked when we got to the door that opened onto the lobby.

"You can request further review."

"Oh. And then?"

"Possibly disciplinary action, depending what the reviewers decide. Do you want to request further review?"

I could see the sun shining outside the police station through the big glass doors. The investigation was done; I wasn't a suspect. So badly I just wanted to walk out there and be done with it all.

"Not right now," I told him.

"You don't feel we've resolved it verbally?" he tried once more.

"No," I said.

I WOKE UP in Kris's tidy bedroom and checked my phone. There was an email from Joanna with her script attached. She invited me to audition and said she welcomed any feedback I had about the script. For the first time since the cops came I felt pure, unadulterated happiness. The joint production had felt like a long shot; this seemed like a real possibility. Kris was naked beside me, I slid my phone back under the pillows and pulled her into me. I rubbed the side of her head where her hair was buzzed close to her scalp. It felt velvety. I ran a hand down her arm and squeezed her bicep.

"You're waking me up," she said.

I lifted her ducktail of dark curls, put my lips on the back of her neck and said into her spine, "Did I tell you about that girl I work with who got funding through Telefilm to make a feature?"

"Maybe." I loved how squeaky and high Kris's voice was in the morning. Other people only heard her husky, fully awake voice. Her hair tickled my face and I sneezed on her. The sneeze whooshed through me without warning and I got snot and spit on the back of her neck.

"Stacey! What the fuck?" She squirmed away. "Disgusting! I'm sleeping."

"Sorry, it was an accident." I wrapped myself around her again and ground my pelvis into her butt. "I'm trying to tell you something."

"I'm sleeping." But she reached an arm behind her and squeezed my thigh.

"She asked me to audition. She sent me the script."

"Very cool, let's just sleep a bit longer."

Frankie was using the blender downstairs.

"A role in a feature, even an independent thing like this would be kind of a big deal. For me." I bit her shoulder.

"Ow."

"I mean, she just asked me to audition, it's not for sure. And it could be for a part with like just one or two lines for all I know."

"It's all work, right?" Kris said, smooshing her face back and forth in the pillow.

"The way Joanna said it, when she mentioned it in person, I feel like she's thinking of one of the bigger roles."

Kris reached her arm further back and spanked me. "You'll get whatever part you want, sure look at ya."

"I mean any part would be cool." I sat up. "You're working today, right? I think I'm going to get on the go."

"You're leaving? I don't work until eleven."

"I need to read the script, she asked me for feedback." I kissed Kris's hand, I put a fingernail coated in bike grease in my mouth and bit down on it, then got out of bed.

My jeans and bra were the only pieces of clothing on her bedroom floor.

"I thought you wanted to fuck," Kris said.

"I do," I said, hauling up my pants. "But I have to go."

I darted down over the stairs. Normally I would have lingered in the kitchen doorway making small talk with Frankie, but I was dying to call Viv. She was the only person who would really understand the significance of the audition. The tops of my new boots were chafing my calves; lacing them up hurt. Outside the sun was shining and the sky was blue. About two feet of snow had fallen overnight. I stomped a path to the road in my waterproof boots.

"What're you doing?" I asked when Viv picked up.

"Cleaning my bathroom."

"Joanna sent me her script, she's holding auditions next month."

"This is the outport thing?"

"Yeah." With every step the back of the boots rubbed the raw part of my calf but my feet were completely dry.

"You think it's good?" she asked.

"I haven't read it yet. It got Telefilm funding."

"So? That doesn't mean anything," Viv said.

"I could have a role in a feature." I was clomping up the middle of Pleasant Street, glancing over my shoulder every few steps to see if there were cars behind me. "That could lead to other stuff."

"I know, I'm glad you're excited."

"God, you don't know anything about the script."

"It's going to be like depressing outport life and like

romantic shots of the majestic coastline. People eking out a living in the destitute bay. Like she knows anything about it."

"It might not be that."

"Anyway, I don't care! I'm excited for you, I really, genuinely am."

On either side of the road people were shovelling out their cars and clearing their front steps, hefting mounds of wet snow into hills on the sidewalk.

"Joanna's not that bad."

"She's annoying," Viv said. "But that doesn't matter, you should do the movie."

"Well, I don't even have a part yet. And it might just be like, a very small part."

"You need someone to run lines with you?" Viv asked.

"You don't have to."

"I want to, I'm being honest, okay? About everything."

"Okay."

THIRTEEN

In March, months after we'd locked the door to Patrick Street and dropped three sets of keys into a mailbox whose rusty hinges squawked, Viv texted to ask if she could borrow my drill.

She asked for the drill because she wanted to remove two plywood figures screwed to her fence. They were both about three feet tall and two across. One was painted to look like a little boy peeing; he was facing away with his pants slid down, flashing his chubby butt cheeks. The second figure was a little girl covering her face with both hands, shocked by the peeing boy.

Viv was sitting on her front step when I arrived.

"Did you tell your landlord you're taking them down?"

"I doubt he'll care."

I laid the hard plastic case on the sidewalk and opened

it up. There was a mound of stubborn snow on the ground below the figures' feet.

"You're going to do it now?" Viv asked.

"Sure."

"I can do it," Viv said.

"It's fine." I looked at the screw in the girl's forehead and plucked the appropriate bit from the case.

Viv hopped off the step and stood next to me as I fit the drill bit into the screw. The screw resisted and I pressed hard on the drill's trigger. The girl's head cracked down the centre, her two hands separating to show the green paint on the fence post behind her.

"It broke," Viv said.

"Fuck, I'm sorry," I said.

The split spread to the middle of the girl's chest but she was in one piece from the waist down. There was another screw between her Mary Janes.

"Should I take the other screw out? It might break her completely."

"I guess we have to, we can't leave her like that," Viv said.

"I won't press so hard," I said, fitting the drill bit into the second screw.

This time I held the drill steady and pressed lightly on the trigger until the screw crunched and then began wobbling out of its hole and finally fell to the sidewalk. Viv and I each took a side of the girl and tugged, her back was still fused to the fencepost, we met eyes and pulled again. We both took a step backwards when the figure detached. Viv let go and I lowered the wooden girl onto the sidewalk. The boy came off easily and stayed intact; I stacked him on top of the girl. Viv picked them both up.

"I'm going to put them in the shed," she said.

"Are they heavy? I can take one."

"Maybe you can open the door for me," Viv said.

I followed her through the muddy backyard to a shed. The barn-style doors were held closed with a wooden latch. I turned the block of wood that held them closed from the horizontal position to vertical and the left door swung open. Inside, the shed was warm and musty; there was a window in the back that looked onto a dogberry tree. There was a biscuit tin filled with rusty nails on a wooden ledge and a gas lawn mower in the corner.

"I'm jealous of your shed," I said.

Viv leaned the figures against the wall, hiding the broken girl behind the boy. I nearly walked into a web with a fat, scab-coloured spider sitting in it. He was surrounded by long-dead fly carcasses.

"I miss living with you," I said.

"I miss it too," Viv said.

She walked out into the yard. I pushed the door, trying to close it, but it had to be lifted.

"Do you know when filming starts?" Viv asked.

"Mid-August, if the second batch of funding comes through."

"Has anyone else heard about funding?"

"Not that I know of."

"No news is good news." Viv held both hands in the air with her fingers crossed and smiled. The sun lit up her orange hair. I slid the piece of wood that held the doors together into place.

"I have some news," she said.

I waited. A warm wind stirred leaves in the muddy yard.

"You're pregnant."

Viv smiled, her irises cranked all the way up.

"Holy shit, you're having a baby?"

She nodded like she was surprised too.

"I'm getting an ultrasound in two weeks."

I wrapped my arms around her.

"It just happened," she said.

"But you want it?"

"I really want it."

Later as I left with my drill case I called to her, "Send me a picture of the ultrasound."

I WAS LYING in bed reading *Chelsea Girls*, another book from Kris. Holly was making curry, I could smell the frying onions and cumin. She was listening to a podcast, two people with bubbly Toronto accents talking about astrology. There was a loud knock on the front door. I put the book down on my stomach. I listened to hear if Holly would go to answer the door — maybe it was someone she'd invited over. Instead, she just turned down the radio. Three more loud knocks. I got off the mattress; one of my knees made a loud cracking noise as I knelt on the floor before pushing myself to standing.

I walked to my bedroom window; the crystal I'd stuck

there was click-clacking against the glass. I pulled the curtain aside and saw a white car idling outside our door with a Domino's sign on the roof. There was a young guy on the doorstep holding a delivery bag with one arm, his other arm was reaching towards the doorbell. I didn't realize I'd been holding my breath until I exhaled when I recognized the Domino's logo. Two sharp rings sounded through the house. I ran down the stairs. Holly was cooking rice now; the air in the living room was warm and moist. She was standing at the bottom of the stairs, looking at the front door.

"It's okay," I told her. "It's a pizza guy."

"I didn't order pizza. Did you?" She was frightened.

I walked past her into the porch and opened the door. The pizza guy started opening the insulated delivery bag. At first I couldn't remember what to say and then it came to me. "We didn't order pizza."

"What about her?" The guy nodded at Holly with his chin. The bag flapped open: inside there were four pizza boxes stacked on top of each other. "No one else here?"

"It must be for the church, is it?" I asked. "Youth on the Horizon or something?"

"It says 2 Clarke Avenue."

"We didn't order it." I opened the door wider and stepped into the frost on the front step in my sock feet. The guy had to back up. I pointed to the double doors on the side of the church. "Try there, they keep ordering stuff to our place by mistake. There's a youth group in there, something Horizons, Wider Horizons or something."

The pizza guy zipped his bag closed and started towards

the church, his car still idling outside our house. I looked for the coughing woman but the fire escape was empty. When I shut the door Snot and Courtney were skulking in the porch behind me.

"Get in, get in." I nudged Courtney's fat side with my cold foot and both cats scurried back into the living room.

"Thank you," Holly said. "For dealing with that."

"It freaked me out too," I said.

"I have to check the rice," Holly said. "I'm making curry, there's lots—if you want some it'll be on the stove."

"Thanks." I started up the stairs but I turned around when I got to the top. Holly was in the kitchen with her podcast turned back up. She didn't hear me walk back in, she was wiping the counters.

"Hey," I said loudly, competing with the radio. "I'm sorry about your glasses."

"Okay, thanks for apologizing." She didn't turn around.

I waited another moment; she lifted the lid of the rice and started fluffing it with a fork. I left the room.

THE NEXT MORNING I woke up to a slab of bright blue sky outside the window. I didn't have to work until the evening and it was supposed to be warm. I could hear the neighbour kids yelling at each other in the parking lot.

I got a shower and made a coffee by pouring boiling water over the partially dried-out grounds I'd used the day before. The paper filter was rippled and yellow where dampness had spread up through it but the coffee turned out surprisingly strong.

I brought my bike in through the kitchen to the living room, leaving a trail of leaves that had frozen and thawed between the spokes of the wheels. Outside there was still dirty snow in the shadows of large buildings and bright white snow gleaming on the side of Signal Hill. For the most part the sidewalks were clear though.

I wore my spring jacket for the first time that year. The next day was supposed to be cold again, but today my baby-pink jacket with racing stripes down the sleeves felt appropriate. The coat was much looser than the last time I'd worn it; usually it was snug around my breasts but now it hung off my shoulders straight down to my hips, where the elastic waistband bunched it up. I'd been entering a thin phase when the cops arrived, but now I was much skinnier. Even though I'd started cooking again the skin on my breasts was slack, the texture of gum that'd been chewed too long. There were stretch marks like dried-up riverbeds on my hips and thighs and butt.

I emptied my knapsack out onto my bed. I tightened the straps over my shoulders. I put on my canvas sneakers, they felt impossibly light after months of heavy-soled winter boots.

The neighbour kids were riding their bikes around the parking lot in long shorts and sweatshirts. The brother had on a Halloween wig, a chin-length, rainbow-coloured bob with bits of silver tinsel in it.

I locked the cats in the kitchen so I could open the front door wide enough to get my bike out. The coughing woman was in her usual spot on the fire escape and there was a younger couple sharing the same side of the picnic table. I'd seen the woman before, today she was wearing a thin grey cardigan over a spaghetti-strap tank top. The guy looked younger, he had a swoop of dyed black hair over one eye, an early-2000s emo look. The woman was smoking and the guy was drinking a green sports drink. He pushed the upturned cap of his drink into the centre of the table and the woman ashed her cigarette into it. They both smiled at me. I lifted my hand in a wave.

I leaned my bike against the side of the house and ran inside to free the cats. When I came out the kids were stopped outside my door, standing on tiptoe with their bikes between their legs, their fingers wrapped tight around the handlebar grips.

"Is that yours?" the boy asked.

"Yeah." I stepped over the crossbar and squeezed the brakes—they were stiff at first but they loosened up after a couple of pumps. I would ask Kris to tune it up next time she was over, but it was definitely rideable.

The girl nodded and kicked off again; she did a wide figure eight around the parking lot, gracefully leaning into the turns. Her little brother careened after her, stomping on the pedals. I could feel the people at the picnic table watching me. It was my first time on a bike since last summer. I was tempted to get off and walk it until I was out of view.

The bike jerked beneath me. The brake pads rubbed against the shiny rim of the front wheel, making a whining noise. The tires were definitely low on air. I pedalled hard across the parking lot, resisting the urge to look back at the people at the picnic table. Finally my legs found a rhythm and the bike glided up over the small hill by the nurses' union.

When I went fast the whining brake pads faded into a measured shushing. By the time I got to Torbay Road my thighs were aching. I rode on the sidewalk to avoid the steady stream of traffic. My knuckles and the backs of my hands were bright red from the wind. There was a knot of pain in the spot where the dog's teeth had pierced me. When I met people walking, I braked hard and the bike shrieked. I scuffed the sidewalk until I could hop off and walk the bike around them.

There was a new burrito place, a chain from the mainland where you choose ingredients from behind a sneeze guard. A group of seven or eight teenagers were squeezed into a booth in the front window, sharing a plate of nachos.

I rode past them, winding between potholes filled with grey water. The wind whipped up ripples in the pothole puddles. I locked my bike to the Our Pleasure sign. The door of the store played three digital notes when I pushed it open. The warmth inside was a relief.

This Our Pleasure used to be a sporting goods store— the ceiling was a grid of tiles punctuated with fluorescent lights. The woman at the counter was wearing a mock doctor's coat. She was tall and skinny with hair that was dyed white-grey with bright purple at the tips. Her eyebrows were painted on thick and her lipstick had sparkles in it. It was just the two of us in there. I was smelly and out of breath.

"Hi," she said. "Are you looking for something in particular?"

I saw the back wall was covered in packaged dildos hanging from hooks slotted into the wall.

"Just one of those." I waved my hand towards the wall.

"Let me know if you need any help."

"Thanks."

The strap-on section was relatively small compared to the long wall of dildos. K-Rock was playing through the store's speakers. People were calling in to talk about bad vacation experiences. Kris had told me the brand name to get. She said other harnesses never worked for her, they dug in at weird angles or slid off her hips. A man on the radio was describing having to leave a resort in the Dominican Republic early because of a tropical storm.

"The thing is, I paid four hundred, almost five hundred dollars for travel insurance that included 'holiday interruption,' that's what they call it, that's their words. Wouldn't you call that an interruption? The power was out—"

"That's one way to end a honeymoon. We're going to have to let you go, David, we've got another caller on the line, hopefully you're feeling more romantic now that you're back in sunny Newfoundland, ha ha."

I found a box with a picture of a muscled set of legs wearing a harness with a dildo stuck through a hole in the front. Kris said get extra small. I had to slide the first three boxes off the hook to get at the right size. Fifty-two dollars. And it didn't come with the dildo; you had to buy that separately. I picked a see-through purple one that was vaguely dick-shaped but not hyper-real. Not the kind with veins and a crease in the head. It came with a small silver vibrator, not much bigger than a lima bean.

"I won't get graphic but I had a very serious case of food poisoning," a woman on the radio was saying. "Couldn't move, basically. It was coming out both ends."

"Well, Gloria, I sure hope you're feeling better now. We're going to let you go. We've got Marie from Paradise on the line, how're you doing today, Marie?"

I carried my boxes to the cash. The woman with the purple hair was standing on a stepstool, arranging packs of batteries on a shelf behind the cash. She had her back to me and I waited quietly for her to become aware of my presence. As the moment stretched on I felt more and more apprehensive about her turning around and being startled, but making a noise to let her know I was there seemed rude.

"Okay, so this isn't a story about me, but my daughter went down to the Bahamas last January with her fiancé and her two sons. They had everything booked, scuba lessons, windsurfing—the boys were really excited about that. And Air Canada lost the luggage. This was January, so they were in long pants. Took the airline four days to get their stuff to them. Four days. Personally, I find that outrageous."

"Thank you for that, we're going to take a break and get right back to you with more vacation nightmares, ha ha."

When the clerk stepped off her stool and faced me, she was totally composed. She'd known I was there all along. Suddenly my own voice filled the store.

"Are you ready to tie the knot?" my voice said through the speaker above the cash.

"All set?" the clerk asked.

"At Dawn's Bridal Parlour we've got options for every bride, from classic to contemporary and beyond. We've got a dedicated team ready to assist you with selection and sizing, free of charge." I remembered repeating those lines into the microphone, experimenting with different intonations. I tried one take as the bride's fun friend and another as a competent, no-nonsense salesperson.

"All set?" the clerk asked again.

"Yes, thank you," I said.

She undid the cardboard tab on the top of the dildo box and pulled out the plastic packaging that held the dildo and mini-vibe. She slit the tape that held the two halves of the plastic packing with a pointed nail. "We test all the vibrators to make sure they're working before you take them home."

"Let us help make your dream day a reality." They'd gone with the first take, the one where I sounded the most like the real me.

The stiff plastic opened like a seashell; she plucked the silver vibrator out of a depression in the packing. She held it between her thumb and forefinger and squeezed. The vibrator shook so hard and fast it seemed to change shape, becoming wider and longer.

"Looks good?" she asked.

I nodded. She squeezed again, it shuddered and stilled. She pressed it back into its plastic indent.

"You'll want to wash both of these with soap and hot water before you use them, I'm sure you know that." She stuffed the plastic packing back in the box.

"Do you need a bag?" she asked.

"No thanks." I dropped the two boxes into my empty bookbag on my way out. I felt them tapping my back with each step I took.

"See, a vacation is all about unwinding, people work so hard they just need to relax every now and then, just need to get away—" The DJ's voice faded as the pneumatic door wheezed shut behind me.

When I got out to my bike I texted Kris: *Got it*. I bent over the bike frame and fit the key into the lock. I felt a buzz in my pocket. I straightened up, leaving my keys dangling from the lock. I was expecting it to be Kris. It was a message from Viv: *Are you still coming over for dinner tonight?*

I'd forgotten. I'd been about to invite Kris over to my place for supper, so we could try out the dildo. Maybe I could tell Viv I was feeling sick. There was a slight incline on the way down the street. The dildo box knocked against my back as I pedalled. When I stopped at the lights I took my phone out of my pocket and typed *shit! forgot I'm working tonight, thurs?* But then I thought about how she'd looked in the sunny backyard, excited to tell me her news. I backspaced the text and wrote *Yup! What time?*

When I got home after supper at Viv's I felt a sunburn tightening the skin on my cheeks and nose. I looked in the bathroom mirror and saw that my face was red and the wind had whipped my hair into curls.

THE EVENING AFTER my dinner date with Viv, I lay in bed with a satisfying ache in my thighs and butt from the bike ride the day before. The dildo box was slid between some summer clothes on the top shelf of my closet. Kris was at a drag show with Frankie and coming over later; I'd left a key in the mailbox for her.

There was a shriek on Holly's side of the wall. Then she called my name. I pushed myself up off the mattress. I stood in the middle of my room, barefoot and braless in my underwear and a T-shirt.

"Are you okay?" I called.

"Come here."

I went through the bottom drawer of my dresser and took out a pair of cut-off shorts. Holly was sitting on the edge of her bed with a Sobeys bag covering one hand. The overhead light was off. She had draped a silk scarf over her lampshade and the room was lit by its dull pink glow. It smelled like incense and dirty laundry.

"I picked my pants off the floor and a mouse fell out of them."

I saw the small grey creature curled on a patch of bare floor, its tail stretched out straight behind it.

"It's dead?"

"It was having a seizure or something."

"It probably crawled in your pants to die."

"I was going to pick it up but I can't." Holly held up her hand; the Sobeys bag was draped loosely over it.

"You want me to do it?"

She nodded.

I put my hand out like I was offering to shake hers. She stood, took the bag off and slid it on my hand, tugging the handles up to my elbow. I made a fist, crinkled the bag in my palm and released it. I knelt next to the mouse and held my hand over it. Its ears were round, its black eyes were open.

"What am I going to do with it?" I said.

"Throw it out the window?" Holly stood on the mattress, putting distance between her and the mouse.

I inhaled: it was like stepping on stage, you just have to believe you're the kind of person who can. I closed my fingers around the tiny body, and as I was turning my hand over, the mouse came to life. Its whole body was one muscle, straining against me. At first my hand closed tight around it; I felt the delicate bones inside it. Then the mouse flew through the air. It landed in the covers next to Holly. She stepped off the bed. The scarf fluttered and slid down the side of the lampshade, making the room much brighter.

"It's alive. It's not dead. It's alive." I jumped up and down. I ripped the sweaty bag off my hand and let it float to the floor.

"Fuck, it's in my fucking bed," Holly shrieked.

"Shake the blanket, shake it on the floor."

The mouse was shivering in a wrinkle of Holly's lilac-coloured comforter.

She lifted a corner of the blanket and the mouse tumbled onto a sock on the floor. It was still again.

"It's dead now," Holly said.

We waited for it to move. It dragged itself forward with its front paws.

"Fuck."

"We have to kill it," Holly said.

The mouse was making very slow progress across the bedroom floor. Its back legs were stretched out behind it on either side of its tail, not moving. The back half of its body got caught on the edge of the sock but it moved from side to side and freed itself.

"How?"

"Drop something on it." Holly said.

We looked around the room. Holly pulled a broom out from behind her dresser. I took the shiny red handle and lifted the bristle end over the tiny creature.

"It's suffering." Holly said.

"What if it doesn't die?"

"Do it hard," she said.

The mouse was inching itself out of the shadow of the broom's black plastic bristles.

"Just get it over with." She was holding the dustpan, ready to shovel up the little body.

I held the handle with both hands near the head of the broom. I tried to imagine the mouse was a windup toy covered in grey felt. A prop. I brought the broom head down as hard as I could. I felt the squish. I lifted the broom slowly. The mouse looked like someone had pinched it; there was a dent in its soft middle and guts had come out of its mouth.

"Scoop it up, scoop it up," I squealed.

Holly came at it from the tail end, pushing the rubber edge of the dustpan under the mouse's belly as she hefted the dustpan. The same motion you'd use to flip an egg in a frying pan. The mouse was briefly airborne again, then landed in the middle of the dustpan. There was a small smear of blood on the floor.

"Oh god, I shouldn't have done that, I wish I didn't do that," I said.

"It's okay, it was dying, it was suffering."

"Fuck. That was disgusting. It was so tiny."

"No, it's good, you put it out of its misery," Holly said.

"Get rid of it," I said. "Please."

Holly opened window and tilted the dustpan, letting the little body tumble into the night. The coughing woman was out there, I heard her rattling breath.

Holly put the Sobeys bag on her hand. She spat on the floor and rubbed at the mouse blood with a sock. She flipped the bag inside out and knotted the sock inside. I lifted the silk scarf off the floor; there was a circle in the centre of the fabric that had been bleached by the light that shone out of the top of the shade. I positioned the slippery fabric so the circle sat in that same spot.

"Do you hate me?" Holly asked, hauling the comforter off the bed and stuffing it into her wicker hamper.

"No, absolutely not," I said. I hated how earnest I sounded.

Bits of the hamper cracked off as she pushed the fabric down into it with both hands.

"Are you moving out?" I asked.

"I don't know."

"Do you hate me?" I asked. "I'm sorry, I know I said I would pay for your glasses, I'm just broke."

She turned to face me.

"I shouldn't have said that, that you might be involved, I shouldn't have said it in front of Dave."

"I don't care about Dave." I picked the knotted Sobeys bag off the ground. "I'll throw this out."

Outside the bedroom it was cold. I ran through the dark downstairs in my underwear, the knotted bag swinging in my hand. I dropped it in the garbage and slammed the spring-loaded lid on top of it. Then I went to bed. I called goodnight to Holly through the wall and she called goodnight back.

I woke, disoriented, to the noise of someone trying to make their way through the mess in my dark room towards the bed. For a minute panic constricted my chest. Then relief, realizing it was Kris undressing at the side of my bed. I fell into a deep, dreamless sleep with her beside me.

In the morning, Kris woke up before I did and went to pee.

"Are you awake?" she whispered when she got back from the bathroom, wrapping her cold feet around my calves.

"I am now."

"Good. Should I fuck you first or do you want to do me?"

"I'll go first," I said.

"Meaning?"

I curled my forehead into her chest and laughed. She dragged her nails over my scalp.

"You fuck me," I said. "It's in the closet."

"Okay." Kris jumped out of the bed and stood on

tiptoes to get the strap-on out from between folded summer dresses and tank tops on a high shelf in the closet.

"Is that what you were hoping I'd say?" I asked.

"Yeah, kinda." Flimsy floral things rained down around Kris when she got hold of the box. She used her teeth to rip open the package with the harness in it. She slid the nylon straps up over her bare legs, then adjusted the plastic toggles. Her bush was sticking out around the fabric in the front.

"Does it fit?" I asked.

"Yup." She pulled the loose nylon straps at the back.

She picked the dildo box off the floor and ripped open the cardboard flaps on top of the box.

"You look hot," I said.

"Play with yourself." Her back was curled, the hip strap of the harness pulled far away from her stomach, doing the awkward work of feeding the dildo through the rubber circle in the front of the harness. I rubbed myself theatrically, grinding and whimpering a little.

"Did you get lube?" she asked.

"No."

"Oh."

I wormed over to the edge of the mattress on my stomach, held her by the hips and made her stumble towards me. Her thighs were up against the edge of the mattress. I put my mouth over the dildo and let it slide into my throat then pulled back. "Is that hot?"

"Yeah." But she pushed me away. I flipped onto my back, and she climbed up on the bed and straddled me. The hard plastic cock hovered over my ribs, her wet crotch against my stomach. She ran her hands over my breasts. My legs were hanging off the side of the bed and my sock feet were on the floor. The open window let in the loud beep-beep-beep of the garbage truck reversing in the church parking lot.

"You want to try it without lube?"

"Let's try it. We can stop if it's bad. Or I mean, if it's not good." I opened my legs, and Kris moved backwards. She spit in her hand and rubbed it over the dildo. "I'm warming it up for you."

I tilted my hips and she nudged the dildo inside me.

"Good?" Kris asked. The longer bits of her curly hair swished around her face; her features were different from this angle. She had one hand flat on the mattress by my ear and the other between my breasts. I nodded. She pushed it in deeper, watching my face. It was thicker than I'd expected: a jolt of urgency shot from my crotch to my lungs. Outside the dumpster crashed back into the parking lot, making everything on my dresser jump.

"Still good?" Kris asked.

I wrapped my legs around her back. She started moving her hips, holding me in place with her warm palm.

After I came Kris loosened the straps of the harness and kicked herself free of it. I stood at the foot of the bed and picked it out of the covers. The velvety triangle of fabric in the front was damp from Kris.

"How does it feel?" she asked, once I had it on.

"Maybe it's a bit low," I said. The plastic cock was pointed at the floor instead of straight out in front of me.

"Yeah, I felt like that at first too." Kris got off the bed and started adjusting the harness on me. I saw the muscles in her forearms shifting beneath her skin. The dildo righted itself.

"Your ass looks so good." She slapped me lightly.

"Get on the bed," I said, trying to sound stern.

Kris smiled and kissed me on the cheek before dropping back onto the twisted covers. I wished I had practised moving my hips. What if I couldn't get a good rhythm going? I knelt in front of her and put my face in her crotch. First I sucked her clit and then I put my tongue in deep, where the taste of her was strongest. The dildo was sticking tip-first into the mattress and the base was digging into me at a weird angle, just below my belly button, but I kept going until Kris pulled me up by my hair.

"I don't want to come yet," she said.

She surprised me by straightening her arms and lifting her hips off the mattress. She guided the plastic cock into herself, balancing with one palm on the mattress beneath her. She rocked against me, squeezing her thighs against my sides. Her breasts bounced each time she smacked into me. Her head was tilted back but I could still see her face: her eyes were closed, brows furrowed. I reached out and rubbed one of her nipples between my fingers. She breathed harder, encouraging. I tried moving my hips—for a moment the rhythm was off, she was pulling away just as I was diving in. Then we found it. I held her narrow body in my big hands and we kept sliding apart and coming back together in tempo.

When I left the house the next day, I nearly stepped on

the mouse. It had landed alongside the front step when Holly dumped it out the window. The entrails blooming out of its mouth had changed colour; they were a less vivid red. It looked stiff, more like the mechanical mouse I'd wanted it to be the night before. I heard the neighbour kids yelling in their porch. The basketball bounced off the inside of their door. I kicked the mouse under our front step and went to work.

ON FRIDAY THE landlord called to say someone was coming by to look at the chimney. A standard inspection—if we couldn't be there to let him in, the landlord would come by himself. The appointment was already scheduled for Monday morning at 9:30, the only time the furnace guy was available.

"I've been trying to arrange this for weeks now," the landlord said on the phone. "You'd think I was trying to get a meeting with the prime minister."

"It's fine, I understand," I told him. "We'll be here." I didn't want him coming in and appraising the state of the house.

Holly and Dave King were asleep in her room when the furnace guy knocked. Kris had just left for work. The furnace guy was wearing a grey jumpsuit and carrying a steel toolbox. There was a cell phone clipped to his waist. I pointed to the basement door, saying, "It's just down there, in the back of the room. Do you need anything else?"

"Should be all good." He reached up and tugged the

cord hanging from the light bulb above the stairs. "This'll only take a few minutes."

I sat on the couch next to Snot and Courtney. I refreshed my email. There was something from Joanna. The subject line said, *An update on funding.* I opened the email. The funding had come through. Filming mid-August as planned.

I wanted to call Viv but at that moment the furnace guy batted the basement door open. He was holding a rag over his mouth with the hand that wasn't holding his toolbox.

"This house needs to be evacuated. Get the animals out. Everyone in the house needs to get out immediately."

"What?"

"Are there other people in the house?" The furnace guy was making his way to the front door. "We need everyone out. There's a carbon monoxide leak. A serious leak. I have to make some phone calls."

"My roommate's upstairs, I'll get her. Don't leave the front door open. The cats will get out."

"The doors and windows need to be left open."

"The cats."

"You can't breathe this in, it's dangerous."

"I've been breathing it."

"Legally, I need you to evacuate. Immediately."

The furnace guy closed the door behind him.

"Holly," I yelled as I dug through the porch closet for the cat carrier. "Holly!"

I ran up the stairs holding the empty cat carrier by one handle and banged on her bedroom door. "The furnace guy says there's a carbon monoxide leak."

I could hear them moving on the other side of the door.

"He said it's dangerous, we need to leave, he said immediately."

Holly opened the door. Dave King was pulling on his jeans.

"Can you help me put the cats in here? They hate it." I held the carrier up.

"Remember I said about that smell?" Dave King said as we jogged down the stairs single-file.

Through the front window I saw the furnace guy pacing in front of the house with the phone to his ear. I went and got the cat treats from the kitchen cupboard. Holly had Courtney in her arms.

"He's all freaked out already," Holly said.

I held the carrier open. It stank of stale cat piss. Holly tried to lower Courtney in, the cat swiped and Holly dropped him. Beads of blood sprang up on Holly's forearm and blurred into a runny line.

The furnace guy opened the door and called in, "I really need you to get out of the house."

"Yeah, we're coming," Holly said, too quietly for him to hear.

Dave picked up Courtney; I came over to him with the carrier and together we managed to force his struggling body into the bag. Once he was inside he froze and I zipped it shut.

"Do you remember me saying that about the smell, though?" Dave said. "That was the smell."

"Carbon monoxide doesn't have a smell," Holly snapped. "It's odourless."

Snot was bunched up on the sofa. He let me pick him up but he pulled his sides in and howled.

"It sounds like a human baby," Holly said.

"It sounds like he's saying hellooooooooooooo." Dave King carefully unzipped the carrier; Courtney stayed curled in the back. I pushed Snot in and closed the mesh door. The furnace man was in the living room with us again. Holly was holding one of Natalie Swanson's J-Cloths against her bleeding arm, dark red spreading through the stiff blue cloth.

"Listen, my boss needs me to confirm the house is evacuated."

"Then what?" Holly asked him.

"You need to leave the windows and doors open. Let the place air out."

"When can we go back in?" I held the heavy carrier against my chest with both arms. The smell of ammonia filled my nostrils. Snot let out another long, low howl.

"I'd give it at least forty-eight hours." The furnace guy opened the front door and waved us out like a game show assistant showing off a prize.

"What about our stuff?" Holly said. "We can't just leave with the windows and doors open."

"I have to get to my next appointment," the furnace guy said.

Holly and Dave King sat down on the front step with the door wide open behind them.

"People die from carbon monoxide poisoning," Dave said.

The furnace guy put his toolbox in the pan of his truck and got in. The automated window on the passenger side lowered and he called "Good luck" from the driver's side before pulling out of the parking lot.

I laid the cat carrier on the sidewalk and sat on the curb. I raised a hand and waved to the coughing woman. I took out my phone and texted Viv, first about the film and then about the carbon monoxide. I watched the screen to see if she would answer immediately, then I stuck it back in my pocket and waited for the familiar vibration to let me know she'd responded.

ACKNOWLEDGEMENTS

Firstly, thank you to my editor, Melanie Little, for your invaluable guidance and encouragement. I'm enormously grateful for the opportunity to work with you, and I learned so much. Thank you to Sarah MacLachlan, Cindy Ma, Alysia Shewchuk, Maria Golikova and everyone at House of Anansi Press for your friendship and for all the hard work you do. Thank you to the Newfoundland and Labrador Arts Council and the City of St. John's, whose financial support gave me time to write, and without which I never would have been able to finish this project.

Thank you to Carmella Gray-Cosgrove and Susie Taylor for reading bits and pieces of this book, for sharing your works in progress with me and for hours of conversation about reading and writing. Thank you to Robert Chafe for helping me hammer out an early version of this story and for blowing my mind with your playwriting lectures. Thank you to Jen Squires for your advice as well as your warmth and generosity. Thank you to Rosellen Sullivan for patiently talking me through some complicated technicalities. Thank you to my aunt Lynn for being a powerful and inspiring force of good in the world and for your help with this manuscript. Thank you to my mom and dad for filling the house I grew up in with love and books. Thank you to Emily Amaral, Theo Crocker, Becky Gibson, Jessica Gibson, Alex Noel, Catherine Roberge, Devin Shears and Jess Tran for your endless support, I love you all immensely.

EVA CROCKER is the author of the critically acclaimed
debut short story collection *Barrelling Forward*, which won
the Alistair MacLeod Prize for Short Fiction and the CAA
Emerging Writer Award; was a finalist for the Writers'
Trust Dayne Ogilvie Prize for LGBTQ Emerging Writers
and the NLCU Fresh Fish Award for Emerging Writers;
and was a *National Post* Best Book. She lives in St. John's,
Newfoundland.